Skating For Grace

Book one

The Royal Skater Chronicles

Anne Perreault

Edited by Annemarie E. Omilian
Edited by Steve Place
Cover design: Natasha Perreault
Cover image: Natasha Perreault

Library of Congress Control Number: 2015950985

ISBN-13: 978-1517072216
ISBN-10: 1517072212

Printed in the United States of America by Create Space, and Amazon company

Published by Anne Perreault

For Natasha, the princess in my life.

Mt 16:26.
For what is a man profited, if he shall gain the whole world,
and lose his own soul? Or what shall a man give in exchange for his
soul?

Chapter 1

Lillehammer, Norway, 1994

In through the nose, out through the mouth, and open your eyes! Tie your laces up tight and stand. Smile! NO! Plaster that smile on your lips. That's right! Now start walking toward the door. Check yourself in the mirror. Yes, you are dressed, good! Keep walking out the door. Smile at the person. Excellent! No! Don't turn around and run back into the dressing room! Keep moving forward. Smile again and keep it up! Stop! Turn and talk to Fiona. Listen to what she has to say. Are you not listening?!

Jacqueline shook her head to clear out the annoying little voice and to try to focus on what her coach was telling her. She saw her mouth moving, but the words did not register. Fiona touched her arm, snapping her out of her half-dreamlike state, and led her through a throng of people to a door leading to the ice. Thousands of faces, bathed in darkness, waited for her. Her stomach heaved suddenly, making her feel nauseous. She half turned and wanted to run the other way. Back to safety, back to the dressing room. She wanted to take these clunky skates off her feet. They felt heavy and unnatural. Fiona's steadying hand stopped her.

"Jacqueline, look at me! We have been through this before. Think of it as just another competition. Just because we are at the Olympics, doesn't mean that the ice is any different," she soothed, but when she noticed Jacqueline staring at the rink and the people, her face turning a sickly white, her voice became harsh. "Jacqueline, you have a job to do! And you have no excuse to feel faint. This is what we have been training for. Now go out there and do your best! They will be calling your name shortly!"

Jacqueline heard her. She heard them call her name.

"Our next competitor is Jacqueline Chevalier, representing Lichtenbourgh."

She saw the door to the rink open, heard the roaring applause of the crowd. Fiona squeezed her arm reassuringly. As she took a tentative step onto the ice, her whole being was transformed. Her skates felt like they were part of her body. Her stomach settled down and the audience was no longer threatening. She didn't have to force a smile this time. It appeared on its own, when she thought of the fun she was going to have in the next four minutes. She stood and patiently waited for the music to start.

When her song started, it seemed as though her body knew exactly what to do. For the next four minutes she was the only one in the whole arena. The music penetrated her body and without thought she was leaping, spinning, flying over the ice. None of the individual moves she made registered. They were all part of her. Then the music stopped!

She found herself at center ice again, breathing heavily with a huge smile on her face. She could not recollect whether she had fallen but by the applause and the lack of melted ice and pain on any part of her body, she knew she had delivered a clean performance. She smiled, curtsied and graciously waved to the ecstatic audience as she left the ice. It was over! She had done her best. The rest was up to the judges and her competitors.

As she went to skate off the ice, she noticed a family in the stands. The children watched her, their eyes open wide and Jacqueline smiled at them and waved. The girl's face split into a huge smile and she turned to her mother in rapt excitement, talking to her and pointing at Jacqueline. Jacqueline smirked to herself. *That is my good deed for the day,* she thought and glanced at her parents, up in their private box. She skated back to the door, receiving a big hug from Fiona who had tears in her eyes.

"Fabulous Jacqueline, absolutely wonderful! You were flawless out there!" The two weaved their way through coaches and skaters still waiting to perform. In passing, some smiled generously while others mirrored the same deer-in-the-headlights look she had worn not ten minutes before. Jacqueline took a deep breath and sat down in the 'kiss and cry' area, waiting for her results.

Someone handed her a large bouquet of roses and a little pink teddy bear. Smiling into the cameras, she waved to the millions of people watching from the comfort of their homes. For support Fiona kept her hand on her arm with gentle pressure. As the announcer's voice rang out, that pressure increased. Jacqueline almost cried out in surprise but her attention was diverted as the announcer began the tally.

"The results for Jacqueline Chevalier for technical: 5.8, 6.0, 5.8, 5.7, 5.9, 5.9, 6.0, 5.9, 5.6, 5.9." Pausing for a moment to allow the applause to die down, the announcer continued. "For artistic merits: 5.8, 5.9, 5.9, 6.0, 5.9, 5.9, 6.0, 5.7, 5.6, 5.8."

Jacqueline's heart raced as she pleasantly accepted Fiona's approving hug.

"Congratulations," she whispered into Jacqueline's ears. "You have done it. I am so proud of you, Jacqueline."

Jacqueline smiled, waved to the crowd and made her way to the changing room. On her way she was stopped by reporters.

"What a wonderful performance, Jacqueline. You must be so happy with yourself right now," a blond female reporter smiled at her, shoving a microphone into her face.

"Thank you so much. The competition is not over yet and there are some very excellent skaters yet to come. The Russians still have two competitors and one of the American skaters, Linda Jones, is still up," she smiled back, imagining that her teeth must be blinding in the bright lights. She almost let out a roar of hilarious laughter, which started in the pit of her stomach, but managed to control herself.

"After your wonderful performance you have set the stage for everyone to follow. It will be difficult for anyone to even come close," the reporter stated.

"Thank you but there is always a good chance someone will perform better."

"We wish you the best!" the reporter smiled at her, showing her own flashing teeth.

Avoiding more reporters, she was able to make her way to the changing room. There was an eerie silence. Some of the girls sat on the chairs, tears running down their cheeks. How she felt for them. How many times had she blown it? The thought of all those years of training, pain, self-denial, culminating into a four and a half minute routine made her sober also. They all had worked so hard and now each would return to her own country. Some would be able to attend the Olympics again in another four years. For others, this had been the last and sometimes only chance. She glanced over to her friend, fellow skater Linda Jones. She sat with a determined and concentrated look as she laced up her skates. Jacqueline knew better than to go and talk to her now. Instead, she sank down on the bench and started to unlace her own skates.

She nervously glanced at the monitor, showing that the first Russian skater had just taken a tumble after attempting a triple Lutz, almost hitting the side of the rink. She heard the audience groan and cheer her on as she rose back onto her feet to finish her performance. She still received high marks due to the difficulty of her program. But her marks were nothing close to Jacqueline's. When Linda made her way out the door, she passed Jacqueline who smiled at her encouragingly.

As she watched Linda glide through her motions on the monitor, Jacqueline marveled at the gracefulness of her friend. She gasped when Linda stumbled after landing the triple toe loop. Linda caught herself and continued as though nothing had happened. By the smile plastered on her face when she skated off the ice, however, Jacqueline knew her friend was crying on the inside. She received very high marks, placing her in silver position. Jacqueline's gold was almost secure with only one skater, the Russian Tatiana Svetlova, still to come. When Linda walked back into the changing room, Jacqueline acknowledged her with a quick nod. Linda needed time to come to terms with her effort. It was only then, that she would be able to accept that Jacqueline had taken the coveted gold medal.

Tatiana's performance, despite her skating well, was just not good enough and Jacqueline slowly realized what was happening. She had indeed conquered the coveted prize! The gold medal! She met Fiona, who hugged her tightly, tears in her eyes. Fiona noticed Tatiana's coach and turned to shake her hand, leaving Jacqueline free to shake the hands of other coaches, some smiling at her, others trying to hide their disappointment. She found herself in a tight embrace as Linda walked up next to her.

"Well done, you deserve it!" she whispered into her ear.

Jacqueline smiled. She felt numb with excitement. She squinted at the bright lights as she walked through the throng of reporters, trying to avoid the multitude of microphones being shoved into her face. She smiled into the cameras, waving to no one in particular. Tatiana, who had just come off the ice, didn't have a chance to work through in her mind that the gold had been taken by someone else. Once that realization hit slowly, her smile did not reach her icy

10

blue eyes, which glistened dangerously with disappointment and shame.

Jacqueline watched, in a very detached manner, what was going on around her. On the ice, workers and volunteers were beginning to set up the red carpet and podium. The arena was well lit as she saw the audience standing in the bleachers, chatting excitedly with one another. Some were capturing the excitement on their cameras while others were eating some food bought from the many vendors around the huge arena. Jacqueline realized in that moment that she had been up for a long period of time. She figured it was way past midnight though her body was taut with excitement, her mind was exhausted and things around her were beginning to go in and out of focus. Stifling a yawn, she turned slightly to see Linda, who beamed at her with eyes filled with excitement.

Chapter 2

A tall blond official, wearing a navy blue blazer, white shirt and red tie approached them. His name tag identified him as Sven Olsen. He bowed and flashed his perfectly straight set of teeth at them.

"Congratulations you three," he said in accented English. "Please to follow me to the changing room. You will wait there until the TV networks okay the ceremony to begin."

Jacqueline suppressed a groan. She did not hold the media in the highest regard. Her whole life she had painfully tried to hide from them as much as possible. Here at the Olympics, it had been hard to avoid them. She found out that she could not sneeze without a network picking up that she had come down with a cold. Jacqueline's parents were also the subject of criticism from the media, since they had decided to keep their daughter away from the Olympic village, and hence the constant hounding of the media. Their intention had been twofold, keeping Jacqueline free from distractions of the media while she practiced at an undisclosed location and keeping a close eye on their still-so-young daughter. The media called them elitists for renting a private house on the outskirts of town, where they had spent the two weeks leading up to her competitions.

Again they pushed their way back through the throng of reporters and photographers until they reached the relative silence of the lockers. A few of the skaters still sat on the bench, slowly and dejectedly putting on their outdoor clothes. Several makeup artists and hair stylists fussed like bees about the three winners, touching up here and there as they saw fit. Delicate hands tucked strands of her chestnut hair back into her bun.

When they finally left, the room once again became quiet. The three winners settled on a bench awkwardly, waiting to be called back onto the ice.

Linda looked at Jacqueline with an excited grin. "What a day!"

"You can say that again," Jacqueline sighed.

"What a day," Linda laughed cheekily. "What are you talking about? You should be jumping for joy!" Linda said to her, playfully tapping her shoulder.

"This is a little overwhelming," she confessed. "And I am so tired. I think I have been running on pure adrenaline for the last couple of days. Now that it's over, I'm exhausted."

"I suppose you are right. I remember the first Olympics I participated in. Granted I didn't make it to the podium and I wasn't a baby like you, sweet sixteen," Linda teased her friend and shoved her shoulder into her softly. "But I remember being totally overwhelmed. My advice is to just enjoy this moment. You may never have another one like it," she said to her.

Jacqueline nodded. "You're right. But all I want to do is go to bed."

13

"My advice to you, honey: make the most of tonight. You can sleep for the next four years."

A little sniffle interrupted their silence. Jacqueline turned to see the tears streaming down Tatiana's face, smudging the touch-up job the make-up artists had just completed. Linda and Jacqueline looked at each other.

"You skated really well, Tatiana," Jacqueline said softly. Tatiana stiffened at her words. She shot her a cold stare.

"Is easy to say for you," she said with a cold voice, making her accent more pronounced. "You are on top. You have gold. I go back to my country in disgrace, no gold."

Jacqueline huffed. "Tatiana, you are at the Olympics! What could be better than that? There is no disgrace in not winning the gold!"

"Jacqueline is right," Linda added, scooting to the other side of Tatiana, who held herself very stiffly. These two were fierce competitors, who had little love for each other. "We have all sacrificed a lot to be here. We have all skated well. Today Jacqueline happened to be in perfect form. It was her day. There have been other days when you have come out on top."

"Uh-huh," Jacqueline grunted. "I am no better than you. It's just that something happened out there today, I can't quite explain it." She lifted up her arms in a stunned gesture. Linda nodded in agreement. A knowing look flashed over her face. They had all been there at one time or another.

Thick tears continued to roll down Tatiana's cheeks, leaving black streaks.

"You are not disgrace. These are your first Olympics," her voice was husky with emotion.

Jacqueline sighed. "This is not the end, Tatiana. There are worlds of opportunities out there for you. You might be back next time."

"No, is over for me," Tatiana replied and then her face hardened. "I hate skating!" She spat these words out, leaving Linda and Jacqueline stunned.

They couldn't comment because in that moment Sven Olsen reappeared in the doorway. "They are ready for you," he said and pointed out to the rink.

"Give us a moment," they pleaded, taking Tatiana by the hand and leading her to the bathroom, where they quickly fixed her smudged face.

They followed Sven out toward the ice, where he held up his hand yet again. He listened to instruction squawking out of his walkie-talkie. The audience, now aware that something was about to happen, started clapping and cheering. Jacqueline heard her name being shouted all over the arena and she smiled and waved at no one in particular. Flashes from the cameras all around the small group blinded her momentarily. She pasted on the smile she didn't quite feel.

"I can't see my parents. I know they are out there somewhere," Linda squeaked. Jacqueline scanned the arena for Linda's parents. She spotted her own mother, looking out through the window of her private box. Once they spotted each other, they both smiled. Her mother said something over her shoulder and the tall figure of her father appeared at her side, smiling brightly and giving a quick wave. Jacqueline nodded back to them and continued scanning the arena.

"There's my mom!" Linda said exuberantly, waving furiously. She laughed when her mother held up a large sign saying: *Go USA, Go Linda!* She jumped up and down and almost fell in her excitement. Jacqueline caught her arm.

"Careful there. They might count that against you." Both girls looked at each other and laughed. It had been a long night.

Chapter 3

"Jacqueline, how do you feel?" she heard someone shout to her.

How should she feel? Tired, she wanted to yell back but instead she smiled graciously. With a nod from Sven the three approached the podium and waited. The audience cheered as they called each skater up onto the podium. She looked down when she noticed that an official of the IOC approached her with flowers. Jacqueline bent down and accepted yet another beautiful bouquet of roses. Then the head of the IOC approached her with a case holding the gold medal. She automatically shook his hand, bending down to allow him to place the medal around her neck. It was surprisingly heavy and she automatically smoothed her hand over the cold surface. One side showed the Olympic rings and as she flipped it over, it depicted a figure skater

Jacqueline felt chills run down her spine. As she stood there, waving and grinning, another thought hit her. She had just made history! She had obtained something no one from her country had ever achieved. *Wow*, she thought as this started to sink in. Again she tried to take it all in, like Linda had suggested, but it was too overwhelming. The crowd applauded like crazy.

From there everything proceeded in slow motion. The flags were raised. Hearing her national anthem being played and seeing her country's flag flying high above the stadium brought tears to her eyes. She could not help it; it was almost automatic. She heard herself sing along with the music as the tears streamed down her face. The pain, the sprained ankles, the hours of stretching her body into impossible positions on two thin pieces of metal, while gliding on a slippery surface all came down to this one moment. Was it really worth it? This was the culmination of every competitor's dream. Was it worth it?

The crowd applauded when the three skaters joined together and waved. The whole arena was cheering for them, three individuals who had been able to defy gravity, to subdue their bodies and to stay on their feet more than their competitors. Then the moment was over.

Before leaving, everyone huddled together holding up their medals, while the photographers took picture after picture. Jacqueline's face hurt more than her body did after the long and tedious session. She glanced at Linda, knowing how hard this moment must be for her. Although her friend wore a pleasant smile, something about her told Jacqueline that her friend was hurting and trying to keep her emotions in check.

They were led back to the changing room, waving as they went. They had to make it past the reporters who were eagerly shouting questions at them. All Jacqueline could do was smile, nod and wave.

In the changing room, they had only a moment for a quick hug from their coaches.

"I am awfully proud of you," Fiona told her, tears streaming down her face.

They held on to each other briefly. Jacqueline remembered the first time she was introduced to this little woman, seven years earlier. They had had their arguments and disagreements. Fiona held steadfast to her belief that Jacqueline could make it to the top of international skating and she was correct. Just last year, she had gained a third at the European Championship and came in fourth in the World Championships, ironically behind both Tatiana and Linda.

Sven Olsen interrupted them and motioned them up a back stair to the makeshift studio of the ABC television station. A tall, harried producer welcomed them and fixed each of them with a microphone. Their hair and makeup was once again touched up to prevent the bright lights washing out their colors. Jacqueline was still wearing her gold medal. It hung heavily from her neck and reflected the bright lights. She smiled as she fingered its smooth surface.

They were introduced to the host and hostess of the show.

"I want to tell you how much I personally enjoyed each of your performances," beamed the anchorwoman, as she shook their hands. Her male counterpart did likewise and helped them settle into their seats. The director quickly explained that they were just to imagine themselves in a room with close friends, answering questions. *Oh yes,* Jacqueline thought, *I am about to share with millions of my closest friends.*

But she knew the drill and smiled pleasantly until the director motioned for them to be quiet.

"In 5, 4..." he whispered and the cameras whirled around and the room became quiet.

"Jacqueline, I know you are very aware of the fact that you have just made history. You are from a relatively small and unknown country, and you are only sixteen years old. You must be very excited."

She smiled sweetly. "Yes, I am."

"For those who have not been following the news," their friendly host explained to his 'friends' on the other side of the camera. "Jacqueline's family is the ruling family of the democratic monarchy of Lichtenbourgh in between France and Switzerland."

Ah, Jacqueline thought, *I was wondering when they would bring that up.*

"Your family must be ecstatic right now," the anchorman said, oozing charm.

"I'm sure they are. I will be hearing from them soon."

"Your parents were in attendance tonight?"

"Indeed, but I have yet to speak to them personally. It has been quite a night," she admitted. She hated this!

"We want to congratulate each of you again for your wonderful performances and hope to see you again in four years. What are your plans now?"

Linda was the first to say that she was looking forward to some time at home outside Denver Colorado, devoting herself to long walks with her two Dachshunds, Fritz and Louisa. Tatiana hesitatingly admitted that she would be retiring after the games. Jacqueline thought frantically for an answer but could only say that she was looking forward to sleeping in tomorrow. Chuckles were heard from around the room. The interview was soon over, and as Sven escorted them back to the locker room, Jacqueline could not stifle her yawn. Her eyes felt droopy and she felt as though her body had been pounded by a ton of stones, yet, she was still upright, walking around in a daze.

Outside the locker room door, the press waited for them like piranhas, hungry for their next meal. The flashes of the many cameras caused her to stumble blindly after Fiona to the front door, where the cheering crowd demanded her total attention. By this time, Jacqueline's cheeks had no feeling anymore. She somehow managed to find her outer clothes and put them over her skating dress. Her black limousine pulled up and the chauffeur doffed his hat with a smile as he opened the back door. She waved one last time at the many cameras, and entered the car. Even before the door had finished closing, she felt herself embraced by both her parents. For a moment they were all overcome with the emotion of the whole ordeal.

By the time they pulled up in front of the rented home, the family had collected themselves and Jacqueline was quickly dozing off to sleep. She startled awake when the door opened and for once she was not greeted by reporters shoving their microphones in her face. The only illumination was the distant twinkling lights of the city and the stars. She breathed in the frosty air and quickly made her way along with her parents to the front door, which was flung open by a butler who struggled to maintain his composure. He quickly removed her jacket as he beamed at her.

"If you would permit me to say," he started in his crisp correct voice, "on behalf of the staff, we want to congratulate you most sincerely." She smiled at him.

"Why thank you. Right now, I am so tired, but I truly appreciate your words. It has been my pleasure to secure this sought-after prize and I will endeavor to continue to represent my country in a dignified fashion," she rambled on, smiling and waving at the crowd, which was not there.

"Come along, dear," she heard the soft voice of her mother and felt her hand on her arm steering her to the stairs.

"I believe it is way past my bedtime, Mother," she started to giggle uncontrollably. Her mother helped her to her room and she just about made it to her bed. She removed the heavy medal from her neck and placed it on the nightstand. As soon as she felt the soft mattress underneath her, she fell into a deep, heavy sleep.

Chapter 4

When she awoke, sunlight streamed into her room. It was well into the afternoon, by the looks of it, and Jacqueline was quite foggy about the events of last night. Then her eyes fell on the medal on her nightstand. Then everything came back in full force. Jacqueline stretched luxuriously. Her whole body felt worn out. She enjoyed her moment of quiet, once again realizing what had transpired. She had done it! She had really done it! All the hard training had been worth it. She squealed in delight, kicked her feet and flung her cozy comforter away from her, only then noticing the time.

"Ahhh," Jacqueline gasped. "Two in the afternoon?! I almost slept the day away!" Then she laughed happily. Who cared how long she slept today? Her eyes fell on the multitude of bouquets in her room. The whole room smelled like a flower shop. Each bouquet had a card attached and it would take hours to read them all. Maybe she would actually have time to go through them leisurely, sipping a cup of hot chocolate.

She dressed in jeans and a sweatshirt, and made her way to the large kitchen. Smells so wonderful made her empty stomach growl. Today she would allow herself to indulge in foods she normally would have to say no to. Jacqueline was sure Fiona would allow her this moment.

"Your Highness, I didn't see you enter," the cook stammered in a heavy accent.

"I'm sorry but I am famished!" she panted as she reached for a miniature quiche fresh out of the oven. Her forwardness was rewarded by a burning sensation in her fingers. She quickly set the little pastry down on the counter and proceeded to blow on her fingers.

"I am so sorry," the poor chef stammered again and rushed to get her ice out of the freezer.

"No matter," laughed Jacqueline. "I didn't think of the consequence of picking up a hot piece of pastry. Please don't fuss," she added, still blowing on her fingertips.

"Do I hear the voice of my youngest daughter?" a booming voice asked from the study, where Jacqueline found her father, a stack of newspapers in front of him. She felt herself enveloped in his strong arms, breathing in a hint of his spicy aftershave and peppermint toothpaste. She smiled up at him.

"You have woken!" he beamed at her. "The whole world is talking about you."

She winced as she saw her picture on the front page. It was a color picture of her, tears streaming down her cheeks as she sang the national anthem, the flag flying high above her head. Her eyes caught a picture of her landing a triple Lutz perfectly.

"Wow, that's a really good one," she mumbled, her mouth full of something extremely tasty. "I knew I was skating well, but I didn't know I was that good."

"Yes, humility is not one of your strong points," her father laughed. Together they poured over picture after picture, story after story as cook plied her with treat after treat. Jacqueline couldn't remember when she had spent an afternoon just with her father, pouring over pictures.

"Here is a good one," her father laughed. "According to this newspaper you are the most talented athlete at these games," he chuckled when she turned bright red.

"That is totally ridiculous. Anyone who makes it here is just as talented. And just because I happened to be able to stay on my feet, doesn't make me the most talented athlete. But I tell you, Father, I am quite tired. I would love to just rest for a bit," she mumbled and didn't manage to catch the yawn that escaped her.

"By all means dear, take a rest. This evening we are having a small dinner party here in your honor," he informed her and she squirmed.

"Father!" Jacqueline tried not to sound too upset. "Why couldn't you have waited? We are here for another two weeks."

"It was not my idea, dear," he soothed, and admitted that the consulate had requested that a small, intimate dinner was held in her honor. "Be thankful that it is only a small affair and that it is not an official state dinner. Only forty people are coming," he informed her and Jacqueline tried not to frown.

She sighed as she made her way up the beautiful oak stairs. Everything in this large Norwegian home was made of huge local timber, cut to exact dimensions by skilled craftsmen. The moment she entered her room, the fragrance of the multitude of flowers overwhelmed her. Her eldest sister would have a very hard time with this and she would undoubtedly sneeze her way out of the room. Jacqueline settled into the warm, cushy window seat, looking at the snow-covered branches of the huge elm tree outside her window. Its bows were heavy from fresh snowfall last night. As she took off the first card, she noticed that the sun was just beginning to reach the horizon. It would soon be quite dark. She shuddered. The long winter nights would be a nightmare for her.

She was so engrossed in her cards that she did not hear the knock at the door.

"Knock, knock," her mother announced.

"Oh, Mother. Do come in."

Her mother, dressed and exquisitely put together, entered and joined her at the window seat. A smile played over her beautiful face. Her mother, although in her late fifties, was still the most beautiful woman Jacqueline knew.

"Look at all these beautiful flowers. Don't you think that we should donate them to a charity here in Lillehammer?" she asked after gazing around.

Jacqueline pasted a smile on her face. She should have figured that her mother would suggest something like this. Always civil minded, she thought wryly.

"If you don't mind, Mother," Jacqueline pleaded. "I would love to keep the roses given to me along with my medal," she attempted to convince her.

"Oh my dear, we have so many roses at home. Think of the joy they would bring another person here," she beamed at her daughter.

What about the joy they bring me? She almost grumbled but caught herself. She knew that if she complained to her mother, she would just receive a sharp reprimand. It didn't matter that Jacqueline had just won the Olympic gold medal. Here she was still expected to do her duty. This time, her duty included giving away all the flowers. Why, oh why, couldn't her mother just leave her be for one afternoon?

"As you wish," she pouted.

"Oh Jacqueline, that face does not become an Olympic Champion," her mother answered sharply.

Jacqueline almost laughed out loud. Did she call that one or what?

"Of course not, Mother," Jacqueline answered and smiled evenly. She was getting thoroughly tired of this conversation.

"You will wear your purple dress this evening?" her mother demanded more than asked. "It will go well with your gold medal."

"Of course, Mother," Jacqueline sighed and turned her attention back to her next card.

"It looks as though you have more correspondence. Tomorrow you have several interviews in the morning," her mother informed her as she dropped a stack of telegrams onto the pine coffee table in the middle of the room.

This time Jacqueline did not manage to stifle a groan. Her mother shot her a disapproving look. Jacqueline hoped she would not lecture her on etiquette and for once she was spared.

"Oh, one more thing, first thing tomorrow morning you need to sit down with the secretary to answer most of these. It would not do to wait too long." She kissed her just above the ear and gracefully glided out of the room.

This time, Jacqueline did not stifle her frustration. She had worked so hard, stayed apart from the whole Olympic experience, that she felt entitled to some pleasure. Now that her competitions were done, she wanted to venture out and watch the skiing, the hockey games, and the bobsledding competitions still to come. She had missed most of the other competitions due to her diligent practice and training. Nine hours of the day had been dedicated to precisely orchestrated strength training, endurance, and dance, not to mention the hours spent on the ice. She was worn out. She needed a break! But she was not going to get one. This evening she was expected to accept the accolades of numerous important people she would never ever meet again, looking stunning and princess-like in her purple designer dress.

She suddenly found it hard to concentrate on the cards. The enjoyment she felt earlier had all but flown out of the window. Answering these had now become a tedious chore that would keep her from enjoying some of the competitions that remained. A knock on her door caused another frown. She was not ready for another session with her mother.

"Are you up for some company?" a cheerful voice turned the frown into a smile.

"Of course, Linda," she laughed. "You are always welcome."

Linda sat down Indian style on the soft area rug, covering the center of the room.

"This is a sweet house, Jacqueline," she complimented. Jacqueline smiled and pointed to all her correspondence.

"Wow, that is a lot of letters!" Linda whistled, impressed. "That's a good thing about staying in the village. There is no room for all these things. I guess I'll have to deal with them when I get back, though."

"I have to answer them by tomorrow," she explained to her friend and her frown increased when Linda laughed.

"Poor baby! Stop feeling sorry for yourself. You are an Olympic Champion! With that title comes quite a lot of responsibility," Linda pointed out grandly.

"I really don't want any more responsibility!" she sulked. "I have enough of that already." She really couldn't expect Linda to understand.

"Sorry, hon, but you got it," Linda replied, not at all sorry for her friend.

Together they made their way through the stack of telegrams.

"Tonight there is a party at the Sheraton hotel. It is going to be a lot of fun. Are you coming?" Linda asked as she waved a congratulatory note from the Australian President in front of her face.

"My parents have arranged for a small dinner here at the house. I won't be able to come with you tonight," she answered miserably. It sounded like it would be a lot of fun.

"That's all right," her friend reassured her. "There will be many others. Tomorrow is pairs skating. You are going to watch that, right? It should be a really exciting competition. I hope my American pals will do well," she added mischievously.

"I hope I can attend," Jacqueline sighed and rifled through more of the telegrams. It took her another two hours to go through the whole stack with Linda's help. By then the sun had disappeared beneath the horizon.

"Got to get ready for the party, girl," Linda laughed and got up off the floor. "Enjoy your dinner," she teased and rushed out the door, barely avoiding the pillow Jacqueline had flung in her direction.

She sighed and got up to ready herself for her own dinner party. She assumed the guests would not arrive until eight so she had plenty of time to get ready.

Chapter 5

Her body felt stiff from sitting all day and she needed to loosen up a little. Jacqueline really could not afford to get stiff at this point. She donned a pair of fur-lined boots, hat and gloves, wrapped a thick scarf around her neck and stepped outside in the bitter cold evening. She stood still for a moment, the cold seeping in through her warm coat. She proceeded to walk down the street and took in the twinkling of the lights in each of the houses. The chimneys were puffing white clouds into the wintry air.

Her face grew cold after only five minutes, but she didn't feel it. This time the previous night, she had paced back and forth with nerves, trying to go through her program in her head. The memory of the applauding and cheering audience warmed her up from the inside out. On the ice she felt alive. Maybe that was why she gave her skating everything. Her parents dinner party would feel empty compared to her time on the ice. With a sigh she turned back toward the house.

Upon returning to the house, she saw in the reflection on the glass in the front door that her cheeks and nose were bright red. She entered the small area beyond the door and shed her layers. She crossed the great room with its masonry fireplace that was giving off a huge amount of heat. She sat down on the stone bench, the heat seeping into her chilled bones. Within moments she was warm again and her nose was running. Comfortable arrays of couches were scattered around the large room, making little cozy areas to gather. It was a great place to sit and relax, as Jacqueline had discovered in the weeks leading up to the games. The wide spiral staircase wound itself behind the fireplace to the second story where the bedrooms were located. The landing doubled as a loft, outfitted with a large-screen TV and more comfortable couches, overlooking the great room.

"You were outside?" her mother asked as she came out of the study to the left side of the great room. Jacqueline nodded when her mother shook her head in disbelief. "You will catch pneumonia!" she said dramatically.

"Mother, I will not catch pneumonia from taking a five minute walk. I had to stretch my legs. My body was getting stiff from sitting around all day," she replied with a sigh. She hugged her mother quickly trying to appease her.

"You went through your correspondence, then?"

"Of course, Mother," Jacqueline answered and made her way up the stairs. She paused and reconsidered.

"Mother, there are a few events I would like to attend. One of them starts tomorrow. I think it would appease the media if I was seen cheering on my fellow skaters," she stated convincingly. She could play at the game very well too. She had been mastering the art of diplomacy her whole life. She was good at it.

"I understand, dear, and we will see what tomorrow brings. You still have interviews and other responsibilities," her mother stated, unconvinced. "We will have to consult your father."

Jacqueline sighed but nodded. "Mother, I would love to attend the events. I have not really had a chance to experience much of these games. I think it would be beneficial if I saw some competitions still ongoing, since I have won a medal and would be representing my country," Jacqueline made the last ditch effort to bend her mother to her ways.

All her mother did was smile and cup her chin in her perfectly manicured hands.

"Don't be in too much hurry to grow up, dear."

Jacqueline ascended the stairs shaking her head. She was sixteen! What was wrong with going to some events here at the Olympics? Who knew if she would ever achieve this level of competition again? It was not the first time she and her mother had disagreed on the level of independence she was trying to achieve. Anything to do with civil activity would gain her mother's stamp of approval. If, however, Jacqueline wanted to spend an evening with friends, who were practically non-existent at this time, she had to present her case as though before a judge.

"Oh, do remember to wear your medal for dinner tonight, dear. And guests are going to be arriving at six," her mother shouted up before Jacqueline closed her bedroom door behind her.

She let out an exasperated sigh! She had forty five minutes. Before she had to meet people she had no interest in ever meeting again, she was going to allow herself a leisurely soak in the tub.

As Jacqueline immersed herself in the steaming water, with sweet smelling bubbles, she once again recalled the events of the past week. The culmination of years of training had all led to this one event. She could still hear the applause of the audience when she stood at center ice. She loved skating! Really there was nothing out there that gave her the adrenaline rush such as jumping through the air and wondering if she would stay on her feet or if she would make a mistake in her takeoff only to land on her butt?

"Jacqueline, are you ready yet?" her mother's voice woke her from her near dream state.

"Not yet, Mother," she replied and watched, with regret, as the nice hot water disappeared down the drain.

She set about blow drying her thick, straight chestnut colored hair. It always took a long time. Once most of it was dried, she set about applying a touch of makeup. She really did not like wearing the stuff on a day-to-day basis. Tonight, however, her mother would insist she wear some. Next she donned the knee-length woolen dress hanging in her closet. She found that it really was a fairly comfortable dress. It looked nice with her blue-green eyes she supposed, and draped a white silk scarf to decorate the V-neck.

"Dear, are you ready? You are late," her mother scolded as she entered her bedroom.

She paused and looked at her daughter. "I suppose we can't deny that you are growing up, can we?" her eyes glistened with tears. "Oh dear," she murmured, "now my mascara is going to smudge."

She quickly dabbed at her eyes and fixed the small smudge.

"Mother," Jacqueline said as she put her arm around her mother. She was rewarded with a quick kiss on the cheek.

"Jacqueline, where is your medal? You are supposed to wear it tonight!" her mother scolded gently.

"Mother, please," Jacqueline rolled her eyes. "The medal is too much."

"No, the medal is a must. And don't roll your eyes at me, young lady!" her mother actually growled as she busied herself with getting the precious medal out of its velvety case to hang around her daughter's neck.

Once again she sniffed and tears threatened to spill out of her eyes. She quickly turned to the door.

"Last night, Jacqueline, was one of the proudest moment in my life." She sniffed one last time, squared her shoulders, lifted her chin, opened the door and smiled back at her daughter.

Jacqueline waited for a moment until the door shut. Her mother seldom complimented her for anything. She was pleasantly taken aback by her comment and it took a moment for her to regain her composure.

She checked herself one last time in the full-length mirror. The dress accented her lean, athletic body. Though she did not have the curves of her eldest sister, she did possess the poise of a dancer. It would have to do, she thought. She had styled her shoulder length hair to curl around her face, framing it softly because she always thought that her face was a little too angular. She blamed her rigorous training schedule and strict diet. During the summer she would allow herself to gain a few pounds.

She was ready to leave the safety of her bedroom. She squared her shoulders, tilted up her chin and opened the door. As she walked along the loft, she noticed that many people had already arrived and were carrying on pleasant conversations with each other. Applause rippled through the guests and by the time she reached the bottom stair, she felt thoroughly embarrassed. Jacqueline could enjoy accolades on the ice after a clean program but here this kind of attention never failed to make her squirm.

She smiled pleasantly and shook numerous hands, receiving air kisses from the women and hand kisses from the men. Everyone ogled her medal, which glistened when it caught the light. Slowly she made her way around the room, finally coming to rest next to Olivia, her mother's cousin. They smiled at each other and the hugs they exchanged were genuine.

By the time dinner was served, Jacqueline felt as though it was past midnight. She sighed as she sat between a young Norwegian businessman and a distant elderly German relative, whom she had just met for the first time. Unfortunately the relative was extremely deaf, so she had to repeat most of the things she said. The businessman on her left chuckled when she almost shouted that she indeed enjoyed skating on a pond. She shook her head and could not prevent a giggle to escape. She quickly reached for her water glass and set it to her lips, disguising her smile.

Dinner was a long drawn-out affair. There was a short speech given by the head of Lichtenbourgh's commerce in Norway, congratulating her and praising her for her resolve and athleticism. It rather embarrassed her and by the end of the speech, her face was thoroughly flushed. By the time dessert was served, Black Forest Cake, her favorite, her eyes felt heavy. Finally her father invited everyone into the great room for coffee. She breathed a sigh of relief and got up.

She longingly thought about the fun her friend was having tonight. And here she was, stuck at a dull party! She stifled a yawn, blinking her eyes. The conversation droned on around her. Why did she have to be the one stuck here with a bunch of old people? When would she ever have the chance to be herself? Only on the ice was she allowed that. The rest of the time she was a pawn in her parents' life.

When the last guest finally took his leave, Jacqueline felt as though she would not be able to make it up the stairs to her room.

"I think I shall sleep here on the couch," she informed her parents.

"In your dress!" her mother asked incredulously, while her father chuckled.

"Of course not," she grumbled and made her way clumsily up to her room, where she practically fell asleep undressing.

Chapter 6

She woke to someone shaking her shoulder. She batted the hand away only to be rewarded by a more persistent shake.

"Give me a little more time," she grumbled again batting at the hand.

"It is past nine. The secretary has just arrived and is waiting for you to answer your well wishers!" Her mother's voice cut through the fog in her brain.

"Mother, can't I wait 'til tomorrow to answer them?" she asked, her voice crackling badly.

Jacqueline shouldn't have bothered, because her mother lectured her about responsibility and duty to her country. Jacqueline rolled her eyes, again, and threw off the covers. She stomped into the bathroom and closed the door none too gently. Within twenty minutes she arrived downstairs in the kitchen to grab a quick bowl of fruit and a cup of hot chocolate, hold the cream.

"There you are, dear," murmured her mother, who sat with her father at the kitchen table by a beautiful picture window. Snow was falling in buckets.

"Father, could I go to the arena and watch the pairs skating tonight?" Jacqueline asked hopefully. "I should be supporting the sport, and since I won a medal, it might encourage my fellow skaters." She could see her father contemplating her request. She smiled into her bowl of fruit.

"I suppose you could sit in our box," her mother finally conceded after discussing the situation with her father.

She shot her mother an exasperated glance. "Oh Mother. Linda is going to be there too." She watched as her mother's face became grave and almost green.

"You can't possibly want to sit in the stands," her mother gasped and pulled a face. "They are dirty and crowded."

"Mother, please. How would it look if I sat high above the crowd? It would seem a little aloof. Think of the press," she explained patiently. *Oh yeah! I know how to push my mother's buttons.*

Her parents agreed to allow her to sit with her friend if she promised to come straight home after the competition. She agreed readily and felt a lot better going into the long session with the secretary, with whom she tediously sent thank you letters for the flowers and the telegrams.

Jacqueline rushed off to change out of her jeans and sweatshirt and donned a very nice navy blue woolen pantsuit and a white blouse. The limousine took her straight to the temporarily studio in the Olympic Village. She endured their endless questions and even managed to make some witty comments. Jacqueline smiled into the cameras, giving them the perfect picture of the *perfect* skating princess. When the lights dimmed, she took a deep breath. It was over!

She politely thanked the young reporter and left the studio. Meeting Fiona as planned to practice for the Gala event, they put together a fun program quickly. After practice, Linda met her at the entrance to the ice.

"I hope you two won't get into trouble," Fiona commented with a smile.

Jacqueline was excited. This was the first time she had been able to get out on her own. Linda enjoyed riding in the warmed up limo instead of once again having to rely on the bus to get into town. Though snow had accumulated on the roads, crews were working tirelessly to clear and sand them.

"What have you been doing all day?" she asked her friend and slowly stretched, feeling her tired muscles complain.

"First I met the captain of the American Hockey team for breakfast," Linda answered and winked. "We had a blast. He's really nice. Then I shopped around Lillehammer. You can't believe how many people stopped me and congratulated me. Then I had lunch with a bunch of speed skaters, and that was a riot, I tell you. What have you been up to?" she asked.

Jacqueline frowned and told her about her day answering questions and working on her program for the gala event. Linda patted her hand sympathetically.

"Just think of the bright side," she encouraged.

"There is a bright side?" she grumbled and winced when Linda pinched her arm.

"Of course there is a bright side. You are now free to do what you want. We are going out to dinner in the town!" she laughed and Jacqueline smiled brightly.

The streets were alive with so many visitors that Jacqueline almost lost sight of Linda. She followed her into a boisterous pub where they sat down to eat. Both were recognized immediately and they signed so many hats, boots, gloves and other pieces of apparel, their fingers cramped. After dinner, which stretched longer than it should have, they had to hurry to make it to the arena in time.

All they had to do was flash their Olympic badges to gain admittance. The Hammer Olympic Amphitheater, where the skating took place, was packed to the full. The event had not begun and both girls found it difficult to get to their assigned seats. Everywhere they turned, admiring fans asked them to sign scraps of paper, programs and clothing and insisted on having their pictures taken with the girls.

"This is really exciting!" Jacqueline shouted above the roar of the crowd.

Linda laughed and nodded. They shook hands with their neighbors and people behind them. The captain of the American Hockey team, Alex Hamilton, joined Linda, and Jacqueline could tell that they got along extremely well. Other skaters came and joined them and soon they were a boisterous, joking crowd. Watching from the stands was a different experience for Jacqueline. She didn't have to worry about anything and she found herself relaxing and enjoying the company of her fellow athletes.

"Jacqueline!" One of the Swedish speed skaters jumped over the seat behind her and plopped down next to her in the vacant seat. "That was very fine skating you did last night," he told her and winked at her. Her eyebrows raised in surprise and she felt herself blush against her better judgment.

"Thank you," she mumbled and took a sip of the huge soda she had purchased from a vendor. She grinned when she thought about what her mother would say about that.

"So, you want to watch me skate?" her neighbor asked looking at her with puppy eyes.

"Eh, I don't know if I can," she managed to reply.

"I would love it if you came," he continued.

"I can't make it to too many events. I really had to beg to get out tonight," she restated with a smile. She excused herself for a moment and grabbed Linda.

"I am out of my comfort zone here, Linda. The guy is getting a little too pushy," she stammered.

"I'll get rid of him for you," her friend reassured Jacqueline.

Very skillfully Linda managed to ask Lars, for that was his name, to get them some more munchies. He bounded off to do so, and Linda deftly inserted herself into the seat, making sure there was someone on Jacqueline's other side.

"Thank you," she mumbled and almost felt bad for Lars who, when he returned, looked longingly at the seat next to her.

The competition soon started and Jacqueline enjoyed the skating of her pairs colleagues. She marveled at the beauty of their moves and loved the way their jumps and spins were synchronized. It was well past midnight when Jacqueline and Linda left the arena. Again they were accosted for their autographs on the way out and found themselves signing anything the fans handed them. Linda looked over at Jacqueline when they finally made their way past the crowd.

"Do you want to come with me to a party?"

She badly wanted to join her friend, but she knew that she couldn't possibly. Her parents would expect her home and she had promised them to return immediately after the competition. While they walked out into the chilly night, she still debated whether to join Linda. In the end she decided that she needed to honor her parent's wishes.

"I need to get back," she grumbled and looked down at the snow around her.

"That's fine. There will always be a next time, kiddo." Linda hugged her and followed her fellow athletes. Jacqueline watched her hook her arm through that of Alex, the hockey team captain. Jacqueline looked after her friend longingly.

The limousine took Jacqueline back to the quiet of the house where she promised herself that soon she would go out and have fun.

Chapter 7

Her chance to go to a party never came. During the day she still had numerous interviews to attend. The evenings were full of social engagements. She managed to watch the downhill skiing with her mother's cousin, Olivia and her children. They cheered and groaned when skiers slid into posts or ended up in piles of skis and poles on the hard slope.

"I am glad I chose skating," she laughed.

"My dear," Olivia frowned seriously, "the ice is just as hard." Everyone laughed at that obvious statement.

Too soon the games were over. Jacqueline was sad when she walked with her fellow athletes to the closing ceremony. This had been an experience she would never forget. She laughed at the antics of her comrades as they hugged each other and blew kisses at the cheering crowd. She didn't join in because she knew her parents would be mortified if she acted in any way other than in a dignified manner. However, part of her itched to throw a snowball at Linda or at another one of her competitors. Watching the Olympic flame being extinguished, she would do anything to be back here in four years.

The private plane was waiting on the tarmac. The tail showed the golden lion, the royal crest.

Jacqueline entered through the small door and proceeded past the pilot and co-pilot, who were busy with pre-flight checklist. This was her favorite of their small fleet of planes owned by the royal family. It was also the newest. The white walls were almost too bright, had it not been for the dark molding and beige seats. This was one of the largest of their planes. The carpet was off white, proudly displaying their royal emblem in golden contrast. As soon as they settled into their seats her father turned his leather chair toward her. Her mother settled into her seat next to her father, pulling the buckle tight. Jacqueline would have rather reclined on the couch, at the back of the plane, but during takeoff and landing, she knew better.

The flight attendant smiled brilliantly when she welcomed them on board.

"Congratulations on your win, Princess. It was such a pleasure watching you and knowing our country was so well represented. It brought tears to my eyes." Jacqueline smiled back at her and accepted the soft drink.

The flight attendant informed them that they were waiting for takeoff and would be on their way shortly. She advised them of a storm off the coast of England. They were in for a very bumpy ride. Jacqueline felt the blood drain out of her face. She hated flying as it was, but flying in a storm was so much worse.

"My dear," he said seriously while they were waiting for takeoff, sipping his drink in a clear crystal glass, brought by the attendant on the dark mahogany tray. "Your mother and I have been thinking about your studies and training. You are going to be studying at home from now on. We have already arranged for a tutor. We know you will not be happy about this, Jacqueline. But the rink has been sitting around unused for far too long and our people are getting upset that you are not there to use it. Since you are now such a celebrity, we think the people would love to see you more. Fiona has agreed to stay in Lichtenbourgh. She will be granted an apartment and, of course, a bonus in her salary," her father continued as they were waiting.

"You see, dear," her mother added quickly as she noticed Jacqueline's stony face, "our country needs you at home, dear."

Jacqueline frowned and looked out the window. Her country needed her at home! It was always about her country, wasn't it? It was never about what Jacqueline wanted. What Jacqueline needed. She enjoyed her time at school in the south of England. She had had some semblance of freedom. If she stayed home, she would have none. She would be at the mercy of her parents and their social schedule.

"Would you please reconsider? I am in the middle of studying for my A-levels and baccalaureates. I would like to apply to university in the United States."

Her parents looked at each other in alarm.

"The United States is too far away, Jacqueline. It is out of the question!" her father boomed resolutely.

Her mother nodded her head. Jacqueline decided that now was not the time to pick a fight. She busied herself with her seat belt as the plane took off. Her body pressed into her leather seat as the plane sped down the runway and she felt the familiar weightlessness and the momentary panic of falling. Jacqueline turned to her parents.

"May I suggest something," she asked quietly and politely. "If I decide to study with a tutor, stay and skate at home, would you reconsider allowing me to go to the United States for university?"

"Haven't I said it over and over again? She is a born diplomat," her father beamed proudly at her. "I will consider it."

"Very well, then I agree," she said slowly, "to *consider* staying home." Her father laughed and his eyes twinkled.

As they ascended through the thickening clouds, she was rewarded with one last look at the snow covered village with the beautiful mountains and lake that surrounded Lillehammer. Within ten minutes they had reached their cruising altitude. The flight attendant was correct. It was a bouncy ride, to say the least. The wind tossed the plane about as easily as a pebble; Jacqueline could feel her stomach grumble and heave.

Her mother saw her expression and put her hand over her daughter's. "It's all right, dear. Think of it as a ride on a roller coaster."

"I hate roller coasters," she mumbled.

"Dear Jacqueline, we would love for you to be able to go anywhere to study, but think on how you leaving again would reflect on our country. There are excellent universities just across the border. Please consider staying after you graduate in the spring," her father continued the conversation they had started and was set to debate with her.

She looked at him and took a deep breath. "Dear Father, I realize that, but you sent me to schools overseas from the beginning. Besides, I am willing to stay here while I study for my entrance exams. With those under my belt, I can go anywhere in the world. I realize that there are more opportunities in the States, since they have a lot more colleges and universities for what I am interested in." she countered with a smile.

She knew her father loved to discuss things diplomatically. It was something the two of them did as often as they could.

"And what, my dearest youngest daughter, could you be interested in that you need to go all the way to the US to study?" her mother asked a little cautiously.

Jacqueline hesitated for a moment, knowing full well that she was about have the discussion she really didn't want to have. She knew that she would have to fight for the dream of her future. She knew her parents would have a hard time accepting the career path she had chosen.

Jacqueline could not keep on skating forever. The life span of a figure skater was limited. After she had retired from the sport, she wanted to do something that, unfortunately, her parents would not approve of. While at boarding school she had begun to work with a local veterinarian. She loved the challenge of the profession and enjoyed spending her days with animals, mostly farm animals. Growing up she had been known to bring home stray animals, patching them up and finding them homes among various family members. Jacqueline absolutely loved horses and had debated with herself on whether to hang up her skates and take up competing in equestrian events instead. In the end, skating had won.

Jacqueline sighed as she considered how to answer her father's question without sending her parents to an early grave. It was in that moment, that the bottom dropped out from under them. Jacqueline grabbed the arm rests as though she could keep them aloft with all of her own strength. Over the next five minutes, the plane began to shudder as the winds tossed it about. There was a great clatter in the small galley as the plane bounced from side to side and up and down. China with the the family crest shattered all over the floor. Her knuckles were white and Jacqueline thought her fingers would leave indentations in the soft, leather armrests. Just as quickly as the plane dropped, it steadied itself again for an instant.

It didn't take long for the plane to take a nosedive again, engines screaming. Jacqueline's stomach swapped places with her heart. Her parents must have felt the same way because soon the cabin was filled with synchronized screams. The Olympic judges would have given them high marks. Jacqueline thought the plane would never stop falling, when it finally leveled out again. Air bags dangling in front of her, hands shakily reaching up to grab hers, she almost couldn't hook the elastic around her head. The compartment was a mess. Contents of the galley were strewn all over the place. As the plane climbed its way back up through the shearing wind in the rear, a violent shudder sounded.

Jacqueline's stomach had no time to settle down when they leveled out and dove toward the sea level again. Jacqueline could see the huge waves below them as the plane struggled to stay barely above the raging sea. It only took another second when they started climbing again. Again her heart and stomach switched places and this time the drink and snack she had consumed before takeoff made it known that they did not like this shift. She wanted to wretch all over the compartment. Her head was spinning as the plane leveled out again only to start climbing up and up. Her mother reached for the paper bag that rested next to her seat. Her father's face was white. It looked as though he might succumb to the turbulence and lose the contents of his stomach in the near future. Jacqueline had barely enough time to reach for hers, when she emptied the contents of her stomach into it. Again and again the plane was tossed about. Her stomach was totally empty and she thought she would pass out if the plane took another dive. It did but she remained conscious. Her head was splitting and during the downward dive she allowed herself to let go of her armrests to hold her hurting head down.

"God in heaven," she moaned desperately, "please help us!"

Her head miraculously remained upon her neck but it was pounding as though someone had taken a hammer to it. Jacqueline was exhausted and she didn't really care anymore whether the plane was upside down or right side up. She wanted to rest her sore head. Tears were streaming down her cheeks. In that moment the screaming of the engines died and there was an eerie silence. The only noise was that of the whistling of the wind. The plane tossed to and fro by the wind that battered it unrelentingly.

"Please, God, if you are out there, don't let us die now," she pleaded and moaned when the plane dove down toward the sea again.

It seemed as though they were almost at sea level when the engines coughed to life and once again the plane climbed rapidly. As the curtain that separated the main cabin from the cockpit swung open, she could see the captain and co-captain fighting to keep control of the plane. Tears streamed down the flight attendant's cheeks. Her eyes were shut tightly and her lips were moving rapidly. She was clutching the picture of her daughter and husband.

At long last the storm relented and the plane leveled out and remained steady. She took a deep breath and wiped her wet face. Her hand came back covered in blood. She gaped at it, not really comprehending what she was looking at. The co-captain turned toward his three passengers, face shining with sweat, and informed them loudly that they would be descending into Hamburg for an emergency landing.

Jacqueline couldn't care less. She was surprised that her head had not split in two. It was hurting her so much she felt that she was cross-eyed. Her mother's face was glistening with sweat and her eyes were scrunched closed. She was moaning softly. Her father placed a hand on his wife's arm and let it rest there. He looked at his wife in grave concern and shot Jacqueline a worried look. Jacqueline was told to recline and the attendant pressed a cool cloth onto the bridge of her nose to staunch the flow of blood.

By the time they landed in Hamburg, her headache had started to subside and she almost felt normal. Her mother, however, was still deathly pale. Her seat was reclined all the way, allowing her to lie back. The flight attendant was hovering about her. Jacqueline swallowed hard. Her mother really didn't look good.

They landed in Hamburg where emergency vehicles stood by and they were rushed to the hospital. By the time the doctors poked and prodded her, speaking in rapid German, Jacqueline was back to normal. She was given a clean bill of health along with her father. Her mother was admitted to the hospital due to her continued headaches.

Her father decided to stay in town until her mother would be released. They were escorted to their usual hotel, which was situated at the beautiful inner city lake. Bellhops scurried about to accommodate them and to take them up to their suite. As soon as she stepped into her room, she collapsed onto the bed and sleep consumed her.

Chapter 8

"Jacqueline, you need to wake up now."

Jacqueline heard through a heavy fog that refused to lift, and she slapped the hand that insisted on prodding her awake. When she finally managed to open her eyes, she had trouble remembering just where she was. Then it dawned on her. The plane! Her mother was still in the hospital! Her eyes focused on the person who had shaken her. Her father was looking down on her, a worried look on his face.

"Are you up, dear?" he asked. She nodded and stretched.

"How are you feeling?" he asked, and put a cool hand on her forehead.

She thought for a moment, stretched again and answered slowly, "I don't think there are any lingering side effects."

Her father patted her hand and smiled crookedly.

"How is Mother?" she asked, as she sat up.

"The hospital just called. She's had a rough night. She is resting in recovery and we will be able to see her this afternoon," he told her quietly.

"What do you mean, resting in recovery? Will she be all right?" she gasped and got up quickly.

"They operated on her for a brain aneurysm. That is all I know at this point. But she is recovering, as I said."

Jacqueline hugged her father quickly. Her father's voice was strained with concern for his wife.

"I'm sure she will pull through, Father," she said softly. He shot her a ghost of a smile and squeezed her hand. Her mother could have died! Jacqueline blinked the tears, burning in the eyes, away. It would not do to succumb to her emotions. She needed to be strong. Her parents demanded it. Her parents and her country demanded it!

"Yes, I'm sure she will. We are stuck here because the plane is under repair. I suppose we could be stranded in a worse place," he chuckled, and pointed out the huge windows overlooking the Alster, the large lake that glimmered in the winter sun. "How about we have some breakfast? Then I am going to the hospital. Do you want to come with me?" he asked.

"Of course I will come," she grumbled, a little offended that he even had to ask. "I am not staying here when my mother is in the hospital, ill."

She bit her bottom lip to keep it from quivering. "I am so glad we made it. I thought we were done for," she whispered and her voice cracked.

Her father nodded slowly and paced back and forth, hands clasped behind his back.

"Yes, I don't think I have ever been so afraid in my life as yesterday," he admitted, as he paced toward the window. Jacqueline knew that it took a lot for her father to admit a weakness. Fear was a weakness!

"You know I even asked God to help us. Glad we are still here," she chuckled. Her father flashed a quick smile at her.

"I know what you mean. It is a good idea to call on the Almighty when all else has failed." The statement hung in the air between them for a moment. Then her father shook his head. He took a step away from her and cleared his throat. "Jacqueline, shall I call for room service or would you rather go downstairs?" he asked as she made her way into the bathroom, her feet sinking into the thick, soft carpet. Their heart to heart was over!

"I think the less people know we are here the better it will be for us," she said as she closed the door. "I opt for room service, don't you agree?"

The hot water felt wonderful. Her body felt as though it had been through a fight or a marathon of 24-hour training. It made her shudder when she recalled the screaming of the engines followed by the dives and the weightlessness. The fear as they plummeted toward the sea as well as when she called out to the Almighty was permanently etched in her brain. She was glad that her plea had been answered, or had it just been chance that they had made it through? The more she thought about it, chance was the more plausible explanation. The thought of an all-powerful being taking care of her - having an interest in her - was just too unbelievable. Jacqueline turned off the water and stepped out to dry off. It felt wonderful to be clean again. In fact, it was wonderful to breathe air. Thoughts fell on her mother.

She hoped that her mother would be all right as she could not imagine her life without her. She was not ready to lose her yet, or for that matter, ever.

"Did you call the family?" she asked as she sat next to her father for breakfast and reached for a toasted croissant.

"Yes, they are very concerned with your mother's state."

Jean, her oldest brother, had offered to come and stay with them, he told her. Her father had told him to stay and mind the home front. He had done so, reluctantly.

Queen Dominique sat pale in her bed when they entered. She looked beautiful with her pallid skin and dark brown hair. She smiled sleepily at them as they entered.

"Oh thank God you two are well. What a frightening experience!" she said as Jacqueline gave her a kiss on the cheek.

"Are you feeling better, dear?" her father asked as he gently took his wife's hand in his.

"I am fine now. I must admit it was a bit of a shock to find myself in the recovery room in the middle of the night. The doctors are very good here, Francois," she told him softly.

After they visited for a while, her doctor came in and explained what had happened. They assumed that she had a previously undetected aneurysm in her brain. The surgeons were worried that it would burst so they had performed the emergency procedure. The doctor assured them that there were no serious complications but that they would monitor her closely for the next 48 hours. He didn't think that they would keep her more than a week.

"Francois, Jacqueline needs to go home," her mother said resolutely, as soon as the doctor left the room. "She cannot afford to stay here with a major competition coming up so soon," she continued, decisively.

"But dear, shouldn't she stay until you are well enough for us to return together?"

"Darling, think about it. She is a representative of our country at the World Championships. Think about the publicity that would bring."

Jacqueline sighed inwardly. Although she almost resented being used as public relations, she was glad her mother insisted she should leave. After a short discussion, her parents decided to send her home as soon as possible. They talked for a little while and her mother closed her eyes for a moment. Her face looked strained and tired.

"Are you in pain, dear?" her father jumped out of his chair to be by his wife's side.

"No. I am just tired," she allowed and yawned. She looked at her youngest daughter.

"You go home and practice. I am counting on you to stay on your feet again. You must win this competition for your country."

Jacqueline almost moaned out loud. She did not need any extra pressure.

"Of course, Mother, I will do my best."

"Good. Now, you two, I need to rest. I will see you tomorrow, all right?" she closed her eyes and sighed.

In the end, her father managed to get a replacement plane. It would arrive in the afternoon, along with her oldest sister Sharon and her fiancé, who would stay with her parents.

When Jacqueline found out that Sharon was on her way she felt a twinge of bitterness. Sharon, the eldest daughter, could always be depended upon in times of crisis. She had always been obedient to a fault to her parents, listening to their advice and following it to the letter, including her choice of husband. *Not like her youngest sister at all*, Jacqueline thought.

Responding to a knock on the door she opened it, allowing her immaculately dressed and styled sister to enter. Sharon stormed into the room with her usual take-charge attitude. Her fiancé, Antonio, Italian by birth, followed her. He winked at Jacqueline as he sauntered up to her father with his usual flair, and shook his hand respectfully. Jacqueline chuckled. She liked Antonio, who had a bit of a come-what-may attitude. What didn't hurt was his dark, good looks. Sharon balanced out that 'bad boy' image with her no-nonsense attitude.

"Jacqueline, dear," Sharon commanded her after a quick hug. "The plane is waiting to take you home. I do hope you make the most of your time. Would you be a dear and fetch me some water, I'm parched." She strode past her and hugged her father.

Jacqueline felt that barb in her heart. Sharon always had the ability to make her feel small, inconsequential and not worth her time. This time, what hurt the most, was that Sharon had not even made mention of Jacqueline's success. So like her mother!

"How is Mother?" Sharon asked as she led their father to a cushy sofa and sat next to him. "Antonio, would you be a dear and call up for a quick lunch for three," she smiled at her fiancé, who was standing by the window staring out into the city.

"Of course, my love, but there are four of us here," he said winking at Jacqueline again.

"Yes, dear, I can count but Jacqueline is leaving. Plus I am sure she is counting her calories again to stay trim and in top shape."

Ouch, that hurt! Jacqueline picked up her small overnight bag.

"I suppose I will get going," she murmured and walked over to her father to give him a hug.

"Wait Jacqueline," Antonio called after her. "I'll walk down to the car with you. There is a mob out there."

He smiled at her when she sent him a thankful nod. He was right. Security tightened around her as reporters swarmed them. Questions about her mother's condition flooded toward her. Oh, how she despised this! Antonio and the security team were able to whisk her through the throng without a comment to anyone.

"By the way, Jacqueline, I just wanted to tell you how impressed I was by your skating. You were great. Everyone at home is so proud of you." He reached out and squeezed her arm.

"Ah, Antonio, I am so glad Sharon is marrying you. You know just what to say," she smiled as she hopped into the back seat of the car and waved as they pulled away quickly.

She loathed the thought of going back to Lichtenbourgh. She would have preferred to return to school, where she actually had some choices, some freedom from the responsibilities that waited for her at home. It was true that she didn't have many friends there either. She had been too busy with her training and her studies to make any meaningful friendships. She couldn't allow herself to trust any of the girls who tried to get her attention. She always thought that they were too catty and fake. Being who she was, Jacqueline was never sure of their true feelings. She had experienced that most of the girls wanted to be her friend because of what she was, not of who she was. It made making friends very difficult. Most of her fellow students had something to gain from making a connection with her family. Skating fit perfectly into her solitary existence. But at least at school she was free from her parents and their endless social obligations. At home she was alone. There was no one for her to talk to while her family was so busy running the country.

Chapter 9

The plane trip home was uneventful. When the plane landed in Lichten, the capital of the mountainous country between Switzerland and France, a country of 100,000 citizens, she breathed a sigh of relief. Jacqueline was glad to be in the limousine heading to the palace. News of her return must have spread, for despite the cold, many of the 50,000 inhabitants lined the streets. Waving to her, trying to get a glimpse of their favorite skating champ and princess, Jacqueline returned their waves and smiles, receiving them enthusiastically. The quaint old town was decked out in celebration. Flags were flying high as she passed down the main street whose charming old houses seemed to lean into the street.

Soon the gates of the palace came into view. As palaces were concerned, it was not a bad place to live. The oldest part, which now housed the official ballroom and offices, had been started in 1650, completed in 1720. Its towers were still beautiful and as a little girl Jacqueline had imagined that she was Cinderella. The newer section of the palace, where the family now lived, was built in the 1800s. Her ancestors must have wanted to placate the Russian Tzar at the time, since it looked like a miniature Winter Palace. As they pulled up to the front of the main palace, a uniformed doorman jumped to open the car door for her. He bowed low as she quickly exited and approached the palace. Once she was inside, uniformed servants scrambled to relieve her of her coat and to retrieve her luggage. She smiled her thanks.

"Where would my brother be?" she asked as a formally dressed butler removed her coat.

"Your Royal Highness, at present he would be with parliament. The session should be out soon. Your sister is in her suite. She has been anxiously awaiting your arrival."

Jacqueline groaned at the thought of Marie anxiously awaiting for her anywhere. As she walked up the grand marble staircase leading to the private living area of the family, she hoped that Marie would at least take into consideration that she had just won the Olympic gold medal and had represented her country well. She walked down the long corridor, passing formal portraits of generations of ancestors, long deceased, making her feel small and inconsequential. She paused in front of Marie's suites and took a deep breath. Sharon was a pussy cat compared to Marie. Marie sat on her bed, a laptop next to her. She smiled without displaying any real warmth as Jacqueline entered.

"There you are, sis," she greeted her. "Congratulations," she beamed, sarcasm lacing her every word. "You actually did something for this country."

"Ouch, I can feel the love," Jacqueline grimaced and flopped down in one of the overstuffed sofas.

"Jacqueline, you are always so sensitive. All that time training actually paid off. I was wondering why Mother and Father allowed your indulgences. It was a smart move on their part. Now we will have tourists flocking to the country and our economy will flourish. Well done, little sis," her older sister said bitterly and patted her on the head.

The two of them had a difficult relationship. Marie was artistic, beautiful and temperamental. She had a beautiful voice but she had given up singing to pursue a more acceptable occupation, accepting the wishes of her parents. As a result, she envied her youngest sister, who could do as she pleased. If Jacqueline could convince her parents to allow her to study in the States, she knew that her relationship with Marie would deteriorate to its lowest point.

"I'm glad I could do my part," she replied graciously through gritted teeth, and shoved her sister's hand away from her head.

"I was trying to figure out how to capitalize on your success. You know I'm developing a web site for the country. What do you think about this photo?" she asked, pointing to a picture at the British Junior Nationals three years ago, where she had ended up on her rear end. Jacqueline smiled wryly and nodded.

"Sure, Marie, if you *don't* want to encourage tourism. I suggest you find something with me and my gold medal, looking princess-like and preferably smiling," she smirked without warmth. "Like that one." She pointed to a picture with her on the medal stand smiling. "Yes, that would be much better."

"Fine, fine; we'll take that one," Marie grumbled and clicked on the picture to upload it to the website. "By the way, Jean wants to see you when he comes home to talk about the reception planned for

63

this weekend," she informed her. "We all know how much you like the attention."

Jacqueline managed not to groan out loud. Her sister was grating on her. Marie was very consumed with who she was. Her attitude was one that the people owed her something. She made sure that everyone knew that she was someone important. Wherever Marie went, she loved being the center of attention. Now that Jacqueline actually made a bigger contribution to her country than Marie ever could, she knew how hard it must be for Marie to have to watch her baby sister take the center stage. Jacqueline, on the other hand, always balked at her public responsibilities. She hated being on display anywhere other than on the ice.

"How is Mother?" Marie asked conversationally, as she strolled to her private bar and poured herself a glass of wine.

"She looked pale and weak," Jacqueline replied. She pulled her face into a disgusted grimace. "Isn't it a little too early for a glass of wine?"

"Jacqueline, wake up to reality. It is never too early for a glass of wine," Marie smirked, taking a particularly large gulp. "You want some?" she teased, knowing Jacqueline would get upset at her. Jacqueline rose and smiled sweetly at her older sister.

"It is killing you that I actually did something that was of more worth than what you do, isn't it? You know, you could be beautiful, if you weren't so green with envy, Marie." Jacqueline watched as the glass in Marie's hand started to shake dangerously. Her sister's eyes darted to her and her face screwed up in a nasty scowl.

"You spoiled little wench," she growled. "I'm going to make sure you are going to regret those words, little sister!"

Jacqueline grumbled to herself and felt anger set in. Somehow Marie always managed to make her angry! She goaded her to be at her worst, whereas Sharon only ignored her and made her feel unimportant. She wasn't sure which was easier to deal with. She hurried down the long corridor. She would do anything to get away from her sister.

She made her way to the huge kitchen to find something to fill her stomach. She settled on some fruit, knowing that tomorrow she would be back in full training.

"Ah Princess Jacqueline, it is good to see you are alive. We were so worried about you. And how is Her Majesty getting along in the hospital? How is His Majesty holding up?" the head chef asked as she was leaving. "And may I congratulate you on your fabulous win. You made us so proud. To see one of our own stand upon the top of the podium was so special."

"Thank you so much, George. I was glad to be there. The whole experience was something I will never forget. It was wonderful."

"The whole palace staff was watching you," the old man's wrinkled face beamed at her. She smiled back.

George had served the family since her grandparents, and she remembered him sneaking her little treats now and then. He had four children himself and was a soft, round man with twinkling blue eyes. Jacqueline always thought he was Santa Claus in disguise. In fact, one time when the children were little, he had dressed up and delivered presents. Jacqueline chuckled as she remembered, grabbing a cup of tea.

Walking thoughtfully back to her room, she encountered well-wishing servants. The atmosphere in the palace was more relaxed when her parents were not there. When they were there a distinct crisp feeling filled the palace. She almost preferred it when they weren't in residence. She supposed that she had learned from an early age, with the attendance of numerous rigid nursemaids and tutors, to abhor anything remotely stiff and proper.

She managed to get out for a long run. It left her winded. Jean caught up with her outside her room just as she was about to head to the shower.

"Little sister," he folded her into a bear hug.

At twenty-eight, he was already showing some gray in his dark brown hair near his temple area. His gray eyes looked tired and worn. Yet he beamed down from his six foot height at his little sister and kissed her cheek.

"Thank you so much for what you have accomplished," he praised her. "You should see the newspapers. They are full of praises. The people love you," he paused, "Let us sit down and chat," he opened her door.

"Jean," she said quietly. "I am standing here dripping with sweat from a run. Would you mind if I showered and changed before we have our little chat?" she smirked at her older brother.

"Oh," he muttered, blushed slightly and stepped away. "So sorry I didn't notice the sweat pouring down. I did ask myself why you were so smelly, but I really took no notice of the sweat thingy," he chuckled.

"Do you mean to tell me that I stink?" she asked him incredulously and punched his arm. He winced and rubbed the sore spot.

"I had to be honest," he grinned. Jacqueline grunted and shot him a disgusted look as she turned abruptly and walked away.

Chapter 10

Twenty minutes later Jacqueline and Jean sat together by the window sipping hot spiced cider.

"You look tired, Jean," she said softly.

He raked a hand through his perfectly cut hair. "Thank you, Jacqueline. Like I needed to hear that. With Mother and Father away I have taken on all of Father's responsibilities. This is a hard job, you know. Everyone is entitled to their opinion and they all have to be taken into consideration and," he looked at his little sister who was rolling her eyes at him. "I suppose you want me to stop complaining, right?"

"I suppose you are entitled to complain some. But Jean, you were born and bred for this job," she smiled as he groaned.

They talked more about how difficult it was to rule a country. She made fun of his complaints. He, in turn, made fun of her. They laughed for a while. Jacqueline felt herself relax a little. She bit her bottom lip, contemplating whether she should tell him of her future plans. If anyone could understand her, it was him.

"I might as well drop my bombshell on you first, Jean. You are not going to like it, but here it is. I want to become a veterinarian. It is your fault, really, that I have chosen this. You and that hawk we had with the broken wing, do you remember?" she asked and lowered her eyes.

On one of Jean's holidays they had come across an injured hawk. They had taken it home and had nursed it back to health. After Jean had returned to school, Jacqueline had released it. Though it remained close to the palace for months, it eventually left one day.

Jean's face turned to stone as he looked at his youngest sister, whom he loved with all his heart. He also knew that his parents had indulged her because she was the youngest. Jean knew that eventually she would have to give up on her dreams as well as the rest of them for the good of their country.

"Jacqueline you can't become a vet," he said seriously. "It is not something we, as representatives of this country, are expected to do. You need to think of something else. You could become a sports reporter for our local television news station," he said hopefully.

"Are you kidding me? Please tell me you are!" She felt her heart start to race and her face get flushed. "I don't want to report on some sports event. Where is the challenge in that?"

"Oh Jacqueline, calm down," he grumbled. He reached out to touch her shoulder and she moved away, face red in anger. "It is not about what you want. You have to remember that we are here to serve the country. It is our duty. There is no *you*. Our parents have been kind to let you pursue your dreams, but eventually you will have to come to terms with the fact that you are a servant of the people," he said sternly through narrowed eyes.

"I don't really care, Jean!" she shot back angrily. He was really making her mad! She had every right to pursue her dream.

"Jacqueline, be reasonable. You are the daughter of the King of Lichtenbourgh. Granted, it is a country not many people know or even think about, but our citizens depend upon us for leadership and representation. That is what your future will be. Patching up animals doesn't do anything to promote this country. It is time for you to wake up and join the family business. We all have to eventually!" he shot right back at her, got up and started pacing.

"I want to go and study in the United States!" she told him stubbornly, her face set and her arms folded tightly across her chest.

"Don't be such a baby, Jacqueline. This is not up for debate," he roared, his face turning red.

"You have changed, Jean. You used to be a lot more fun," she growled and turned away from him.

"This is me, Jacqueline." He pointed at himself. "Wake up to reality! You are not free to choose what you wish to do. There are responsibilities waiting for you. If you want to be a vet, why not take care of children? I have heard it said that they are almost the same as animals."

"You have got to be joking!" she snarled angrily. "Children or animals?! There is no difference!? I can't even talk to you about this right now! I'm leaving!" she growled and rushed out of the room.

She stormed back a moment later. "Never mind, this is my room," she grumbled and locked eyes with her brother.

She was steaming mad! But as she started to calm down, she realized how ridiculous they were and she cracked a smile, which turned into a wide grin. Jean stared at her and his face cracked into the same grin. They both began to laugh. After a moment or so she had tears running down her cheeks. She flopped down onto her sofa and wiped her face with the back of her hand.

"Jacqueline, Jacqueline, what are we going to do with you?" Jean gasped when he had a chance to take a breath. "You must try to be more accommodating, please."

"You can't expect me to do something just to appease the family. Look at Marie. I just realized why she is always so grumpy. She is miserable."

"Don't be ridiculous. She is not. She loves her study at the university. And her university is in Switzerland; twenty minutes away! She didn't insist on following her own desires. You need to get with the program. You are not a child anymore," he grumbled. They sat quietly for a long time.

"Jean, I am already not just skating for myself," Jacqueline said slowly, realization setting in. "Do you think that I am out there six to eight hours a day for my own satisfaction alone? Granted I love to skate and find it satisfying but going to the Olympics made me realize that I am representing my country. And to tell you the truth, that brings me pleasure at the same time," she explained and they sat in silence again. "I'll tell you what," she continued as an idea hit her. *Ever the diplomat*, she could hear her father's voice in her head. "If I promise to continue skating until I get too old, too injured or just don't do well

71

anymore, will you and the family reconsider allowing me to become a veterinarian and to study anywhere I want?" she asked quietly, looking her brother straight in the eyes. He regarded his sister for a long moment.

"I'll tell you what. If you do become a vet, you have wasted your natural talent," he muttered more to himself and smirked. "You were born to be a negotiator. You have stated your point. I will talk to the parents about it. All right?" he held out his hand. Jacqueline grinned brightly and shook his hand.

"Well, I had better turn in early. I have an early session with the trainer. Ugh, we are now back to the grind. Eight hours of sheer torture," she complained.

The alarm clock woke her bright and early at 5:30 a.m. for a session with her personal trainer. Since she was hurting from the torture, Jacqueline slowly made her way back to the kitchen to scrounge up some food. As she was finishing her breakfast, Jean strolled in.

"How was torture today?" he asked good-naturedly.

She growled at him, cheerfully.

"Mother is expected to be released in a day or so, Sharon has informed me. I have a day of playing with the press. You want to change places?"

"No thanks, brother. You do that so well. I am off to my next session, dancing. How about you come with me?" she grinned, when he in turn frowned at her.

"The press and I will do all the dancing I can stand on a weekday," he replied and she laughed at him.

Jacqueline liked dancing. She loved music. But Fiona would also push her through her paces mercilessly on the ice today. She knew she would probably not be able to walk by the end of the day. Ahhh, a perfect day!

Chapter 11

The palace was filled with anticipation and activity. Her parents were arriving today, after being away for more than two months. Jean looked anxious as he paced the front hall. They had received word that the plane had arrived safely and they were en- route to the palace. The front doors opened to admit the the King and Queen along with Sharon and Antonio. They were talking excitedly. Her mother still looked a little pale and leaned on her father's arm.

"There is my Olympic Champion," her father boomed and embraced her. Her mother followed suit, ever reserved.

"Jacqueline, I'm sure you are aware that we are hosting an official reception here tomorrow evening," her mother said as she walked slowly toward her office.

"Mother, you are not going to work now, are you?" Jean asked incredulously.

"My dear Jean, I do have work to do," she said resolutely.

Her father followed her into the office they shared. Things were back to normal.

"I need to speak to you about your dress for the reception," Sharon said hastily and tapped her foot, while she waited impatiently for her youngest sister to follow her into her suite. For the next half-hour, she endured a change of many dresses. They finally settled on a beautiful baby blue dress. It was one of her favorites and Jacqueline was glad Sharon had allowed her to pick it.

The reception was a success. Everyone seemed to love her family. The country was proud of their royal family, especially after Jacqueline's victory. The guests lined up for hours and Jacqueline was exhausted by the time dinner was served. Her feet were killing her from the high heels she was wearing, so she slipped out of them when she sat down at the table.

"Your Highness, I am so glad to be seated next to you," the head of the board of education beamed at her. "Would you be willing to come and speak to our tenth graders? Here you are, barely a year older than they are, and an Olympic Champion. It would give them something to strive for."

Jacqueline smiled and answered that she would consider it after the World Championships.

Time flew by and Jacqueline found herself in Chiba, Japan. She had arrived a week earlier and was comfortably settled into a rented house near the skating venue, the Makuhari Messe Arena. Since no one was allowed to skate on the actual rink until the day of the competition, they practiced at a nearby local rink. Her training time was 7:00 a.m., and she shared the ice with several other skaters. Jacqueline was focused on getting her landing right when one of the other skaters almost crashed into her. After that, her skating was very tentative. The training session was not the best, and she had a number of falls and near misses. Feeling discouraged, she wanted to quit practice early.

"Oh no, you aren't going to go get depressed on me," Fiona admonished her. "Tomorrow will be a better day," she reassured her.

"I hope so, Fiona," Jacqueline said quietly.

She felt the pressure on her. The photographers lined the outside of the rink, snapping away as she crashed after her triple Lutz.

In that moment Linda appeared at the rink and she rushed to meet her friend.

"When my session is over let's have lunch and explore the town," Linda suggested enthusiastically.

"I will check with Fiona first," she said rather hesitantly.

"Jacqueline, have some fun," her friend chided her and got ready for her practice session.

When Jacqueline brought the matter up with Fiona, her coach frowned and sighed.

"You know I would let you have your time," she began slowly, "but your parents charged me with keeping a sharp eye on you. After today I think we need to find a quiet place to go over some jumps. Perhaps we will be able to rent some private rink time from a friend of mine. Let me call him right now and check with him. If we can't skate until later, I will allow you to go off a few hours with your friend. How does that sound?" she asked.

Jacqueline smiled - a huge smile.

"I knew there was a reason I took you on as coach. Thank you, Fiona," she snickered.

Waiting for Fiona to reach her friend was agony. Finally she got through to him and was able to set up a training session. The only time available was in the late afternoon. Jacqueline was jubilant and quickly told Linda that they could go out to lunch.

The afternoon was cold and blustery. The two set out on foot, Jacqueline promising Fiona to be careful and to be back at the rink at 2:00 p.m. They even managed to sneak out the back door, avoiding any photographers and reporters. Jacqueline giggled as she buttoned her winter jacket up to the top. Her hat disguised her, but the two girls stood out in the crowd of Japanese. She felt like she was in a spy movie, trying to keep away from the enemy.

Soon the press caught wind and followed them. The girls darted in and out of people to get away, and escaped into the entrance of a shop. They hid themselves among the wares in what happened to be a butcher shop. Jacqueline thought it a riot as they avoided large masses of something dead hanging from the ceiling. She examined the carcass and came to the conclusion that the animal hanging from the meat hook in front of her had been a sheep. Linda wrinkled her nose and looked rather pale.

Jacqueline peeked out of the shop and found that they finally had lost the reporters. The girls emerged, and looked around. People were hurrying to and fro, heads tucked into their scarves, their eyes not looking at anyone but focused on the ground.

"I don't know where we are," Jacqueline grunted and the butterflies in her stomach started fluttering around. The color had drained out of Linda's face and both stood in the sea of people hurrying past them. Jacqueline felt dread rise up in the back of her throat.

"What are we going to do?" she whispered. She didn't want to feel this afraid. Usually she had people around her who could point her in the right way. Here they were all alone! She swallowed hard.

Linda took a deep breath and grabbed her hand. "It's not like we are in the middle of nowhere. There are tons of people who can help us. Let's just ask for direction."

She stepped up to an old wise man standing in a doorway and smoking a pipe.

"Excuse me sir," she said. "Could you direct me to the Makuhari Messe Arena? My friend and I are skaters and we got lost."

The man stared at her as though she had sprouted three heads. Linda groaned and turned to Jacqueline.

"He doesn't speak English," she whispered.

"There has to be someone who speaks English," Jacqueline grumbled and pointed into the crowd. Her voice sounded unnaturally high pitched.

They spotted a group of giggling girls, about Jacqueline's age, and walked purposefully up to them. Linda repeated her plea and the girls looked at them shyly. For a moment they chattered in Japanese, pointing this way and that, when the oldest girl bowed respectfully.

"We will take you there," one of them said quietly, her voice in clipped and precise English.

Both Jacqueline and Linda breathed a sigh of relief. Within thirty minutes they were outside the entrance to the arena. Neither of them thought of eating at this point but they sincerely thanked the girls. Jacqueline thought of how best to express that thanks when she saw the rink manager standing on the other side of the door. Biting her lip, she rushed through. After talking to him, he didn't seem too impressed by her appeal.

"Please, sir. Can't we give these girls some tickets for their time? They really helped us out."

He nodded and Jacqueline grinned triumphantly. She went back to the group and told them that they would have tickets. The girls bowed respectfully and retreated, giggling and chattering excitedly.

"Not a word to Fiona," Jacqueline whispered, when they made their way to the rink. "She will never let me leave her sight again."

"You have my word," Linda said and held out her hand. They laughed as they searched for their coaches.

After a satisfying session at Fiona's trainer friend's rink, she felt a lot more settled and ready for the competition. Fiona thought it might be helpful if they held all their practices at the private rink. She talked to her trainer friend, who was also among those watching. He was a very charming fellow, about Fiona's age, and smiled with pleasure when asked if they could come back.

"It would be my pleasure," he grinned.

The next day Jacqueline put on a raincoat when she went outside for her morning run. The streets were wet and she returned home drenched. The house had an indoor sauna and pool and after warming up in the sauna, she swam.

"Well done." Fiona watched her come out of the pool, puffing hard. "I love the fact that you are so self-motivated. Do you know that is why I took you as a student? You were always pushing yourself, even in the beginning. That was when I knew you would go far. I am so proud of you, Jacqueline. We are at the World Championships! You, from a country people don't hear about usually. And me, who really hasn't had many top skaters. We should enjoy these moments."

"Yes, I am trying to," Jacqueline replied as she stood dripping wet next to the pool. "It is just a little hard when you are continually training."

"Aww, poor baby." Fiona had no pity on her.

Chapter 12

Over all, Jacqueline felt on top of her game. Everything was coming together so effortlessly. She began to have high hopes of a successful championship. She just hoped that on the day of the competition, she would not be overtaken by nerves. That was always a danger. Her program was strong in all sorts of jumps, spins and combinations.

The days flew by quickly, filling up with training and sightseeing. Fiona and Jacqueline took the opportunity to visit the countryside, which was quite beautiful. The weather turned nasty, and Jacqueline was no longer able to run outside. Instead she worked out and swam indoors. Linda joined her for workouts, making them more enjoyable.

The day of the competition came swiftly. Jacqueline had a very satisfying training run in the morning. It was the first time she was allowed to skate in the actual arena where the competition was to take place. She developed a feel for the length of the rink and the ice. It was also important for her to find her place on the ice for the jumps. If she got lost, it would disrupt her concentration. Every rink was slightly different and it was important to get used to it. She skated together with Linda, a German skater, an Italian skater and a Japanese skater. Linda also looked really good and Jacqueline knew her to be a fierce competitor. She would have to be at her best tonight, she thought as she exited the rink, surrounded by reporters.

"How do you feel about tonight?" they shouted at her. She smiled back and shoved her way through them as quickly as she could.

"Well done," Fiona told her back in the locker room. "You are looking strong out there."

"I'm not the only one," she sighed as she unlaced her skates. Fiona frowned at her and laid a hand on her shoulder.

"You know how it goes. Intimidate the competition. Even Linda will do that, remember. Out there she is not your friend, but your competition! It is Linda's competition to lead. She is chasing the World Championship title. With Tatiana out of the picture anybody can get it. You are the Olympic Champion! Just remember that! Now, let's get out of here!"

They retreated to their waiting car and drove home. Jacqueline spent the afternoon in the sauna, keeping her body nimble and relaxed. Too much depended on her staying injury free, and anything could happen when you train with weights. A pulled muscle was all she needed. After a very light and early dinner, it was time to get to the arena. Jacqueline started feeling butterflies again and her hands were sweaty.

Jacqueline was competing somewhere in the middle. She was glad not to be at either end. It always made her more nervous. Tonight was the short program, the technical part of the competition. She had a strong program with which she had delighted the audience and judges at the Olympics. Would it be enough here too? It was only a matter of time to find out.

The minutes ticked by slowly, while Jacqueline kept her muscles warm and limber. Her stomach was starting to act up again as it became closer to her performance. The time came for her group to warm up before their competitions. She was to be the first skater after the warm up. Her breath came in short bursts and butterflies had now taken residence in her stomach. She did not remember the order of her program. She started to panic!

"Go and tighten your skates," Fiona told her gently. She mechanically did as Fiona told her, and by the time this was done, the Zamboni had finished cleaning the ice.

"Do your job! Give me a repeat of Lillehammer," Fiona told her sternly as they locked gazes. "Focus on the music, focus on the ice. It is just another competition, nothing more! Don't forget to stay on your feet!" she said through clenched teeth and hugged her.

Jacqueline tried to take a deep breath but she was unable to do so.

"They are announcing your name. Get out there!" Fiona whispered into her ear.

She managed to make her way to the gate and hesitantly took a step onto the ice. Once her skates touched the slippery surface the world felt right again. She felt the familiarity and welcomed it. The audience began to fade as she made her way to the middle. Jacqueline waited for the music to begin. Once it did, her body took over. Her first move, a triple toe loop, sent her soaring through the air. This was why she trained so hard. The landing was hard but solid. She absorbed the landing in her hips, knees and ankles, speeding off to the next sequence. She was nearing the end and was preparing her landing after her double Salchow, double Lutz combination, when the ice became just a bit more slippery or her blade suddenly seemed thinner. Her foot and ankle wobbled dangerously. As she forced her right arm out from behind and extended her left hand in front of her to fight for her balance, she heard the crowd moan in anguish but she fought for the landing. It took all her strength and concentration to continue smoothly and not to end up on her butt. When she came to rest after the final spin, she had indeed reason to smile. The crowd showed her their appreciation and was on their feet clapping wildly. After taking a bow in all directions, Jacqueline picked up the nearest bouquet and headed breathlessly, to the exit.

The crowd settled down while Fiona and Jacqueline waited in the kiss-and-cry area. Fiona beamed at her and patted her knee. Jacqueline took a sip of water, waving to the fans who were yelling her name in unison. She decided to enjoy every moment of these World Championships.

"A bit slippery out there, dear?" Fiona whispered through clenched teeth.

"Just a little bit. And these skates seem to be narrower than I remembered from this morning. Somebody must have taken my skates and switched them," she giggled in return.

Her marks put her way ahead of everyone. She was pleased that she had a wide margin, since some of the tougher competition was still to come. Jacqueline smiled and walked to the changing area. Reporters were there to greet her, while photographers tried to capture her every move. All right, maybe she was not going to enjoy every part of these Championships, she thought wryly.

"Well done," said Fiona through gritted teeth, when they were alone behind the curtain, separating them from the rest of the world. "One question though: Are you trying to give the competition a better chance? If you are, you are doing a fantastic job. Your marks would be so much better had you not done that little stumble there at the end. What, were you tired? Is this all a little too much for you?"

When Fiona got going there was not much that could stop her.

"Because I thought you wanted to win the title. You know, it might go well with your other title. But if you are just playing around out there, fine. Have fun. Let me know when you are ready to compete!" she barked dangerously.

Jacqueline knew better than to interrupt. Fiona would be done venting soon and then they would be able to talk about the program and what may have gone wrong. The blunder cost them a lot actually, and Jacqueline hoped that tomorrow night would be better.

Meanwhile on the screen, it seemed that some of the competitors were having difficulties. A girl from Germany missed her landing, smashing onto the ice. One competitor from Australia completely missed a combination and had a fall on another. When the last seven skaters were busy warming up, Jacqueline could not help but wonder what was in store for them. Linda was among them as well as another top American skater. Linda was the first to go and had a wonderful skate until her double Lutz double Salchow. She under rotated, coming down on the ice wrong and ended up taking an extra step. The crowd sighed but Linda finished her program and smiled. Because of the difficulty of her program, her marks were not bad but they were nowhere near Jacqueline's. The skaters that followed skated well without major mishaps. At the end of the night Jacqueline was in the lead, followed by an Austrian skater and Linda.

The following night's competition would be fierce. Jacqueline knew that Linda would not just give up. They would be fighting to the end.

Again, the next day started early. Jacqueline spent a good portion of the day in the sauna to keep her muscles supple and relaxed. She got to the arena early for her warm up. Linda smirked at her when she entered the changing area and busied herself with her skates. Jacqueline sat next to her and did the same.

"Whatever happens tonight, no hard feelings, right?" she muttered as they both finished.

Linda regarded her for a moment. "I don't think I could be mad at you for fighting hard," she concluded and hugged her quickly.

They walked to the ice together; focused on what was to come. Jacqueline had difficulty just thinking through her program, as her stomach started to heave again, her hands sweaty.

"I will tan your hide if you don't focus!" Fiona growled and took Jacqueline's chin firmly in her hand. "Who is the Olympic Champion?" she asked making Jacqueline focus on her dusty brown eyes.

"I am," she winced and tried to move her head, but Fiona only tightened her grip.

"I can't hear you!" she hissed.

"All right, you have made your point!" Jacqueline hissed back. Fiona released her chin and grabbed her arm instead.

"Stop comparing yourself with everyone out there. You have every right to be here, Jacqueline. You have the talent. You fought for your place here. Got that?"

"Yes," she replied demurely.

"They are calling your group for warm up. I want to see you practice that jump you almost missed last night. Go over it a couple of times," Fiona instructed loudly.

Jacqueline nailed the jump the first time! And the second time. By the third time, she was feeling like she owned the ice again. She tried a few other combinations and steps to make sure she was solid on those. She nailed them every time. In fact, she was getting more and more air on her jumps than she had recently, making the rotations easier. Her landings were smooth and absorbing the shock of the height of the jumps easily. She felt rather confident about herself.

"Now don't feel too confident!" Fiona warned. "Stay on your guard and watch yourself. But I like the height of your jumps," she told her as they were coming off of the ice.

Jacqueline had plenty of time to wait while she watched one skater after another fall or miss something in their program. Since she was the skater with the highest marks she would be skating at the end of the night. What a disaster! Jacqueline started to feel that the whole competition was a mistake and thought that it would be nice if they allowed *do overs*. She watched skater after skater coming off the ice, tears in their eyes. Many of them were unable to hold back their emotions.

Jacqueline really felt for them. These were the top skaters of each country. They had worked hard to be here. The jumps they did could not be performed by just anyone. They had trained so hard to do these feats of athleticism and now they were at the top. Some of them would not be back next year. They would retire and go on to do something else.

Jacqueline watched as the last few of her competitors took the ice. None of them had a major fall. Linda in particular had a great performance, making her the lead skater. Her jumps were bold and high, her movements graceful and flowing. She beamed when she exited the ice. Linda received high marks, taking up the lead in front of everyone else. Jacqueline could feel the butterflies, the nausea and unease inside her body. She stumbled to the door of the rink, breaking out in a cold sweat.

As she made her way onto the ice, all the discomfort once again disappeared. She had to wait a few moments, though, while the little helpers were clearing up the rink from Linda's exquisite performance. Finally the ice was free and she took her position.

The music started and just like always, she allowed it to take over. She was so focused that she didn't miss a beat, not a step. Her jumps catapulted her high into the air and she landed softly and elegantly. Too soon the music ended, and she found herself wondering how she had done it again. It seemed too easy, too effortless. The audience was beside themselves. They were hooting and hollering. Jacqueline felt as though tonight had been something very special. Her performance had been beyond what Jacqueline had expected.

Fiona hugged her over and over again when she finally made it off the ice amid roaring applause. She smiled as she felt herself being crushed again and again. The kiss-and-cry area was waiting for them and Fiona, for once, could not contain her enthusiasm. The next few moments were tense, but to Jacqueline it didn't matter what scores the judges would give her. She had done her best out there. Jacqueline had allowed her body to take over and because of the rigors of her training, it had performed wonderfully. The scores came and she was rewarded with high marks for her performance. It put her just ahead of Linda by a mere two tenths of a point. Jacqueline felt a wave of satisfaction flow through her. Yes, she liked how that felt. She waved and exited. Skaters shook her hands. Hugs were given, some with tears.

"So, here we are again, eh," smiled Linda when they received their medals. "Do you think it will always be like this with us?"

"I hope so, for my sake, but I don't think so. I think I will have to let you win a few just to keep you from pouting," she laughed and waved to the audience. They both cracked up at that.

"Next competition I am coming up on top," Linda warned.

"I hope you know that you are going to have to train really, really hard," she sassed back. It was all in good fun because they both knew that the other had just as much right to the title.

"Wow, World Champion," Jacqueline sighed contently when the medal was presented to her. She thought that she could get used to this.

Again the three winners were escorted to the broadcast studios and for the next few hours, they were congratulated in different languages and asked what they would be doing next. At 3:00 a.m. she finally fell into her soft bed.

Chapter 13

After spending the next day with the media, Jacqueline's became excited about returning home because Linda agreed to come for a visit on her way back to the states.

"Are you sure it will fit into your training schedule?" she asked for the tenth time.

"Yeah, we don't really have anything big left to compete at," Linda grinned sheepishly. "I have always wanted to stay at a palace."

"I see. You like me only because of what I am. This is a very shallow relationship," Jacqueline laughed merrily, teasing her friend. It was funny how she knew that Linda was a true friend. She trusted her!

"I have never been on one of these things," Linda whispered and looked around the plush compartment on their flight from Frankfurt, where the private plane picked them up.

"I hope it's not the same plane as before," Jacqueline mused.

It was! The flight was only thirty minutes long and nothing unpleasant happened.

"A girl could get used to this," Linda laughed and looked out the window upon approach. "So this is your country! These mountains can give the Rockies a run for their money. Oh, look at that Lake! It's so charming! Is that the city?" she asked when they flew over the capital. "I love those quaint houses! It's like stepping back in time!"

"Don't let my family hear you say that," Jacqueline flinched, warning her. "They are trying to modernize." She couldn't help but chuckle.

It started to snow when they entered the waiting car, but that did not stop the citizens of Lichtenbourgh from coming out in full force to greet their favorite skating champion. They waved flags and shouted greetings from the side of the road that led to the palace in the center of town. Linda was beside herself. Jacqueline could not help but laugh at her friend's enthusiasm.

"You know what this reminds me of?" her friend asked her. "This reminds me of the really old towns you see in movies. I love the brick houses and cobble-stoned streets! I half expect a horse and cart to come around the corner. I can so see you in this town! This is a princess kind of town. I could get used to this place." She frowned at Jacqueline, who continued to laugh.

Linda looked around and then back at her friend. "All right, all right. Can I tell you something?" she lowered her voice and looked around suspiciously.

"Are you going to have to kill me?" Jacqueline giggled and dodged Linda's quick hand striking playfully at her arm.

"Ha-ha. Be serious! I compete so that I can visit these beautiful cities with great architecture. Isn't that goofy?" Linda confessed and waited for her friend to come back with something smart.

"Actually it's kind of nice," Jacqueline admitted softly and then added grinning, "but really, really strange!"

They both laughed until tears were running down their cheeks. Linda became quiet when they approached the palace, flanked with tall columned arches and high entry doors. Two footmen opened one of the doors and helped them out of the car. Linda stared all around her while she tripped up the stairs. The footman prevented her from falling. She blushed deeply but made it the rest of the way without any more incidents. The huge door opened and Jacqueline's parents greeted them in the large foyer beyond. She stared at the beautiful columns flanking the large marble staircase leading up to the second story landing. She almost fell backward when she gaped at the large chandelier in the middle of the room.

"Linda, what a wonderful surprise. I am so glad you have decided to visit," Queen Dominique said as she hugged her and gave her an air kiss.

King Francois smiled at her and greeted his daughter with a genuine hug and kiss on the cheek. "You have done us proud again," he whispered.

Jacqueline showed Linda around the palace.

"Compared to Buckingham Palace, this place is tiny," she laughed as Linda toured it still gaping at the beautiful architecture. They first headed to the oldest section of the palace, which was connected to the more modern palace by a covered walkway.

"My family's offices are down this corridor," she explained and felt like a tour guide.

Linda loved the old part of the palace. She squealed in delight at the numerous shining suits of armor standing as if in attention. In the giant ballroom she grabbed Jacqueline and the two waltzed around the room until they both collapsed against the wall, gasping and laughing.

"If you look down this way, you will see the crown prince slouching around, wandering aimlessly, staring into space," she intoned and received a frown from her older brother. She introduced him to Linda.

"Ah, Jacqueline's competitor," he grinned and shook her hand. "Jacqueline you did well again," he smiled at his younger sister. "We were all jumping up and down during your performance."

They proceeded to walk toward the guest suite, when Jean seemed to have remembered something. He grinned, but somehow the smile never made it to his eyes.

"Sharon is having a tea in your honor this weekend."

Jacqueline groaned. She glanced at Linda, who commented that that was out of this world. Well, a tea was better than a whole reception line. She loathed those. They finished their tour and Jacqueline felt her strength fading.

"Do you mind if we go and rest. I am exhausted."

Linda agreed that she too was tired. Jacqueline showed her to her room. She again gawked at all the paintings that seemed to stare at them as they made their way down the hallway toward the living quarters.

"This room is bigger than my apartment," she said in awe. "Thanks for having me."

"I am glad you are here. Now I don't have to go to the tea by myself," she grinned and turned to the door. "Sweet dreams. If you are hungry just dial 99. Someone will be here before you can hang up the phone."

Chapter 14

The week flew by. Linda loved the rink on which Jacqueline practiced. They took time each day to go for a run and to skate. Jacqueline still had to work with her tutors every day. Linda took this opportunity to do some sightseeing, escorted by either Jean or Marie. Jacqueline was blown away when the two of them came back from shopping, laughing like they had been friends for years. She felt a twinge of jealously run through her. How dare her sister try to inch in on her friend! Marie, after all, had a slew of them, while Linda was Jacqueline's only friend.

"Jacqueline," Linda said sheepishly when she came to her at the end of the day. She was wearing something new and expensive, looking like she stepped out of the pages of a fashion magazine. Jacqueline could not but stare at her.

"Do you mind if I go out with Marie tonight? She has invited me to her club to meet some friends of hers and have a few drinks."

Jacqueline wasn't sure what to say but she could feel anger rising in her like a raging beast again. How dare her sister! She knew Marie was doing this on purpose. She swallowed it down and smiled sweetly at her friend.

"Of course not. I was just going to go to bed early anyway."

Linda beamed and rushed out of the room to meet Jacqueline's sister. Jacqueline paced up and down in her room, anger and frustration chasing her wherever she stepped. How dare her sister! She would show her! How? After all, Marie had at least ten friends she could call on to come to her rescue. How many friends did Jacqueline have? One! And the one she did have was being coaxed into the enemy camp! Jacqueline choked down the tears of bitterness and anger that burned in her eyes.

On the day of the tea party at Sharon's, Jacqueline was moody. Linda and Marie had spent the morning at the spa, while Jacqueline had to study at home for her upcoming exams. Later, as the limousine sped them through the miles of farmland to the tea, Linda seemed oblivious to her friend's mood.

"I can't believe you complain so much about living this life, Jacqueline. I would trade it in for mine in a heartbeat," Linda muttered, not taking her eyes off the large farm they passed. "To live in a country this old and represent its interest would make me very happy."

Jacqueline growled softly. "Linda, you are on vacation. You are getting a quick snapshot of my life. I am not free to choose my life. Everything I want to do I have to fight for. I never said I don't like this life. I just don't like being on display... and I don't like having to prove myself all the time."

They fell silent until they drove through the gates of Sharon's estate. Linda gasped when the hunting lodge, a wedding present from her parents, came into view. It was surrounded by meadows and fields, where the spring flowers were trying to make an appearance. Linda squealed in delight at the huge stork's nest on top of the beautifully restored thatched roof.

"Let's hope that it means that there will be lots of nieces and nephews coming," Jacqueline chuckled and Linda grinned.

Again uniformed footmen opened the doors and helped the girls out of the car. Both smiled and thanked them. The door exposed a cozy entryway. The great room had a soaring cathedral ceiling with windows reaching 20 feet from floor to ceiling framing room, with a breath-taking vista of the snow-covered mountains. Flowers bloomed in the sun coming in from the windows. A huge fireplace dominated the center of the room. Just like in the rented house in Lillehammer, there was comfortable seating all around the room, which was decorated in a tasteful country style. Hunting pictures donned the walls.

"There you are, sister," Sharon welcomed her with a quick, business-like smile.

"And welcome to you, Linda," she smiled. "The guests should arrive soon. Please make yourself at home." She turned to her sister and patted her shoulder.

"You did well again, Jacqueline. We are beginning to get used to this winning streak of yours. Will it continue, do you think?" she asked quietly.

Jacqueline felt the pressure rise and her mood almost reached another low. Then she realized that Sharon had paid her a compliment and she allowed a slow smile to spread over her face.

"Your guess is as good as mine. I did promise Linda she could win some too. It would not be fair," she chuckled and then turned serious when her sister did not laugh.

"I want to thank you for doing this," she whispered to her sister, after she talked to her cousin for a while. "I forgot how nice it is to have family around."

"There are others coming too," Sharon told her. "I couldn't just do family. The wives of some of the members of parliament have accepted my invitation. They should be here shortly," she stated and glared at Jacqueline when she sighed. "You know, this is not only for your own enjoyment, dear!" she hissed.

Despite the many different guests paying way too much attention to her, she began to enjoy herself and her mood improved. Linda also received her share of attention and took it like a seasoned professional. When Jacqueline found out that Sharon was meeting Antonio in the States, she managed to get Linda a ride home on the family jet. Linda beamed brightly when they discussed her travel plans to go home.

"Traveling on a private jet is certainly more comfortable than flying commercially," Linda drawled and acted as though flying privately was becoming the norm for her.

Jacqueline smirked ruefully. "Except when you are in the middle of a storm."

Linda ignored her friend.

The next day, her parents discussed her schedule for the following weeks. Several local TV stations were lined up for interviews. Several women's associations also asked for some of her time. And then the head of the board of education had reminded them that she had offered to come and talk to their students. She grunted and pouted. She did not want this. Jacqueline realized that most of the competitions were over but she needed to get ready for next season's competitions. And then there was school. If she wanted to start college courses in the fall, applications would need to be filled out.

Linda's visit was soon coming to an end. Jacqueline was counting the days when she would be alone. She loved her friend, but toward the end of the week, Linda was spending more and more time with Marie. Jacqueline was sulking, allowing her jealousy to shape her moods. Linda didn't understand what had caused her friend's moods, and by the end of the week, they were barely talking.

Soon after Linda left, Fiona returned from a visit with her family - it was time to get together with a choreographer and shape the next year's program. It would take a couple of months until the program was perfected to meet their standard.

"Jacqueline we need to talk of your future plans," her father cornered her one morning after breakfast. "When do you have some time to come and speak with us about it?"

Jacqueline wanted to bite out a sarcastic *never*, but instead smiled and answered, "I am busy throughout the morning but right after lunch I can take a break. Why don't we talk then, say around one?"

"Very well," her father nodded.

Throughout the morning, Jacqueline dreaded the passing of time. She knew her parents would forbid her to leave the country to study in the States. Moreover she knew that studying veterinary medicine was out of the question.

She was unfocussed during the initial meeting with Amanda Royce, the choreographer, who was also her dance instructor. She and Jacqueline got along very well with each other.

"What is wrong with you today?" Fiona hissed when she once again did not heed their direction. Jacqueline just shook her head and apologized.

"Could we possibly postpone this? I can't seem to concentrate on this today. I'm so sorry." The two women looked at her in astonishment but nodded.

"Of course, Jacqueline. You have a lot on your plate this week," Amanda answered.

Chapter 15

Amanda was right. After the meeting with her parents, she would be whisked off to the center of town to be interviewed by the local news. Then she was expected to sit for down with an American journalist at the palace. After that she was to finish her last test before sitting for her A-levels and baccalaureates. But first, the meeting with her parents. She entered her parents' shared office.

"Sit, dear, sit," her mother greeted her while she was filing some papers.

Her father nodded and waved at her as he was still on the phone. She sat a while, thinking of how she used to dread coming here even as a child. She felt intimidated by her parents when they asked her here. She could feel the power in this room and it made her feel inconsequential and small.

"Tea, dear?" her mother offered.

Jacqueline shook her head. No tea for her.

"Let us get down to business," her father looked up and put the phone gently back onto its cradle. "You are looking to study in the US. Quite frankly we are entirely against this. We believe you need to spend time in your own country to get to know the people again and for them to get to know you. You have been propelled to popularity. We need to encourage this. Your wins have put this country on the map. Already tourism is on the increase. Our citizens love you. You need to be seen."

"You know how much I loathe all those things," she complained. "I don't want to be paraded in front of people. I don't want to be a celebrity. What I do want is to go and study in the US and live in obscurity," she growled, knowing full well that those demands would never be met.

"Yes, of course, but couldn't you study it here, or in Switzerland. You have been away at school for so long. Now it is time, Jacqueline," her mother replied briskly. "No more little princess. You are grown up. You handle yourself very well in difficult situations. It is time to come and partake in the family business."

"I can't," she gasped.

"What were you looking to study, anyway?" her father asked laying a steadying hand on his wife.

Jacqueline closed her eyes for a moment. *Here is comes. They are going to be furious.*

"I would like to study biology or pre-veterinary medicine. I would like to go to vet school in the US."

Her parents stared at her, then at each other.

"A veterinarian. An animal doctor," her mother finally managed to say. "I don't even know what to say. It is totally against who we are, Jacqueline. We don't spend our days in muck tending to animals."

And there it was!

103

Of course her mother understood that her youngest daughter would never be satisfied with only practicing on small animals, surrounded by white walls and assistants. No, Jacqueline longed to spend her days with the large animals, rolling around in the muck, as her mother so eloquently deduced. She grinned when she thought back to the numerous hours she had spent with the vet in England, up to her knees in mud and manure. It was not a picture she was going to paint for her mother willingly.

Her mother's face had lost all its color and she turned to her husband speaking in rapid French, something she always did when she was upset. He put a calming hand on his wife's arm.

"There is always a first, Mother," Jacqueline smirked trying to lighten the situation.

"Yes, well," was all her father managed as he sat studying his perfectly manicured fingernails. "I don't think we need a veterinarian to run the country."

"No we don't. But I won't be ruling the country either. Jean will be. We still have horses that need medical care!" Jacqueline couldn't believe those words had come out of her mouth, laced in sarcasm.

"Yes, we hire people for that," her mother answered coldly. "The family does not need a veterinarian."

"And you didn't need a skater either, and now look at what you have," she said, making the most of the positive points of her skating. "I remember I had to beg and beg to be allowed to skate. You thought it would be too common. But yet look at me now! The economy is up because people are coming here since they have seen me skate. I know in my heart of hearts that being a large animal veterinarian is what I would like to do. Once I am done with skating, I long to do something, I feel is of value. You have always taught me to do something has significance. This does."

"Why not a doctor? We can always use more doctors. Humans are more valuable than animals. They work in nice and aesthetic environments. And don't come home smelling like pig or cow!"

Jacqueline frowned at her father. She almost rolled her eyes but thought better of it. He was her king, after all.

"If not a doctor, then a lawyer. Very respectable," her mother piped in when she saw the look on her daughter's face.

Jacqueline grimaced at her parents. This was degenerating into a stand off! There was no way she was going to concede. She spent the next hour defending her position. In the end, nobody yielded and the negotiations came to a crashing halt, like she had predicted.

"My dear parents," Jacqueline sighed. She got up and started pacing back and forth. She had one more ace up her sleeve and she was ready to use it. "I spoke to Jean about this and I would like you to consider it. If I dedicate the next four years of my life to skating and winning everything I can, barring accidents, do you think you could consider allowing me to study in the US to become a veterinarian?" Her parents regarded each other for a long time, and then looked at her.

"Where will you study in the meantime?" they asked.

"I have heard of long-distance programs. If I stay here for the next four years, get my degree this way, skate and do well, does that sound agreeable?"

"You would go to the States after that?" her father asked.

"Yes, I would like that," she answered quietly.

"We will consider it."

And with that statement, Jacqueline was free to go. She felt as though she had been through a very rigorous training session for three days. She went to her room and put on a movie and promptly fell asleep.

"Your Highness, you are wanted at the TV station," a voice broke through the fog.

Jacqueline struggled to open her eyes.

"Thank you, Therese, for waking me," she scrambled around the room and found her jacket and shoes and ran out the door. The car whisked her to the TV station where she arrived five minutes late. She apologized profusely.

"Don't worry, Your Highness. We have calculated for these possibilities," her handsome TV host told her with a bright smile.

For the next twenty minutes she answered from a list of prepared questions. She felt like she was totally in control of what she was allowing the host to see: a perfect picture of her family. There were no skeletons in their closet, were there? When her time was up, she thanked the host and was transported quickly back to the palace.

When she arrived she was hurried to the official parlor where visitors were received. It was a large room with a fireplace that now crackled happily. The windows gave a beautiful vista of the sprawling lawn, still covered with snow. In the distance the snow-covered mountains stood majestically. She was greeted by a producer who introduced her to the host of the show, a smiling Charlotte Walton. She quickly drew Jacqueline out of herself by telling tales about her stay in London, just days past. Apparently it had been a disaster and Jacqueline soon laughed along with her.

"So this is how it is going to play out," the producer told her in a hurried voice. "Charlotte and you are just sitting in your living room, having a nice chat. Be yourself, and don't worry about the camera. Have fun with it. Just pretend you two are long buddies playing catch up."

Jacqueline winced and nodded her head. Right!

"Quiet please, in 5, 4, 3 ..." and the cue was given for Charlotte to start. She smiled into the camera with the blue light and greeted her audience.

"We are guests at the beautiful palace here in Lichten, the capital of the country that has made news so much lately, with the most recent figure skating World and Olympic Champion. Thank you for sitting down with us," she beamed at Jacqueline. Jacqueline smiled back and replied that it was her pleasure.

"As I look around here, I am astounded at the beauty of this place. These mountains are just so breathtaking," she beamed at

Jacqueline as though Jacqueline was responsible for their beauty. "Tell me how you got started in figure skating."

"I was seven years old and my parents wanted me to accompany them to a gallery opening in Switzerland. Of course at that age I didn't want to be at a gallery opening and so I put up quite a fuss, in a very princess-like fashion," she laughed and Charlotte smiled knowingly. "My mother finally bribed me with a skating lesson after the opening. I had been bothering my parents for a while to allow me to try skating but they had yet to give in to my demands. After the lesson, I was hooked. It was my first year at boarding school and my parents agreed to allow me to continue. I really loved it and much of my spare time was spent on the ice. A year later my coach introduced me to Fiona, who saw something in my very awkward beginning and we started to practice earnestly and to attend small competitions. At that time, I really didn't think it would lead to such success. My ambition was to make it to the Junior Nationals and maybe the Junior European Championships. We accomplished that a few years later."

"What was it like to win your first competition?"

"It felt wonderful, empowering. Everyone in my family is incredibly talented. My sister, Marie, is an amazing singer. Sharon, my oldest sister, is an interior designer. Jean was a soccer player. It seemed that I had joined them by winning my first competition. And then my second, and so on. When I made it to the Junior Worlds, I couldn't believe it. I placed third."

"At sixteen there is a lot riding on your shoulders," Charlotte stated seriously. "Do you feel the pressure on and off the ice?"

Jacqueline wanted to leap up and run away. These questions were getting too personal.

"I won't deny that I do. My life is even less private now that people recognize me everywhere. I am a very private person and so that is hard for me," she added honestly, glancing toward the door, expecting her mother to appear and frown at her.

"It is hard to be someone everyone knows. I understand. Do you get much time to hang out at the mall with friends? Go to the movies like a typical teenager? What is a typical day like for you?"

Jacqueline almost gave a sarcastic laugh. Movies! Mall! Those things implied that she had a life! Which she didn't. "No mall. Movies are mostly at home. I get up around 5:30 in the morning, start out with a three-mile run. I eat a very healthy and non-fattening breakfast, which is followed by a work out session. I meet Fiona and we have our skating session. That can last a good three to four hours. I also dance every other day for about an hour. After a healthy lunch I return to the rink for another two hours, after which I sit down with my tutors and go over the day's work and usually fall into bed at night. Right now I am preparing for the A-levels and my baccalaureates so I get to bed around midnight."

"Wow that is a tough schedule. Most adults would be able to keep up with it for about a week. And on days like this, you take a break?"

"No I already had a training session with Fiona. We are preparing for next year's program. It takes a while to sit down with the

109

choreographer and iron out any glitches. But that is actually the fun part. I get to pick the music and we go from there," she smiled back.

"What are you passionate about?"

Jacqueline was glad for the caked on makeup that prevented everyone from seeing her face blush with the question. She had seen that question on the list but now that she had been asked it, she felt uncomfortable and didn't want to answer.

"I love to skate," she managed to say and smile. *And I want to go away to the States to study veterinary medicine!* But she couldn't say that.

"What about your future? Are you going to continue to skate or will you go into something else?"

"I hope to study and have a normal life," she laughed.

"Normal life, you say. I don't think you were meant to have a normal life. It must be hard to maintain friendships of any kind," Charlotte asked sympathetically.

Jacqueline suppressed a groan. These questions were entirely too personal!

"I had some friends at boarding school but because of the schedule I am home now. I just had a visit from a friend recently."

"Yes, I understand Linda Jones, the silver medalist, stayed with you for a while. You two are good friends off the ice?"

"Linda and I just got along right away when we met last year at the World championships. She is a fierce competitor. She makes me be at my best if I want to beat her," Jacqueline grinned.

The interview went on for a bit and Jacqueline gave a tour of her rink and training facility.

"People probably think that I have it so easy being royalty" Jacqueline explained. "My family works hard. We all are out there doing what we can for our country."

Finally the lights went out and the interview was over. Charlotte shook her hand and smiled genuinely.

"Thank you for being so honest and open with me. I hope to talk with you again."

Jacqueline felt so worn out she stumbled to her room. As she poured herself a glass of water, there was a knock on the door and Marie walked in.

"So how is our little star?" she asked and plopped herself down next to her sister.

"Not now, Marie, I am not in the mood to argue with you," she said tiredly. "Why are you home anyway? It's not the weekend."

"Who wants to argue with our golden child? You can do no wrong. Hey, you want a pony? Now is the time to ask. The world is at your feet," her sister replied sarcastically. "I'm home because I felt like coming home today. I am just staying for the night."

"I just want my bed," she said as she made her way to the bathroom.

"Don't be ridiculous. It is 4:00p.m. Have a little fun. Let's you and I go out on the town tonight," Marie teased.

Jacqueline poked her face out of the bathroom door wearing toothpaste around her mouth.

"Are 'ou ki'ing me?" she asked and quickly turned toward the sink to spit out the toothpaste. "I am tired. I was up early, ran three miles, had a tough work out session, had a meeting with the parents, did an interview in town, then came here and did another interview. I am exhausted," she declared, and picked up the phone to call the kitchen for a quick bite to eat. "Besides I don't like the people you hang out with. They are not my style."

"Excuse me, Your Highness," Marie sneered. "Who are your friends?"

"I don't have many and my only friend just left to go home. Oh wait. You managed to steal away my only friend!" she growled and blinked away the tears that sprung to her eyes. "Please go away, Marie," she pleaded and felt the tears coming.

Jacqueline was thankful Marie left without witnessing her breaking down.

Chapter 16

Jacqueline awoke when her alarm clock went off. She smashed the snooze button and tried to get up. She found it extremely hard to do this morning. Perhaps it was because of the aftermath of the previous day. She hit the snooze button three more times before she was able to rise out of bed and reluctantly crawl into the cold shower. Looking outside, she discovered that snow was falling thickly.

"Swimming or bed?" she mused and then decided that swimming would be the wiser choice. After her swim, she was famished and devoured her breakfast.

"You did not have dinner!" Chef scolded her as she poured herself a cup of hot tea. She looked at him apologetically. She stole a freshly baked croissant out from under his nose and grinned when he rebuked her in good fun, as she went off to her next agony session. Out of all the things Jacqueline had to do, weight training was her least favorite. She endured a lengthy, exhausting session and stopped back at the kitchen on her way to shower.

"You are back to steal some more croissants?" George glowered. He had his rolling pin in his hand, which he brandished as a weapon. His face and apron were covered with flour and Jacqueline turned her face so he would not laugh.

"Actually I just came for a glass of water," she coughed, "and to steal whatever is cooking in that oven. It smells delicious!"

"Aha, away with you!" the chef yelled swinging his weapon. Jacqueline retreated only to pick up a spoon. She pointed at the man, grinning from ear to ear.

"You know I could so beat you. I just bench pressed fifty pounds. Yeah, you better put down your weapon and surrender. What is in that oven?" She advanced dangerously, swinging her little spoon. George laughed and put down his rolling pin. He raised his hands in defense.

"I surrender! I surrender! Please not the spoon!"

Their laughter could be heard in the hallway. George rewarded her with another croissant and allowed her a quick peek into the oven, which was filled with several geese. Jacqueline could feel her mouth water.

"Yummy, yummy," she gasped.

"And stay away from my geese, or I will cook yours," he threatened as she slowly made her way out the door, laughing hysterically, tears running down her cheeks. She ran straight into her brother who was talking on his phone, not watching where he was going.

"Ouch," she complained as he stepped on her foot. He looked up in surprise.

"So sorry, sis," he quickly apologized and hung up. "And may I congratulate you. The interview you did yesterday has aired in the

States and you are being praised as the next Grace of Monaco," he smirked.

Jacqueline rolled her eyes at him.

"Great, just what I wanted," she said as she slipped past him.

"Wait! There is a dinner tonight. We are entertaining the president of an oil company and his family. They are from that place there in the desert, what is its name?" he thought for a moment. "Oh yes, it is called Dubai. Never mind that. Be sure to come presentable. No jeans and T-shirt," he grinned and pinched her arm.

She curtseyed genteelly, and hurried for a shower. A dinner she dreaded, but the goose.... yum!

The goose was tender, moist and tasty; Jacqueline was in heaven. She savored every bit of her portion along with root vegetables and lemon meringue pie, which melted on her tongue. Dinner was a formal affair with uniformed attendants. The president of the oil company was quite pleasant and complimented her on her success. He had brought his family, who cast furtive glances at her from time to time.

She was quite surprised to see that Aisha, his wife, was an Arab, while the president, John, was quite the blond-haired American. Jacqueline spent the evening making small-talk with their twins, who were roughly her age. Grace was petite and well, graceful. She had a heart shaped face, framed by thick, dark brown hair flecked with red streaks. Her hazel eyes were framed by wireless glasses, which she continually pushed back on her nose. Grace was a skating fan. Brian,

115

her twin, was a good foot taller than his sister, towering over her protectively. He was a spitting image of his mother, with thick, curly black hair and dark, almost black eyes that sometimes twinkled mischievously when he spoke to his twin in hushed Arabic.

They were both preparing for college in the fall. Grace was going to a college in the East of the United States to study literature and journalism, while Brian was going to study zoology at a university in California. That got Jacqueline's attention and they spent some time in the evening discussing different courses he would be taking. Jacqueline thought longingly about her own studies. All in all, the evening was not a complete bust. She got along just fine with her dinner guests and actually enjoyed talking to them.

"Do you think I could come and watch you skate tomorrow?" Grace asked tentatively. She blushed when she asked.

Jacqueline almost groaned. She liked the twins but she was not ready to have them invade her inner sanctum, the only place she could retreat to.

"I'm not sure my coach would be so happy about that," she said slowly and quietly hoping her mother had not heard them.

She knew Fiona would not have a problem with her having guests at the rink. She, Jacqueline, just didn't want them there! Grace's face fell. Jacqueline almost rolled her eyes and took a deep breath.

"Jacqueline, why don't you take tomorrow off," her mother suggested. She had overheard their conversation! Jacqueline looked at her mother and shook her head.

"I don't think I can, Mother," she said quietly, trying to hold on to her privacy as long as she could. With her mother getting involved, she knew that she was fighting a losing battle. "There is the program to work out."

"Pish-posh, Grace wants to go skating," her mother smiled and looked at their guests.

Then she turned toward Jacqueline and cast a warning glance at her daughter. Jacqueline understood her mother's look. These people were important to her country! She nearly voiced her displeasure, anger festering just below the surface, well aware that with one look, her only sanctuary was being ripped away from her. Instead, she turned to the two young people and smiled.

"It would be my pleasure for you two to come and skate. Have you done any skating at all?" she asked them using the best public relations voice she could muster.

Of course they had! They both skated in their free time. Brian had played on a hockey team and Grace had taken some lessons when she was younger. They were thrilled to be able to join her in the morning.

"Well, that is wonderful," her mother beamed at everyone. "And while the young people are entertaining themselves, why don't I show you around our country." Her mother invited the older folks as they left the dining room to adjourn in the parlor.

By now Jacqueline wanted nothing more than to curl up on her bed. Her eyelids were heavy. The fire was roaring and the room was too warm. It was a recipe for falling asleep. And she did. Her brother bumped her arm just as she was losing the fight. She jerked awake and couldn't help but yawn.

"I am sorry, but it seems that it would be best for me to retire," she said as she got up.

It was indeed getting late and everyone excused themselves. Morning would come too soon, she thought as she walked sluggishly along the hall to her room bumping into the wall sleepily here and there.

She rounded the corner and bumped into something softer than the wall, Brian!

"Excuse me," she stammered, her face turning bright red. Then she looked at him again. "Are you lost?"

"I think so," he admitted scratching his head in a bewildered way. His hair stuck up in all different direction, making him look a lot like a dark Peter Pan. "I forgot where my room is."

She feared she would laugh and quickly cleared her throat. "Hmm, that would be a problem. Where are you supposed to stay?" she asked as she continued down the hall toward her room.

"Some blue room," he answered and ran his hand through his rumpled hair.

"Ah, no problem. I actually know where it is," she laughed. She motioned for him to follow her. "You are not the first one to be lost in these halls. It is said that one of my ancestors got lost after a night of heavy entertaining. He was never found!" she whispered mysteriously and laughed along with Brian. "We have many such stories to scare our guests. In fact, that might be the reason we don't have too many guests," she pondered and pointed to his door. "Don't hesitate to ask for help. I wonder if your sister found her room," she whispered and smirked at him.

"She is probably wandering these halls, just as I was. Is there anyone who would help her?" he asked as he opened his door.

"Actually," she giggled and turned to go, "we have a group of dedicated servants who comb these halls at night looking for lost guests. Perhaps they will find our long lost ancestor in the process one of these days."

"I am much relieved then, good night," Brian grinned and closed his door.

Chapter 17

When her alarm clock rang the next morning, she threw it across the room. But then it only rang again and she had to get up to turn it off. By this time she was barely awake and grumbled as she made her way to the back door. She jumped when she heard a noise coming from behind her as she passed the room Brian was supposed to be inhabiting.

"Good morning," he said surprised.

"You are up early," she grunted while she gave her heart a chance to settle down again. Usually there was nobody around at this hour in the morning.

"Yeah, I couldn't sleep. I guess I am suffering from jet lag," he answered. "I thought that if I can't sleep I could go running. Would you like to join me on my little run?"

"How little? I usually go three miles and that's it."

"All right, I guess I could go *only* three miles," he goaded her and waited. "You coming?"

It turned out to be a fun time. Brian complained that she was taking her time, but at the end of the three miles he was huffing and puffing harder than Jacqueline.

"All right, I am not in shape anymore," he wheezed.

"And here I thought I was holding you back," she said as she opened the back door, trying not to breathe heavily.

After such a strenuous exercise, they craved food – breakfast sounded really good. Jacqueline showed him the way to the kitchen.

"If you smile at chef, and thank him and make him feel as though he is the best thing since ice cream, he will eat out of your hands and anything you want is yours," she advised him quietly as they approached their target. The staff was busy trying to get a presentable breakfast ready and they did not even notice the two. George was grumpy as he bumped into Brian.

"I'm sorry, sir, but I need to ask you to leave the kitchen. This is no place for you right now," he complained and frowned as Brian smiled and complimented him on the delicious goose. "Have you been taking lessons from her?" he pointed to Jacqueline with a wooden ladle dripping with pancake batter. She knew better than to stay around when George was in a bad mood.

"Well, no, eh, yes, I suppose. I am just hungry," he stammered.

Chef growled and pointed him toward a bowl of fruits and a few steaming rolls, sitting on the counter, fresh out of the oven. He shot Jacqueline a grumpy look and was on his way.

"I think he got up on the wrong side of the bed," she whispered as they stole out of the kitchen, each with an apple and a piece of bread. "He is usually a lot happier."

"Well, thanks," Brian grinned as he took a bite of his hot roll. "Mmm, this is really good. I'll see you in a bit," he told Jacqueline.

"Wait, you are going the wrong way!" Jacqueline laughed.

"I don't think I will ever find my way in this labyrinth," he grumbled as Jacqueline pointed him in the right direction.

She was off for yet another torture session. By nine o'clock, she was dressed and clean and appeared in the dining room. The guests were already seated and were conversing with her brother, who was sitting with them.

"So the young people have an exciting day planned," Jean joked as he poured himself a cup of coffee.

He looked at his sister and, knowing how difficult it was for her to share her ice with strangers, he smiled. Jacqueline ignored her brother's peacemaking gesture. She was not looking forward to this at all.

Their mother walked in late and apologized for her tardiness and explained that her husband was occupied but would join them after their trip around the country. When Grace appeared, Jacqueline chuckled and hid her face behind a napkin. She felt Brian's eyes on her and avoided looking at him. Apparently Grace had indeed found her way around the palace. She was dumbfounded that her brother had gotten lost. He took it in good humor, when Grace shook her head at his confused wanderings and teased him mercilessly.

Jacqueline felt as though she was going to jump out of her skin. Her usually sedate rink was filled with laughter and shouting from an impromptu hockey match the twins were participating in. Brian was chasing his sister across the rink with a broom. Grace shrieked in pleasure and avoided him as much as she could. He finally swept her off of her feet and she fell with a loud *thump*, landing on her rear. Grace glared at her brother who circled the rink in victory, making it look like he had just won the medal.

Jacqueline swallowed hard. This was the only place in the whole world where nobody could follow her. And here were these two, laughing and teasing each other when she only wanted to get on the ice and let the music soothe her already tangled nerves. She groaned inwardly and thought that her mother had asked a little too much of her youngest daughter today.

"Hey Jacqueline," Brian's laughing voice cut into her self-pitying thoughts. "Are you just going to sit there or are you going to come out here to join us?"

Jacqueline huffed. She didn't just go out onto the ice to play! Her time was too valuable for that.

"You know we have skating rinks in Dubai," Brian said proudly and smirked when she made a surprised face.

"Really, in the desert?" she bit out sarcastically.

"Well, no. They are in a building," he told her seriously, and Jacqueline burst out laughing.

"This is going to be so much fun," Grace giggled, when she sat next to Jacqueline to tighten her skates. "Can you show me some moves?"

Again she swallowed a groan. *Show her some moves?* Who did Grace think she was? Some two-bit skater, who had nothing better to do than to *show her some moves?*

Jacqueline swallowed her ire and got up on the ice. She showed her a few easy jumps, which Grace mastered surprisingly quickly. Brian joined them and tried to do the same, in hockey skates. Jacqueline bit her bottom lip. She didn't want to admit that she might actually be starting to have fun. When Brian attempted a spin and landed in a loud thud on the ice, even she couldn't hide her grin. Grace stood over her twin, laughing and teasing him remorselessly. Jacqueline was caught by surprise to find herself finally warming up to the twins.

Fiona arrived and glared at her.

"We don't really have much time to fool around!" she grumbled. Apparently everyone around her was in a bad mood today, Jacqueline thought. It was rubbing off on her.

"Five more minutes, and then I am going to expect you to do some practicing," Fiona warned.

Jacqueline was only too happy to comply. She really didn't have the time to be racing around the rink after the twins. Watching her guests as they attempted a hockey match using whatever they could find, Jacqueline envied them. She grinned when Brian attempted to get the *puck*, a piece of crumpled up paper, away from his sister using a long paint roller. Where he had found that, she didn't know. Grace guarded the puck with her broom. She let out a blood curdling war whoop and charged at her brother. Brian skated out of the way quickly, leaving Grace to chase him. Jacqueline chuckled. Suddenly, it wasn't so bad to have people sharing her ice.

Jacqueline tried to settle down to work. Brian and Grace stayed on the ice but were instructed to stay out of the way. That would have worked out wonderfully if only she could have stayed on her feet during this relatively simple training session. Unfortunately it seemed that gravity worked overtime today and she landed with a thump on her rear end, again and again. She moaned in pain and was about to get up when she was covered by a spray of ice. She sputtered and glared up at a laughing Brian.

"I'm sorry, but I just couldn't resist," he laughed out loud and bent over. Then he held out his hand to help her get up.

She tried to get up as elegantly and dignified as she could, but all the illusion was lost. Her face was covered with ice, which was melting down her neck. Her rear end was coated in ice. As she skated away she tried to brush the ice off her butt with as much poise as she could muster. She heard roaring laughter behind her. After two hours she felt her muscles were finally giving out, her brain shutting down. Fiona could tell that Jacqueline had had enough.

"School is out for today," she yelled and Jacqueline sighed in relief.

"Thank you, I am beat. It was a long night last night and it has been a long day," she told her coach when they got off the ice.

"It looks like you are getting along just fine with your guests," Fiona tried to hide her smile behind a steaming cup of tea.

"Mother made me!" Jacqueline pouted quietly.

"But of course, whatever you say, dear," Fiona grinned and
sauntered away.

Grace skated over to her beaming. "That was so much fun! I
wish I could skate like you. But I think I lack a little bit of discipline."
She bit her bottom lip and twirled the end of her pony tail. "Brian was
telling me that you were up early this morning and beat him in a three
mile run," she said and her face was unreadable.

"Well, it really wasn't a race," Jacqueline corrected her, feeling
like Grace was trying to make a point. "But he did seem a little winded
at the end." She looked down at her skate to hide her smile.

"You have to come and skate in Dubai," Grace said, watching
Jacqueline take off her skates. "You would love it there! The weather is
great, unless you come in the summer, and the beaches are beautiful.
Our house is right at the beach. The water is warm and blue," she
enthused.

"But aren't you moving to the States?" Jacqueline asked.

"Not yet," Grace told her. "We are both going after the
summer. Aren't you going too?"

"Well, no. It hasn't been decided yet," Jacqueline answered
quietly.

Grace prodded her for an answer. Again, Jacqueline had to
swallow down her anger. Yes, she liked the twins, but she wasn't ready
to share her thoughts with them. Especially not with someone her
mother wanted her to entertain because of a business deal for her
country. Grace prodded her long enough that finally Jacqueline told her

her fight against her parents' aversion for her future plans. She felt irritated and frustrated all over again.

Grace pursed her lips and looked at Jacqueline for a long time. "I know this is really strange, but I have found that sometimes it helps if I pray about it." She turned to face Jacqueline earnestly.

"You mean like to God?" Jacqueline asked.

"Yeah of course to God, silly!" Grace answered smiling. "Who else?"

Jacqueline had to admit that she really hadn't thought about it. She felt a little bit embarrassed.

"Just try it and see what happens."

Jacqueline thought about this statement for a while. She remembered the fear during the almost fatal flight.

"I just... might try it. I'm not in the habit of doing that kind of stuff, mind you."

"Hey, that's all right. I wasn't either until last year. A friend of mine invited me to go to a meeting. Let's just say, it was eye opening," she said enthusiastically. Brian came up to his sister's side, his skates flung over his shoulder. His hair stood up in true Peter Pan fashion. Jacqueline found herself fighting a smile.

"I see she is talking to you about her new religion," he teased.

"It's not religion, Bri, it's... It's a relationship," Grace reprimanded her brother seriously. He turned away from his sister to make a face at Jacqueline.

Chapter 18

"I'm famished," Jacqueline stated. "Let's pilfer the kitchen. This time Brian, try to stay out of chef's way. Grace, he is usually a pussy cat, when you get to know him," she laughed at Brian's disbelieving face. "You must just rub him the wrong way."

The three made their way to the palace and soon found themselves outside the kitchen. Again it was a place of fevered activity and shouts could be heard through the closed doors.

"I tell you what," Jacqueline suggested. "We steal in, grab a sandwich and steal out. No problem. Follow me!" she whispered and opened the door a crack.

She felt like they were on a very important mission. Several cooks were bent over steaming dishes. The pastry chef was busy pounding some dough into shape. Jacqueline opened the door all the way and the three stepped into the bright room. It was steaming in there!

"Your Highness," she heard George shout. "May we help you? I tell you what. You tell us what you want and we will deliver it to you. That way you are out of my way," he growled.

The three ordered sandwiches and decided to eat them in the sun room, which was wonderfully warm at this time of day. Jacqueline looked at her watch. She needed to be studying and not playing board games with her parent's guests. She felt her nerves tingle as she tried to concentrate on pushing her piece around the board. Her thoughts were on equations and species.

As the sun started to go down, the room became cooler.

"Why don't we move into the living room," Jacqueline suggested. "There is a fire there!"

They reconvened in the living room in front of the roaring fire. She leaned back against the back of her chair and laughed at the way Brain was systematically destroying Grace, one simple move after another. Grace was not taking it too well, either, and the game ended rather abruptly when the board went flying across the table.

"Oops," Grace said innocently. "Did I just do that? I guess it's a tie, brother of mine!"

Brian threw his head back in roaring laughter. They settled on the couch and talked about their studies coming up. Jacqueline felt envious. They could pursue their dream, while Jacqueline had obligations to her family and country to fulfill.

"So where are you going, now that you are finishing up with your exams?" Brian asked and ran a hand over his hair, causing it to stand up yet again.

"I'm not sure," she muttered and lowered her eyes.

"It's complicated," Grace answered for her.

"You girls! It's always complicated," he grumbled.

"That's right," Grace answered and made a face at her brother.

"Whatever, Grace. You and your drama. Your day is not ever complete without at least one dramatic thing happening."

"Oh, that is not fair. I don't need drama every day!" Grace replied with feigned dignity. They bickered in good humor back and forth, while Jacqueline couldn't help but laugh at them.

"You must be happy to have an older brother, who is dignified and nice," Grace winced when Brian pinched her arm.

"You'd be surprised," Jacqueline answered quietly.

Finally it was late enough for her to excuse herself to get ready for dinner. Yes! Shower and food, she thought, and then bed, please. On her way to her room, her mother intercepted her.

"How was your day, Jacqueline?"

"It was very nice. I like them, actually. They mentioned that they have a skating rink in Dubai. Perhaps I should go and skate there. How would that be for business?"

"That would be excellent, dear," her mother smiled and hugged her quickly. "We are close to making a deal. Your father and Mr. Spencer sequestered themselves after lunch. I want to thank you for stepping up, Jacqueline."

"You're welcome, Mother," she answered sincerely.

The shower felt so good after a day of pushing her body to its limit. She emerged feeling a different person. She combed her hair and put it into a ponytail. She donned a simple green pantsuit and beige angora sweater. Looking into the mirror and nodding to herself she though, *Yep, that will do.*

Dinner was excellent, as usual. Jacqueline thought that it was a shame that she had to watch what she ate because the food at the palace was so good. On the other hand her self-discipline was probably a good thing, she thought, as she dipped her spoon into the scrumptious cream of mushroom soup.

She watched as Grace and Brian told their parents about their day, laughing with them. What amazed her most was that the parents interacted with their children so casually. Her own family never shared such intimacy, such carefree openness. If they sat down to eat together the atmosphere was usually forced, stiff. In fact, she spent most of her time when she was not busy studying, skating, or presenting at some sort of social function, alone. She felt as though she was missing something very important, and her breath hitched. She had to choke back sudden tears that sprang to her eyes. It would not do for her to start crying.

After dinner she excused herself, bone weary and unable to entertain anymore. The twins also chose to retire to their rooms.

"Now, you will be able to find your way to your room, right?" she teased Brian and he assured her that he had marked the way with breadcrumbs. She turned to him seriously.

"Er, that didn't work out so well for Hansel and Gretel, you know."

"True, but they were in the forest," he chuckled.

"Hmm, have you thought of the palace personnel? They are absolutely ruthless when they find any little debris on any surface, especially the floor," she replied and smirked back. He winced and looked around.

"I suppose I may be wandering around like your ancestor. Please look for me in the lost galleries or the dungeons by the morrow," he stated dramatically and kissed his sister on the cheek. "Good bye, fair sister. No, no, don't cry over me. I will battle the haunted rooms, dust bunnies and other monsters I come in contact with on my travels."

"And you called *me* dramatic!" his sister hissed, raised her eyebrows and made her way to her room. "You could just follow me," she laughed over her shoulder. "I know the way."

Merrily they bid Jacqueline good night. Jacqueline chuckled as she made her way to her suite. Feeling guilty over not studying, she tackled her chemistry book. She turned moles into atoms and balanced equations for the next two hours until the words on the page became fuzzy. Her alarm clock told her it was nearing eleven.

"I guess I exaggerated a little bit when I said that I would study until midnight," she murmured sleepily and set her alarm clock.

It seemed that she had hardly closed her eyes when her alarm went off. Grumbling she hit the snooze, repeatedly. As it didn't make the annoying noise stop, she reluctantly got up, groped around for her running attire, and looked out into the bleak predawn darkness. *Why am I doing this?* She asked herself. *Who in their right mind gets up at this vile hour?*

She must be out of her mind, she chided herself as she opened the door to the frigid outdoors. The wind was blustery and the rain had made the snow slippery. She took one step outside and decided today would be a swim day. As she turned around, Brian emerged from the dark palace. He was bundled in a warmup jacket touting his future university. He wore a woolen hat and had earplugs in his ears. He grinned as she almost stumbled over him.

"Wow, you are up early again," she coughed. "I am scrapping my run this morning."

"What?" he shouted, removing the plugs.

"Look around, Brian. It would be impossible not to fall in this weather," she pointed to the frozen slush.

"Ah, point taken," he agreed. "Oh well, so much for getting back into shape," he uttered sadly. "I thought since you are up, I might as well join you."

"Well, we do have a pool," she said quietly. Why was she offering him to join her? She craved her privacy even more this morning after all the time they had spent together the previous day.

"Of course you have a pool," he laughed, slapping his forehead lightly. "Why didn't you tell me this before? I can do the pool. Meet you there?"

She hesitated, fighting with herself. She knew her parents were counting on her to be the entertainment and she was getting used to his easy going style. She suppressed her sigh.

"Sure. Do you know where it is?"

"Ah, no. Not really." Brian scratched his head, which caused the hat to slip into his eyes. He pushed it back onto his head.

"Get your stuff and meet me in the front hall then. If you can find that," she teased.

She was surprised when Brian beat her to the hall.

"I assume you have managed to navigate on your own," she teased and received a mysterious grin in reply.

Brian turned out to be a much better swimmer than he was a runner. This time she really had a hard time keeping up with him. After forty-five minutes it was she who was out of breath.

"I could go on like this for a while," Brian told her when she got out of the pool.

"Good for you," she grumbled and toweled off.

He grinned back at her in reply. "What is next?"

This time she was not able to suppress a soft groan.

Brian's eyebrows shot up. "Unless you don't want company," he said quietly.

She managed to recover by faking a cough. "No, by all means."

Before they made their way to the weight room they once again decided to try to get some food. It was becoming a habit.

They stopped outside the kitchen door. "I'm not sure whether your Chef will pommel me if I show my face again," he whispered.

Jacqueline laughed at him. "He really is harmless. You will see."

The kitchen smelled wonderful. George was busy rolling some dough, when he spotted them.

"And still you return," he growled and frowned at Brian.

"Be nice George. Brian has to eat after the workout he just did!"

The old man scrutinized poor Brian, who stood stock still, as though he were prey, waiting to be devoured by its predator. Then his face turned pink for just a split second and he returned the old man's scrutiny. It seemed like ages when the chef finally grunted, nodded and turned to wipe his floury hands.

"What is your pleasure?" he asked.

"What do you recommend?" Jacqueline replied and nudged Brian.

"I could just go for a bowl of cereal and some fruit," Brian replied.

"Cereal!" the chef sputtered and stared at the young man stupefied. "He comes into *my* kitchen and asks for cereal!" he muttered as he shuffled toward the fridge. "I can whip you up an omelet, like you have never tasted. Crepes, egg soufflé," he paused a moment and thought. "That might take a while. You will not have cereal!" he commanded.

"All right," Brian stammered. "I will have an omelet with cheese, mushrooms, peppers and onions."

"Chef, didn't you hear me?" Jacqueline growled. "The poor guy's going to have major cramps if you make him one of your omelets. We are on our way to the weight room!"

She rummaged through the fridge and emerged with a container of yogurt, two bananas, and some strawberries. She pulled out two bowls, ignoring the muttering chef. She spooned yogurt into both, topped it with fruit, and poured some granola over the top.

"Here you go," she grinned as she handed Brian a bowl. "I don't know what is wrong with him," she pointed her finger at the muttering chef. "He is usually much less intimidating."

She led him to a high-top counter surrounded with tall chairs. "Enjoy your breakfast."

"Thanks," he answered and dug greedily into his food. "You know, I will have to try some of his omelets now," he stated with his mouth full.

Jacqueline smiled and they talked their way through breakfast. She put her bowl into the industrial size dishwasher.

"You do dishes?" Brian marveled as they walked out.

"I wouldn't call that doing dishes," she called over her shoulder.

When they met again, Jacqueline showed him the way to the weight room. It was equipped with the newest equipment.

"Nice setup," he complimented. She grimaced.

"This is my least favorite part of training," she confessed quietly as the trainer entered the room.

Chapter 19

The training session was more to Brian's liking than hers. After a few minutes, she was thoroughly tired of the whole thing. She toweled off her sweaty brow and winced when she looked at her reflection in the full-length mirror surrounding the room. Her face was red and glistening with sweat; her hair had come partly undone from her pony tail and was sticking out at odd angles. She was still huffing and puffing.

She escorted him back to his room, explaining how to get there. Brian grinned and thanked her for a fun morning. She groaned. Then she hurried to get cleaned up for her next training session.

She sat down on her bed and pulled her warm socks over her warm up pants. A thought came into her mind. She remembered Grace saying something about praying to God when she needed things. She chuckled. It was cool to think of having a genie, who would grant her every wish, but somehow she didn't think God was like a genie. He would probably want something in return. Maybe she should give it a try. She had tried it when the plane was tumbling out of the sky, why not now? This time she would do it proper-like, though.

She knelt by her bed and folded her hands demurely, looking out her picture window into the sky, where she assumed God was watching from. She took a deep breath.

"God, thou art great and mighty. I," she paused looking for just the right word that would catch the Almighty's attention. "I beseech thee with my request. I wish to become a veterinarian. Wouldst thou please look favorably upon me, a humble servant?"

She rose and dusted off her pants. She had done it!

She dragged herself to the rink again. This traveling back and forth between her room and the rink added to her exercise, she mused. She figured she walked about two miles every day, between the rink and the palace. She pushed the door open and froze in place because Grace was sitting in one of the chairs, lacing up her skates. Was she never to have a day to herself with these two around? It was like they had attached themselves to her! Permanently!

She tried not to let her irritation show. Grace was waiting for her, stifling a yawn.

"Sorry, but I just got up. I am definitely not a morning person," she admitted as she moved to sit next to Jacqueline while she put on her skates.

"That is nice for you!" Jacqueline grumbled. She really didn't need this hanger-on! "But I don't have the luxury of sleeping in, except on Sundays. That is when I don't do too much."

"Oh," Grace said and stared at the ice. "I don't know how you keep up this pace, Jacqueline. Don't you even have a moment when you just relax?"

"Sundays," Jacqueline grumbled and stepped on the ice. *Or if nobody is here on my ice with me,* she wanted to say. Instead she smiled sweetly when Grace joined her on the ice. She chose to ignore her and started to warm up. It was soothing to glide across the smooth ice. She almost forgot about Grace.

"How do you do it?" Grace shouted when she landed a triple axel flawlessly.

"Practice, falling, more practice, more falling," she grinned against her better judgment. "You get the point, right?"

Grace laughed. "I would love to be able to just perform like you. I think I would die from nerves."

Jacqueline tried to focus on her practice, but something didn't let go of Grace's last statement. She finally gave up. She sighed and turned toward where Grace was trying to do a spin, not too badly either.

"Tell you what," she said to her. "It's not that hard to put on a small performance. Why don't I help you with that for tonight?"

The words were out of her mouth before she realized she had said them. *You only have yourself to blame, Jacqueline!*

"You would do that for me?" Grace beamed.

Jacqueline plastered on her smile. "Of course, why not?"

"Okay. When can we start?" she asked.

Jacqueline thought for a moment about this added responsibility she had just taken on, voluntarily. When would she ever fit it into her schedule?

"There is no time like the present," she sighed and discussed some possible elements Grace would be able to perform. Grace blushed and thanked her over and over again.

"I never thought I would do anything like this."

139

"Inside all of us is an ice princess, don't you think?" Jacqueline chuckled.

When they were satisfied with her progress, Jacqueline led her to a small room off the back of the rink, filled with exquisite costumes.

"Wow, would you look at all these!" Grace whispered and gently ran her hand over the soft material.

"Yes, well one must be prepared for all occasions," Jacqueline explained. She pointed to a glittering red and orange costume.

"I wore this one to the Junior European Championships. It looks like fire. I think it is one of my favorite costumes." She held it up to Grace. "Go ahead. Try it on," she encouraged her.

"I don't know if I could wear something like this," Grace stammered.

"We'll see how it looks," suggested Jacqueline and shut the door to the room so Grace would have privacy.

"You look fabulous," she beamed, when Grace emerged a little while later.

"I feel like I'm not wearing anything," Grace admitted. She tugged on the short skirt, trying to make it stretch. "Do I really have to wear this? It is absolutely beautiful, but I really don't feel very comfortable in this."

"That's fine," Jacqueline said, wondering why Grace felt that way. She never had a problem with her costumes. "You can wear a sweater and jeans, if you would feel more comfortable."

Grace thanked her, almost apologetically. "I would be more comfortable with that. I mean, I can't wear something this short anymore."

"How come?" Jacqueline looked at her in surprise.

"Well, I just don't feel comfortable in short skirts anymore. When I became a Christian my life changed and I became more aware of how things I do affect others around me."

"That's nice, but what does that have to do with the clothes you wear?"

"I just try to wear more modest clothes," Grace mumbled.

Jacqueline thought about that. She never had a problem with the clothes she wore. She found them acceptable and her costumes were functional.

"That's fine, Grace. I'm not offended. Just thinking about it."

"Good," Grace grinned. "You see," she panted, suddenly feeling the need to explain. "I used to not worry about what I wore, but since I became a Christian, things have changed. I am aware that I carry some responsibility not to make my brother stumble when I show up in something short and tight."

"Your brother has a problem with what you wear?" Jacqueline was a little astounded that Brian would have a problem with his sister's clothing.

"I'm sorry, that didn't come out right," Grace giggled. "My brother, Brian, doesn't care about that. But there are other young men out there and I just don't want to make them uncomfortable. Do you get the picture?"

141

"Oh," Jacqueline replied slowly as she started to realize what Grace was talking about. "I never thought of that. You put it in words I have never heard. I mean I don't go around wearing clothes to gain the attention of men, but if you put it that way," she continued slowly. "So, this is something new to you too?"

"Yeah," Grace admitted sucking her lip and twirling her pony tail. "You see, when I became a Christian something inside me changed. I thought less about me anymore and more about Christ, who saved me. For example, I used to go out and party with my friends all the time. I never cared about what my parents thought. Many nights my late nights would keep them up, worrying about me. I don't want to do that anymore. It's not that I am not allowed to do that, but I just don't want to do it anymore. I wasn't honoring my parents by going against what they thought was right for me. There are other things I used to do that I just have no appetite for now."

"So you want to please an invisible God now?" Jacqueline asked sarcastically. She wasn't sure if she wanted to talk religion with Grace.

"No," Grace answered slowly. "It's not just about pleasing God. I can't do that, not really. It's not about doing good. And really I can't be good enough to wipe out my sins by myself. That was already done for me. By Jesus' loving act of taking on my sins when He died on the cross, I am now free to act according to what He is directing me to do through His Spirit. Does that make sense?" she asked looking at Jacqueline seriously.

"Not really. You have a dead guy directing what you are doing with the help of a ghost? That sounds a little strange to me. I guess I have not really heard it the way you put it. I always thought that if you are good enough, you end up in heaven. If you mess up enough times, down into hell you go."

"That is not exactly the way it goes. You see, nobody deserves to go to heaven, because we are born with sin. Sin separates us from God. Because God knew that, He made a plan and sent His son to act as a blood sacrifice for us, to take on our sin and punishment by dying for us. When we trust in Jesus as our Lord and Savior, we start to make different choices because the Holy Spirit, our counselor, starts directing us. Then we start reading His love letters to us, the Bible, and we see that God expects to direct us intimately, kind of like you and I are talking right now." She pursed her lips for a moment. "So when was the last time someone died for you?"

Jacqueline laughed softly and shook her head. "A body guard would die for me."

"Yeah, because he is being paid to watch you. However, Jesus died while we were condemned already. In reality He took our punishment. The punishment of death. The one we deserved. He didn't deserve the punishment. He showed love by following what God, His Father, asked Him to do, even to the point of dying on the cross."

They walked outside to make their way back to the palace.

"Hmm, you have given me a lot to think about," Jacqueline murmured softly. She looked at Grace and smirked. "So, no costume for you."

"Thanks so much for understanding," Grace uttered quietly. "You would be surprised at how many people look at me and shake their heads."

When they talked to both families, they laughed and accepted the girls' invitation for the evening.

Chapter 20

Her parents summoned her back to their office in the afternoon. They both looked up from their paperwork when she walked in. Her father set down what he had been working on and looked at his daughter.

"You have been incredibly useful with helping us secure a very good deal for our country. In return we would like to grant your proposal and are allowing you to study whatever you wish. We would like to encourage you to reconsider your chosen course of study, but if you think you would like to pursue this kind of work, we will not stand in the way."

"Really?" Jacqueline shouted and clasped her hands over her mouth.

"Yes. You wanted to skate... and look at the favorable publicity your crazy hobby has produced," her father answered with a twinkle in his eyes. "We are starting to realize that we really can't hold you here, if you want to fly away. But we would like to keep you here as long as we can," he laughed.

Her mother sniffed and turned her head.

She couldn't believe it! Her parents had granted her request! Against all odds they had granted it. She pursed her lips and twisted a strand of her hair that had escaped her pony tail. Then a slow smile played on her lips. That was the second request God had granted her. Could this be possible?

Jacqueline wanted to tell Grace and found her in her room.

"You will never believe what just happened!" she laughed loudly. "My parents have agreed to allow me to study whatever I want. I took your suggestion and I prayed. I want to hear more of what you have to say," she grinned.

Grace sat down on her couch and closed her eyes for a moment. Then she looked seriously at Jacqueline.

"Well, as you begin a relationship with Christ you have to come to the understanding that you are a sinner. No, don't look so shocked," Grace quickly added, "we are all sinners before a Holy God, before we take on the likeness of Christ. So you are in good company." She pursed her lips and crinkled up her eyes, trying to think. "You see, what would happen if you were driving along and accidentally hit and ran over a child, killing it? You didn't mean to do it, of course. You would come before a judge and he would sentence you according to your crime. But what if there was a complete stranger in the courtroom, who in the last moment stood up and took your punishment? You see God is a very just God, and nobody can come before Him without fault. When Jesus came to earth, being one with God, He took on your punishment, your guilt, your sin, so you can now stand before a just God, covered by His blood."

146

"But I haven't done anything bad," Jacqueline argued. "In fact I try to help our people, I don't steal, and I don't lie. I'm not a bad person."

"I know you aren't. But look at it from God's perspective. How much do you give credit to Him? When was the last time you acknowledged God as King, as Lord? When people come before your parents they bow down and they honor your parents' wishes, don't they? They understand that your parents have authority over their lives. Well, God put them into that authority. It is the same thing with God. He would like complete say in what you are doing in your life. He wants you to come before Him and give Him your heart, your future, your past and your present. He wants to live with you in that heart of yours. That is what you have to come to understand," Grace said earnestly.

"It may take a week. It may take a long time for you to understand and agree to it, but when you do, your life will change and you will be a new creation when you are born of the Spirit. The stains of your past are no longer a part of you. Christ's blood has washed it clean. And then, your life really begins and you will have someone on your side, keeping you accountable to Himself."

"Wow," Jacqueline whispered. She bit her bottom lip. "I have never heard this before. I always thought I was a Christian because I go to church now and then."

"Not really," snickered Grace. "You have to come to understand the evil that is in your heart and that without a Savior, Christ, you have about a chance in a trillion of making it to heaven. In fact, the only way to be reunited with God is through His Son, Jesus Christ."

"Well, I have a lot to think about. Where did you hear all this?"

"At the revival meeting I went to last year in the States. Boy, I tell you it was something else. But if you are really interested you should start reading the Bible and praying. And you can always call me with questions."

"Yeah, I guess so," Jacqueline replied quietly and her brows knitted in thought.

The show for the evening was scheduled before dinner. The Spencers laughed when they entered the arena where Grace was waiting on the ice for them. Jacqueline had the lights down low and only the rink was lit up.

"This is a really nice setup," she heard Mr. Spencer exclaim as he took a seat on one of the cushioned seats off to the side of the rink.

"We like to keep Jacqueline happy," her brother Jean joked and she heard Brian snicker.

Once their guests were settled comfortably, Jacqueline thanked them for coming, feeling very formal and proper, and announced the debut of a previously yet unknown skater. She chuckled to herself as she left the rink and motioned Grace to take her place on center ice. The music started and Grace skated very nicely. She almost fell after the only jump she attempted but recovered nicely. Not bad for only one afternoon's work, Jacqueline thought. Grace bowed elegantly to the applause, the *audience* standing at their seats, cheering enthusiastically.

148

They sat down quietly when Jacqueline glided up and took her place. She skated as though she was performing for the Olympic judges and from the look on her audience's faces, they thoroughly enjoyed it.

"You really need to come to Dubai," her guests remarked happily.

Jacqueline looked at her parents. They looked very pleased, as though they had just enjoyed a particularly scrumptious and unexpected meal.

Chapter 21

All too soon the visit was over. Jacqueline couldn't believe that she was sad to see the guests leave. She had gotten used to both of them being around her all the time, and when she found herself at her rink the day they left, she was lonely. Their resounding laughter was missing from the rink.

Her life returned to the crazy schedule she kept. She had been contacted for a lot of public appearances and reluctantly obliged. Her packed calendar put a lot of pressure on her, leaving her feeling overwhelmed and overextended. On the ice she found herself making mistakes she had not made the previous year. Her attention span was getting shorter and shorter and although she had major examinations coming up, she found that she could not get any facts into her brain. She felt helpless. It was as if she was being swept to and fro and felt as if she had no control of her life.

"You don't look yourself!" Fiona gazed at her with concern one afternoon after she had spoken to a group of high school students. "Are you feeling all right?"

"I don't know, Fiona, I am so tired all the time."

"Sit down a moment. What is going on?" Fiona pulled her to the side of the rink. "We can't go on skating like this. You are so distracted that you are making some very serious mistakes. I don't think that the schedule you keep is all that good for you. We need to think of eliminating some of your activities. You are taking on too much."

"I know," Jacqueline sighed. But she felt obligated to placate her parents. They had agreed to let her study whatever she wanted. She owed them. "I feel like I am running on empty all the time. Everyone around me is ordering me around. It would be nice to have some time to breathe."

"I want you to make a list of your activities. What is the most important thing for you right now? I don't need my star skater burning herself out. All right? If I have to speak to your parents about easing up your schedule, I will. We will discuss this tomorrow. For now, go and skate. I'm going to leave you to it," Fiona patted her shoulder and walked out of the rink. "I'll be in my office if you need me."

Jacqueline took a deep breath and looked at the expanse of the ice. She breathed deeply and allowed the music to calm her raw nerves. The CD was playing Handel's *Messiah* and the powerful notes flowed out, washed over her and touched her soul. She was soon gliding across the ice, allowing the music to direct her movement. After a few moments she began to have fun. The jumps became bolder and higher, her joints absorbing the force of the landing without any flaw. Soon the music stopped and she slid to a halt, panting but elated. This still was what she wanted to do. She felt alive on the ice.

151

Sudden clapping echoed from the entrance and Jacqueline half-expected Fiona to be standing in the doorway to the rink. Instead a tall, lanky man in his late thirties started toward her on street shoes. He was dressed in a dark suit, his blond hair combed neatly, his steely gray eyes measuring her and her surroundings.

"I had to come and see it for myself," he said in slick, oily French. "You really are as good as I have seen on TV," he chuckled.

"Eric La Pelle, what in the world are you doing on my ice?" she scowled as the stranger chortled and came closer. She had trained with this man for a short while once. He made her skin crawl. His students were usually a mess of nerves. Jacqueline had seen him give his last student such a dressing down, that the poor girl was unable to finish her program.

"This is not a public rink. You have no right to be here. I am going to ask you to leave," she told him, her green eyes growing cold and weary as he came ever closer.

"You are not even going to give an old friend a warm welcome," he asked in a malicious voice.

"I don't see any friends around here," she growled.

"But Jacqueline, think of all the fun we could have had. You and me," he grinned and stepped closer. The insinuations of his words, the way his eyes calculatingly raked over her, made her feel like she had just invited a cougar in for a tasty morsel. The rink became a few degrees colder and Jacqueline suppressed a shiver, as she remembered... Her stomach flipped unpleasantly, making her feel nauseous.

"Stop right there! You are no friend and as you can see, Fiona is doing just fine without any help from you or any other trainer."

"There is always time to change," he said and walked a circle around her, looking her up and down, a malevolent gleam in his eyes. He clicked his tongue softly. "Yes indeed. You have grown up nicely, little princess."

Jacqueline thought she would hurl on his very expensive shoes.

"Leave or I will call security. Better yet I will call Fiona. She is like a bear mother with her cub when it comes to me," she threatened, heat rising to her face.

"I don't see Fiona. I think you are bluffing. You are all alone." The cougar stepped forward.

Jacqueline shook herself and straightened her spine. This was her rink, her territory. He had no right to be here and she knew that on the other side of the door was a large contingent of security officers, who were already itching to take someone down.

"Whether I am alone here is of no matter to you. I asked you to leave!" She raised her voice. Her body was tight with tension. *God, I need You to help me,* she thought.

"You have developed such a natural flow, that I will have to thank Fiona for her work. I think it is time I took over now," he sneered at her, a victorious look on his face. She could smell his breath of garlic and wine, his favorite food groups.

"Get out Eric! There is no job for you here," she said loudly holding her head up high. She managed to met his glare without flinching. She didn't want to remember what happened two years ago, when Fiona had to take some time off to tend to her mother and sister. His inappropriate words to her, his stares... she shuddered. They made her feel... hunted.

"I say! What is going on here?" she heard Fiona's voice coming from her office. She walked toward the rink, assessing the situation.

"Ah Eric, what an unpleasant surprise. I think it's time for you to leave, now! You might want to do so on your own two feet or else I can have you dragged out the door by security. All I have to do is shout and they will cart you out of here quicker than you can think," she drew herself up to her full five feet, looking quite imposing, Jacqueline had to admit. She would have laughed, had the situation not been so unsettling.

"Well, I can see I am not wanted here. All I came to see was if you were in the market for another coach; one who could bring you to a new level. I can see that you are not ready for me. I will wait!" he sneered, and circled around her one last time. Then he turned toward the door, whistling to himself. He bumped against Fiona on his way out and touched his brow.

"Always a *pleasure* to see you Fiona," he grinned.

"The pleasure is all yours, let me assure you," she spat out, barely keeping her words civil. His whistling became fainter as he exited the building. Fiona looked at Jacqueline, who had gone pale. She moved over to her and touched her shoulder. She drew her into a hug. Together they walked off the the ice.

"Stay right here. I want to make sure he leaves the grounds and we will leave a message that he is not to be admitted under any circumstances." Fiona hurried back to her office, while Jacqueline took a moment to let her breathing steady. Eric La Pelle had done a job on her with his insinuating stares, inappropriate comments. She had been fourteen at the time, and horrified by him. On numerous occasions he had insisted that the reasons she couldn't get enough air in her jumps was because she was overweight. For months, after Fiona had assumed her role as coach, Jacqueline had refused to eat, almost ending her up in the hospital. And that was just one of the many things Eric had done to her to almost quit skating. Fiona had to restore her very gently and it too a long time.

Fiona returned with a cup of steaming hot tea.

"Drink this," she shoved the beverage into her hands. Jacqueline's hands had gone stone cold. "What in the world was he doing here? Are you all right?"

"Yes," she breathed the steam off the cup. "He wanted to see if he could entice me to come and train with him, or so he claimed."

"Nobody deserves him as a trainer. I thought his license had been revoked."

"Thanks Fiona. I am glad you came when you did. I thought he was going to devour me like a lion," she shuddered and took a sip of the tea. "This is hitting the spot."

"Drink it all, my dear," Fiona said seriously, then allowed a grin to spread across her face. "It is what we British do best. I am glad I came down when I did. I don't know what it was but I just felt the need to come and check on you."

Jacqueline calmed down talking to Fiona. She had a lot to think about. The fact was that this was the third time she had prayed and God had answered. Maybe there really was something to this. She would have to consider carefully.

"I'm off. Got to hit the books. Exams are next week. I hope I'm prepared," she sighed. "I have more speeches to make. I hate that!"

From then on, her parents promised to think about lessening her social schedule. It would be a challenge, because the calendar was set up for a month in advance. Jacqueline had to sit for her exams. She knew that would take every ounce of strength and concentration she could muster. Fiona agreed to suspend practice while she was taking her exams and she thanked her for it.

It seemed that since the visit by Eric La Pelle, Fiona was watching her like a hawk. There was also a security guard with her at the rink. Fiona made sure that she had enough sleep, which Jacqueline scoffed at. With one final push before the exams, she was getting only five hours or less a night. Her skating was atrocious! She was making mistakes she hadn't made in years.

And then there was her sister's wedding! Her mother reminded her of her session with the seamstress. She was surprised to find that it turned out to be painless and relaxing. All Jacqueline had to do was remain motionless. She was so tired that it didn't take much for her to just stand still. She jerked awake when the seamstress told her to stop swaying. Sharon's beautiful dress also underwent a last scrutiny. The dress itself was a masterpiece of lace and silk and intricate designs of pearls and flowers. The train was ten feet long. The veil matched the dress with designs of pearls and silk flowers throughout. It also trailed behind. Sharon would make a beautiful bride. She was practically quivering in nervous anticipation.

"Now, Jacqueline, you know that you are to be at my house Saturday morning at 9:00 a.m., correct?" Sharon asked her for the tenth time.

Jacqueline smiled at her sister and squeezed her arm. "I'm sure Marie and I will be there with bells on our feet," she chuckled.

"We are not having bells, dear."

"Of course not, silly. Relax Sharon. We'll be there. Anyway, it is appropriate for the bride to be late."

"Not this bride," her sister chided her.

Jacqueline sighed in relief on the day of the wedding. The sooner she could get back to her uninterrupted schedule, the better. She had to admit that she enjoyed watching her sister glide toward her waiting bridegroom. Sharon looked lovely in her beautiful, extravagant wedding gown. Antonio looked beyond handsome. Jacqueline envied them when they exchanged vows before a thousand guests. Her heart jumped when she thought that one day she would be standing next to the love or her life, promising to love only him. That was in the distant future, she chided herself, and forced her attention back to the couple.

157

Chapter 22

The next week flew by in a flurry of activities. Jacqueline was even busier than the week before. She was preparing for her exams. She was cramming! By the time Friday came around, it felt as though she had just poured a month into a week. She was as prepared as she could be. Her body was tired and her mind threatened to shut down. She collapsed into bed and reached for the phone. Linda may just be awake now, she thought, as she dialed her friend's number. They hadn't really left on the best of terms, but Jacqueline longed to talk to her.

"Hello?" a sleepy Linda answered.

"Wake up, sleepy head," she chuckled. "Why are you still in bed? Time to skate!"

"Uh, Jacqueline, I am tired. It's 4:30 in the morning! I know you don't get up at 4:30a.m either. So leave me my half an hour of sleep," her friend yawned and chuckled. "It's good to hear your voice. How are you?"

Jacqueline shared with her friend what was going on. She didn't sugar coat the fact that she felt worn out. Linda sympathized and told her to prioritize. For her it was most important to keep up with her skating and her studies. All else had to come after that.

"You know how my parents are," complained Jacqueline. "I have to make at least one public appearance a week. It is so exhausting."

"Poor, poor princess. Are you done complaining, because I am about to come over there and slap you! You are acting like a spoiled brat. All this is part of life. Act like a princess and not a brat."

Jacqueline was quiet for a moment. She could feel the sting in what her friend had said.

"You are right," she murmured. "I just had to have a sounding board."

"It's all right, Jacqueline. You do have a lot of responsibility but you need to allow yourself not to be dragged down by that. Take it as a challenge for the future. You don't know what's ahead for you."

"So wise, dear friend," she chuckled and heard Linda laugh on the other end. They ended the conversation but Jacqueline felt just as worn out as she had before.

The first week of her exams, Jacqueline slipped into auto mode with daily testing that lasted for three to four hours. She woke up and studied, skipped her run and training time only to study more before the examinations, barely managing to make it to the rink once. She felt out of sorts completely by Friday afternoon when the last exam of the week was completed. Jacqueline thought in horror about the next week of testing ahead of her, taking the weekend to look through the experiments she had performed in the past.

By the time Friday came around again, Jacqueline's head was swimming. If she saw another Bunsen burner in the foreseeable future, she would scream. But Jacqueline felt a great deal of pleasure; her exams were completed.

All she wanted to do was go to her room and relax. She felt as though her nerves were about to snap. Jacqueline found herself pacing back and forth in her room, unable to relax. Groaning, she threw herself onto her bed, waiting for the chance to relax, which never came. What was wrong with her? She leaned against the headrest and closed her eyes.

Jacqueline didn't wake up until well into the next day and blinked blearily, rubbing her head. She was sporting a massive headache and tight shoulders, which could only remedied by a massage. Perhaps she would venture out of the palace for a massage.

Her mother caught her in the front hall on her way out, making Jacqueline almost felt guilty that there weren't any social engagements scheduled for her.

"You look worn out, Jacqueline," she said as a matter of fact. "I think it is time to take a rest."

Jacqueline's eyebrows shot up in surprise. Her mother never suggested that anybody take a rest, always demanding more and more from her family. She stood still for a moment, waiting for her mother to continue.

"We have a standing invitation to visit the UAE, remember?" her mother smirked, something she also never did. "As I recall you got along very well with some twins when they visited here."

Jacqueline had forgotten about her new friends in the frenzy of the past month. She looked at her mother. Did she have something up her sleeve? She looked almost too smug for her own good.

"Mother, what are you suggesting?"

Her mother took her by the arm and led her toward the office.

"Your father and I have been thinking. You have been working so hard and we would like to acknowledge that hard work. You have done invaluable work for this country, Jacqueline. Your father just received the paperwork on the oil deal with Dubai. It was partially due to you that we have this deal. So, how would you like to take a vacation? We can go to Dubai, you can do a little skating if you like, and then we are going to the States. It has been a long time since we have visited Miami. On the way home, we will visit Bermuda, which should be a lot of fun this time of year. It is time for you to relax."

"When are we leaving?" she sighed, overcome with relief.

With school done and the weather turning nicer, Jacqueline found herself spending a lot more time outside. As she was riding her Hanoverian mare through the woods behind the palace, she thought about her upcoming month. She would be seeing the twins in a few short days. The thought filled her with nervous excitement, though she wasn't sure why exactly, since their presence had irritated her when the twins first invaded her private space.

She suddenly remembered what Grace had said to her the night of her little performance. In the frenzy of the past few weeks, she had forgotten their conversation about God. She remembered calling out to

161

God when Eric threatened her, and Fiona showing up almost right away. Jacqueline was beginning to think that there was definitely something to this whole God-thing. She thought it was really cool, if not a bit creepy, and glanced up toward heaven to see if she was being watched. Visiting with Grace would allow her to learn more about it.

And there was skating. Fiona had contacted the local skating association in Dubai, and they were excited about her arrival. Her appearance would coincide with their big spring show, Fiona informed her. They were waiting for her with open arms. She groaned. *So much for a vacation*, she thought.

It was time! They were off. She waved to Jean, who watched from the front door as they drove out the gates. Jacqueline couldn't help but chuckle at what was packed in her luggage.

"To think that I am going to the desert with my skates," she mused as she watched her luggage being taken from her.

Chapter 23

This is amazing, Jacqueline thought as their plane circled Dubai International Airport. On their approach, Jacqueline had caught the first glimpse of the city. This was not some little camel-trading oasis, much to her surprise, but a large bustling metropolitan city. The city was alive, even at midnight, and there was noise all around them as they were escorted to their waiting vehicle. As she stepped out of the air conditioned building, she was aware of the warmth of the night. It was as warm as any summer day in Lichtenbourgh. Countless people were shouting, vying for their attention and addressed them in broken English, realizing that they were Europeans or Americans. They were hustled into the waiting limousine, air condition running.

On the drive through the city, Jacqueline was amazed at this city in the desert. Indeed the streets were wide boulevards, divided by beautiful palms, luscious green grass and delectable flowers. To imagine that this had been desert not long ago was astounding. They rounded a large round-about, something she had not seen since England. In the middle, a fountain gushed a column of water. People were milling about and visiting with each other. Men in white flowing gowns walked side by side with women, some of whom were covered completely in long black cloth.

Cars darted in and out of traffic. Horns tooted all around them. They crossed a bridge over a wide river. The four-lane road was crowded on both sides. The lush vegetation surprised Jacqueline.

"This is an amazing city," her father mumbled as he also inspected the sights.

"I did not expect it to be so green," she admitted and he nodded.

"Yes, it is very beautiful here. And look at all the traffic. Did you see all the people about? It's as though it is in the middle of the day," he mused. Jacqueline nodded.

What was more amazing was that the only green areas were around the roads. Once you got fifty feet from the roads, however, it was all desert. Buildings were scattered helter-skelter throughout the desert. They drove past tall skyscrapers, which towered over older tan structures with flat roofs, which almost blended in with the desert that surrounded them. As they moved to a less congested area, Jacqueline noticed the sea shimmering darkly, sometimes hidden just behind the single residences, which were hidden behind tall walls. After continuing to travel on the four-laned road, the distance between houses stretched further and further apart. Houses turned into large mansions, scattered throughout the desert and along the beach. The car slowed down and turned into one them.. The driver punched a code into the security keypad at the fence and the metal gate slowly opened.

They entered the compound into a luscious park. Exotic plants and birds in cages surrounded the drive up to the house. The house itself sat against the dark sea and as Jacqueline stepped out of the car, she breathed in the sea air mixed with the exotic fragrance of diversely blooming flowers. The front door swung back, revealing a large foyer with marble flooring and rosewood stairs leading to an upper floor. Mirrors gave the impression of an even larger expanse.

A formally clad butler bid them welcome and led them through the foyer to the sitting room, where the family was gathered watching TV. Beautiful Berber carpets covered the black marble floor here and there. Paintings of Bedouins on their camels and horses, ancient and deadly looking weapons hung on the oak paneled walls. Their hosts rose from their comfortable couches. Grace must have fallen asleep, but she bounced right up when she heard the commotion.

"Welcome, welcome, friends. Or as they say in this country Saalam Alaykum," Mrs. Spencer greeted them with a warm smile and shook their hands. Grace hugged Jacqueline and giggled excitedly.

"Please, you must be tired." Mr. Spencer motioned to the soft leather couches and asked the butler to bring some sweet tea as refreshment. The twins took hold of Jacqueline and dragged her to the corner of the room, where a separate sitting area was nicely arranged. They bombarded her with excited questions. Jacqueline could only smile from one to the other as they shot their questions at her.

"What do you think of our town?" Brian asked proudly. "It sure is different than you expected, isn't it?"

"I can't wait to show you around. You came at a good time. It is not too hot and not too cold right now. Tomorrow we can go swimming. Oh, the water is so nice right now. And later on we will take you to the skating rink," Grace told her excitedly, talking rapidly without taking a breath. "They have been advertising you all week long. I can't believe you are here," she squealed and clasped Jacqueline's hands in hers. Jacqueline felt herself once again overwhelmed. Here they were again, invading her privacy. She wanted to go to bed and Grace was jabbering on and on.

"I suppose my whole week has been scheduled?" she sighed. She didn't want to sound ungrateful, but she was here to relax and it looked like she was not going to get to do that.

"Oh sure. We have a lot scheduled. You won't have time to be bored. You are going to love it here, you are not going to want to go home." Brian beamed at her. "It is good to see you again. You can keep Grace off my case!" he teased and was rewarded by a gentle punch. He flinched and rubbed his shoulder.

"The best part of this whole stay is that you get to stay in my room!" Grace squealed and hugged her again. "I asked mom if we could share a room so this way we can catch up, right? And, like, at first she didn't want to but then she kind of changed her mind, agreeing that we could have a lot of fun," she giggled and winked at her.

Jacqueline wanted to run away. Grace was in overdrive, it seemed. All Jacqueline wanted was to maybe hang out at the pool and the beach and get the skating over with. That was all she could handle!

"Sure, that sounds like a lot of fun," she managed to reply.

"I think we should turn in," Mrs. Spencer suggested. "I'm sure our guests are tired. I hope you will find your accommodations adequate. It is not a palace, but we do have plenty of room," she smiled.

166

Grace's room faced the sea and was indeed spacious. It had an airy quality to it. Posters of landscapes dotted the white walls. The marble floor was again covered with an ancient Berber carpet. A large canopy bed stood against the far wall. The large windows were partially opened, allowing the cool sea breeze to come in. The light curtains fluttered in the breeze.

"Nice room," Jacqueline told Grace upon entering. "I love your bed."

"You get to sleep in it. I am going to take the couch. It's okay," Grace added quickly when Jacqueline was about to protest. "It is almost as comfy as the bed. It pulls out, you see," she giggled at the fun of it all.

Jacqueline had to admit that she was tired. She had fallen asleep on the plane but it had not been enough. She yawned.

"Bed time, I think," Grace smirked and the girls got settled for the night.

Chapter 24

Sun streamed into the room as Jacqueline sat up straight in bed. She had overslept! She looked around her, confused for a moment. Then she realized that she was not at home but was on vacation! No exams awaited her, no training was scheduled, and most importantly, her time was her own. Sort of. There were no interviews to be given, no ribbons to cut. She glanced over at Grace, who was sleeping soundly. She almost giggled when her friend emitted a slight snore. A warm breeze stirred the air. Quietly Jacqueline slipped into shorts and a T-shirt. A quick brush through her hair and she tiptoed out the door. A glance at the clock on the wall told her that it was only 7:00 a.m.

The house was quiet and cool. The only noise came from the far side, where Jacqueline assumed the kitchen was located. She quietly opened the sliding doors in the sitting room and stepped out onto a sprawling patio made up of broad flagstones. She heard waves softly washing onto the white beach below. The sea sparkled a brilliant blue and the beach stretched for miles and miles in both directions.

She took a tentative step onto the warm sand. For 7:00 a.m. it was already quite warm Jacqueline observed, as she gingerly walked across the hot sand toward the water. The waves were small, gentle, and the water warm and inviting. Jacqueline waded in up to her knees.

She was amazed when she spotted little gray fish darting about here and there in the emerald sea around her.

"You're brave," a cheerful voice greeted her from the beach. "It's still too cold for my taste."

"Morning, Brian. You're up early again," she turned and greeted him when he approached her.

"I'm a morning person, I guess," he said. "I heard my dad leave just now and so I thought that if he could get up and go, I should get up too."

"Ah. Your place is gorgeous. This water is wonderful. And the beach, beautiful!"

"Yeah, I know. I love it here," he replied looking about him a little sadly. "Anyway, I sure am glad you came. There is so much to see. How do you feel about the zoo? We have a zoo here. In fact, I worked there while I was at school. I may come back to work here when I graduate."

"Really? Ice skating rinks and zoos in the desert. What else do you have?" she teased.

Jacqueline joined Brian as he walked the beach, water splashing at her bare feet. It felt good. Brian told her a little bit of the history of the place. His eyes shone when he talked about the extravagant projects planned for the near future. He laughed and told her that the locals liked to show that they could keep up with the world.

Jacqueline allowed his voice to wash over her. She didn't care what he talked about. As she walked through the water, she suddenly felt the pressure of the past half year. It was as though it threatened to crush her and leave her buried. To take another step would be too much for her. She felt her strength drain out of her, and she slowly sank down into the wet sand. She sat there gasping for breath.

Brian, who had stopped talking, continued to walk until he realized that she was not next to him. He turned to find her sitting on the wet sand, head in her hands, gasping for air. Quickly he was by her side.

"Hey," he said softly and put a hand on her shoulder. "Are you all right?"

She couldn't answer. Jacqueline buried her face in her arms as tears streamed down her face. She didn't have the strength to talk. Brian just sat next to her, arms wrapped around his knees, until the tears stopped and her breathing returned to normal.

"I'm sorry," she gasped. "Am I too young to have a nervous breakdown?" she croaked and shot him a crooked smile. "I don't normally break down in front of people like this."

"It's okay," he mumbled. "With your schedule I'm surprised you are not in the nut house. I don't know how you do it."

"Me neither," she whispered and wiped away her tears. Her parents would be mortified if they knew that she had fallen apart like this.

They sat side by side, not talking, and Jacqueline felt the strength slowly returning to her limbs. Her feet started to tingle from the cool water. She looked out to the sea, enjoying the quiet.

"I am so tired," she whispered. "I just want to sit and watch the waves. I don't think I can do anything else. Isn't that horrible?"

"No," Brian answered. "I guess I can understand it completely. What you do is pretty amazing."

"Not so much," she sighed and leaned back onto the warm, wet sand. It felt so good. For a while all she heard was the rushing of the waves. She felt her eyelids get heavy and she closed them.

She woke up with a start. Brian was poking her shoulder, trying to get her attention. She rubbed her eyes and winced. Her hands were covered with sand, which stung her eyeballs.

"How long was I asleep for?" she croaked.

Brian grinned and leaned over her. "Not long enough, Jacqueline. Can you get up? The tide is starting to come in." He pointed at her legs, now fully immersed in water.

She squeaked and tried to get up. Brian held out a hand and she accepted his help. Her legs felt wobbly. It seemed that just standing was almost too much for her. Jacqueline followed him to the house, stumbling over the hot sand.

"Wait right here," he said with a slight smirk on his face, and shot into the house. She snorted. As if she was going somewhere.

Brian returned with a tall glass of something green. She pulled a face and looked at him.

"You expect me to drink that?"

"Drink it. It'll give you a ton of energy. I try to drink one every morning." He sat down on the chair next to hers and watched expectantly while she sipped at the drink. It was surprisingly sweet! And good!

"What in the world is in this?" she gasped and downed the whole cup.

Brian laughed and told her his mystery ingredients. She shot him a thankful look and closed her eyes again. She was still tired and she knew she could not possibly go anywhere or do anything for a while. She needed to figure out how to regain control of her nerves. She rubbed her temples. The constant headaches were back!

"Have you ever thought of slowing down?" Brian asked and stretched his arms. "It looks to me like you are running on overdrive, Jacqueline. How can you possibly keep up with the demands you put on yourself?"

She chuckled ruefully. "I'm not the only one who puts demands on my time. Remember who my family is?"

"Ah, there is that too," he grinned. "I did forget for a moment that you are not like the rest of us peasants." He playfully shoved her shoulder with his.

"That's right and you didn't approach me correctly, so off with your head," she said and closed her eyes again, trying to force the headache to stop.

As long as she had her eyes closed, the pain in her temples eased. Brian sat next to her, keeping quiet. She found him watching her when she opened up her eyes from time to time. A curious look was on his face. It was almost as though he was trying to figure her out and couldn't.

"Why do you do it?" he finally asked. She startled at the sound of his voice. She had almost forgotten that he was there.

172

"Why do I do what?"

"The whole thing? Why do you really do it?"

"Because it is what is expected of me!" she whispered and her eyes stung with tears.

When everyone roused themselves Jacqueline and Brian were still sitting next to the pool. She still didn't think she had the energy needed to move. Grace was excited and chatted at her nonstop. She closed her eyes as the headache returned in full force.

"Gracie, whoa. Slow down," her brother warned.

Jacqueline was glad for his intervention and gave him a thankful nod. He didn't acknowledge it. She was beginning to feel cross-eyed. She also appreciated that he hadn't mentioned her little breakdown at the beach.

By the end of the day all she had accomplished was to change into her suit and take a dip in the pool when the heat became too much for her. Other than that she sat in the shade under a black cloth tarp, drinking green smoothies, as Brian called them, and eating snacks that were brought out to her.

The adults joined the young people at the pool and shared laughs and stories. Jacqueline couldn't believe that her parents were sitting down with her, without making demands on her time or her person. She found that it was pleasant to spend time with her family.

She turned in early. Grace put a movie into the player and it held her attention for a mere five minutes.

"Morning," she heard behind her as she stared at the waves crashing onto the beach. Jacqueline suppressed a smile. She kind of knew that Brian would meet her out here, early in the morning.

"Are you feeling better?" Brian asked and came alongside her. She nodded. The weariness in her body and mind was still there, but she was able to fight it to function.

"Would you like to take a drive with me into the desert?" he asked quietly. His eyes were shining with excitement. "Today would be a perfect day to take a quick trip to the desert. It's only a couple of miles away."

"I'm not so sure," she hesitated.

"Now is the right time to get out there before it gets too hot," he explained, tapping his foot while he waited for her to reply.

"I'm not sure," she said tentatively again. She was hoping to just relax again today, to get her strength up and to settle her frayed nerves. Going somewhere was not to her liking today.

"Come on," he finally urged. "I promise you will never forget this. It will be an adventure," he beamed and waited impatiently for her to reply.

Finally Jacqueline acquiesced. She felt that she had enough energy to take a trip into the desert; this was after all, a chance of a lifetime. She sluggishly climbed into a battered red four-wheel-drive vehicle. For a moment she felt a twinge of guilt weigh her down. She had not asked permission from her parents.

With the top down, the warm wind blowing on her face felt refreshing, as they accelerated out the gate and down a straight, four-

174

lane road. The wind tossed her hair about and slowly the guilt about not telling her parents where she was going blew off her. This road had no cultured vegetation on either side or in the middle. The only vegetation along the road were scraggly bushes and dry looking patches of grass. The scenery flew by as they sped down the smooth road.

"This is not really the best place to drive around in the desert, but it will be fun," Brian grinned, as he slowed the vehicle down just enough to take a turn into the desert.

It was flat, with houses dotted here and there. They sped down the dirt road - at least it looked like a dirt road to Jacqueline - and soon they were surrounded by sand, sand and more sand. Jacqueline squealed with excitement, as she saw a lone camel wandering around the outside of the housing complex.

"We have to be careful of those guys," explained Brian as he pointed out another camel. "They just wander around everywhere and if you hit one you can pretty much say goodbye to your life. They tend to fall into the vehicle," he added seriously.

"Thank you for that bit of information," she muttered dryly.

Brian grinned at her and took off into the middle of nowhere. As they sped over a few bumps, Jacqueline could not help but hold on tightly to the roll-over bar to steady herself. She tried to keep her hair out of her face, but it was to no avail. She had to admit that this joy ride was not something she was able to do every day. It was fun! The further they got from the houses, the higher the bumps became and soon they were speeding up some pretty steep dunes. Jacqueline felt her stomach flip as the earth in front of the vehicle disappeared. She squealed and grabbed the bar above her head as they flew down the steep dune. Brian laughed at her until he flew down one dune and tried to get back up another only to find himself stuck!

"Oh man!" he grimaced as he turned the engine off to look at the damage. The front tires were stuck in the rise of another shallow dune. He kicked the tires and scowled at the vehicle. Jacqueline got out very slowly, looking at her surroundings.

"So how far away from civilization are we?" she asked.

"About five miles as the bird flies," he grumbled in reply.

"Should we be walking back to get help?"

"No, we can't really," he replied and kicked the tires again.

"Okay, kicking the tires won't help us get out, will it?" she laughed, thinking that this was pretty funny. Brian glared at her.

"Do you have a better idea?" he asked. "Because if you don't there is the shovel, the piece of board, and you can push too, you know."

"Grumpy, grumpy. Hey, you wanted to come into the desert. It's an adventure, you said. Well, I guess we are having an adventure. I really didn't need *this kind* of adventure, though. Did you bring any water? I am getting thirsty."

Brian looked at her and sighed. Then he grabbed an old rusty shovel out of the back of the vehicle. He also fished out two dilapidated boards of ply wood. He grumbled to himself as he took the boards and laid them next to the vehicle.

"Here, make yourself useful and start digging the sand away from the side of the tires. I will push these boards under the back of the tires and back out. Hopefully it will work," Brian huffed.

Jacqueline took the shovel and got down to business. She noticed that it was getting warmer. By the time she accomplished her task, her face was covered in sweat and her hair clung to it in clumps. Brian handed her a bottle of water. She downed it in a second, grimacing because the water was almost as warm as the air. Brian was ready with the boards and he got into the driver's side.

"Jacqueline, you need to push. Otherwise we may not get out of here today," he grinned at her. She sighed and took the position at the front of the vehicle. So much for a leisurely trip into the desert. Brian started the engine and slowly added gas.

"All right, start pushing," he yelled.

"What do you think I'm doing?" she grumbled as she pushed with all her might.

"I guess all that weight training is paying off now," she shouted and panted.

Brian laughed and slowly but steadily the vehicle freed itself. Brian whooped as it finally got out. Jacqueline was sweating bullets. She jumped back into the vehicle.

"I have to admit, that was unique," she mumbled and wiped the sweat from her brow. They both had a good laugh as they made their way back to the road.

"You do know how to show a girl a good time," she teased him.

177

She was covered in sweat and fine sand. Her scalp itched and felt gritty. She even had sand between her teeth. Once they reached the road and were racing down the double lanes, her sweat problem disappeared. Instead her whole body felt crusty.

"I think I don't like the desert too much," she admitted. "It is a little too sandy," she chuckled.

Brian scowled. "I love the desert. You never know what you are going to get. Hey," he continued when he saw her face. "It could have been worse. It's always best to be prepared," he laughed. "We could have gotten really stuck."

"You don't call that getting really stuck?" she asked incredulously.

"Of course not. We got out of that too easily. Trust me, I've gotten stuck and couldn't get out for hours. I had to walk out one time. That was interesting. I was in the middle of nowhere and luckily someone picked me up and I was able to get help. Now *that* was an adventure," he chuckled. He looked at his passenger and couldn't help but laugh at her.

"Did you know that your face looks a little, well, dirty? You still have sand between your eyes." He handed her a paper towel. She tried to wipe her face as best as she could.

"I was wondering where all the sand disappeared to," she laughed and couldn't wait to get into the shower. "Thank you for showing me such a good time," she said sarcastically and smirked. "And allowing me to do my work out. I really appreciate it. What would I have done without you? I would have missed my weight training."

"See, if you had not come, your whole exercise regimen would have been disrupted. I am so glad to be of service."

They continued to banter back and forth until they reached the house. They had passed a couple of camels walking along the road. Brian was careful to give them a wide berth.

Chapter 25

The shower felt wonderful as all the sand washed down the drain. Jacqueline really felt as though she had worn the whole desert. When she got out of the shower, she realized that she was starting to feel normal again. Figures that she had to get stuck in the desert for that! Grace was just stirring... beginning to gradually wake up.

"Wake up, sleepy head," Jacqueline teased and tickled her nose softly. "I have already had a huge adventure while you were still sleeping, studying the inside of your eyelids."

Grace grimaced, shoved Jacqueline's finger out of her face, while she tried to keep her eyes from falling shut again.

"What was your adventure?" she moaned with a yawn.

She laughed when Jacqueline finished retelling her take. "I should have warned you not to go out into the desert with my brother. He is sure to get stuck. It's pretty funny though."

Once Grace got up and dressed they trudged downstairs to have some breakfast, which consisted of fruits galore, fresh bread, and jam. It was delicious and Jacqueline ate her fill. Brian shared the excitement of the morning with everyone at the table and her parents looked at her in alarm.

"Mother, Father, it was a lot of fun," Jacqueline assured them. "I'm sure we were never in any danger."

Her parents turned to face each other with raised eyebrows. "We would prefer you not to go and attempt anything so dangerous again."

"It wasn't dangerous. The most dangerous part of the whole thing were the camels. Really, we were fine," she grumbled and could feel her ire rise. They frowned but didn't pursue the issue.

After breakfast, Grace suggested that they put on their suits for a day at the beach. Jacqueline was only too happy to comply, since the trip into the desert had been taxing. The two of them giggled loudly as they raced up the stairs to change. Jacqueline paused for a moment as she put on her suit. She had never giggled while running up any stairs. But doing so with Grace, was almost therapeutic.

The beach did, indeed, prove to be restorative, warm and inviting. They strolled through the soft sand toward the brilliantly blue water, where they reclined onto their beach towel, soaking up the sun's heat. Between the soft splashing of the waves to shore and the distant call of seagulls, Jacqueline began to relax, the tension leave her body.

Grace poked her just as she was dozing off, and pointed to the sun. "You need to slather on suntan lotion... you are already starting to become nice and crispy on only your first day. It doesn't take long for that to happen here."

Later in the afternoon Grace and Brian suggested that they head into town. Jacqueline reluctantly agreed, not really wanting to go out again. She still felt tired and didn't have much energy.

"This is where you will be skating," Grace informed her as they pulled up to a large complex. Tall palms surrounded them, giving the necessary shade.

"We are going in?" she asked as they got out of the car.

"We figured you would want to look at the place where you will be skating. It is a really nice rink. Trust me on that." Brian held the door for her. She rolled her eyes at him and he gave a little bow. She heard a snort behind her.

"Such good manners, Brian," she heard Grace hiss at her brother. "Where have you been hiding them?"

The rink was indeed impressive. It was a regular-sized hockey rink with plenty of room for spectators. She was pleasantly surprised and started to feel herself getting antsy to skate. She met the rink manager, who was thrilled to have her visit his facility and invited her to skate any time. She thanked him, telling him that her coach was the one who would set up her practice times.

When they left the rink and drove toward the center of town, Jacqueline was amazed by the juxtaposition of the old and new architecture. She was astounded at the tall skyscrapers that towered over the small, worn old buildings. There was not an ounce of trash anywhere on the streets. She gasped at the number of new sports cars that passed them, some of them driven by men wearing their traditional white robes while others sported designer suits. Down by the river she saw a fleet of overburdened wooden Arab sailing vessel, the dhows: some carrying sheep, others boxes of unknown cargo.

The twins took her to an Arab open-air market called a souq. Here the streets were tight, narrow, and twisting through the old section of town, so different from the business district, where the streets were wide and straight. They darted in and out of shops and walked down the busy, narrow streets until they came to a markedly different section. Here, the streets were still narrow and tight, but instead of fabrics and clothing or housewares, shops here were filled with gold, bracelets, rings, and other expensive baubles. The gold almost looked fake, there was so much of it and it shimmered so brightly.

As they walked along, peddlers advertised their wares in loud, guttural tones. This was indeed a strange, mysterious land. Again she marveled at the strange attire of the local people. Women walked behind their men, inspecting gold bracelets, rings and other shiny objects in the stores. The men haggled over the prices and struck their deals with a handshake. Children scurried in the narrow streets, laughing. As they came to the end of the souq, she had to admire the line of luxury vehicles waiting at the traffic light right alongside the small, beat up Japanese made sedans.

"This certainly is a strange place," she told Grace.

"Yes, but I totally love it. I mean, where else does old meet new in such an odd and mysterious way?" Grace grinned at her and threaded her arm through hers. "Come with me to my favorite gold store. The owner knows us really well and he always gives us a deal. Let's see what he has in his store today."

Grace dragged her to a small store at the corner of an alley. Brian rolled his eyes as he watched them enter the store and reluctantly followed. When she entered she almost had to squint at all the bright jewelry, which almost looked phony. Jacqueline's eye fell on a simple ring, made out of gold with a small ruby in the center of the delicately shaped golden flower. The design of the ring was simple and dainty, she had to admire it.

"Ah, I see the young miss has good taste," the shop keeper zeroed in on her with his dark eyes staring at her knowingly. Jacqueline felt rather uncomfortable at his intense gaze.

"I make you a special price. For you only one hundred Dirham. For you, such a special young lady," he said with his heavy accent.

"I am not really in the market for this," she answered shyly and turned to go.

Brian was leaning against the doorway, hands in his pocket. He was trying not to pay attention to the girls. "You're not buying?" he asked astounded.

"I have no reason to buy right now. I really don't need another ring. It would be a waste to purchase it. I have to admit it is rather lovely. I have yet to see another ring like it."

The store keeper quickly engaged her again. "Miss, for you I will make it ninety Dirham. It is a good deal." The shop owner's eyes shone. He was enjoying himself trying to convince her to buy the ring.

"No, really, I am not trying to get a lower price," she mumbled. "I really should not buy anything right now. But thank you so much."

"Just for you, because I have yet to have such a lovely young lady in my store today, eighty nine Dirham," he urged.

Jacqueline shook her head and walked toward the door. The owner's face fell disappointed but turned toward Grace, who was eying a lovely ruby pendant.

"Young miss has a good eye," he flattered her and over the course of ten minutes Grace was the proud owner of the pendant. Both parties were obviously very satisfied with their deal and the shopkeeper bowed to them as they left the shop.

The friends made their way to a huge hotel that loomed over the old souq. Here they walked through the huge and ornately decorated lobby. Brian and Grace showed her the small, oval skating rink in the belly of the hotel. Parents were helping their little ones get their feet under them, a group of teenagers were hanging around, chatting. A young girl was just doing a sit spin in the middle of the rink.

"This is really cute," Jacqueline stated.

"If you want to, we could skate here," Brian suggested. They looked at him.

"Really?" Grace said, sarcasm lacing her tone. "Have you looked at us? We are wearing shorts. It is cold in here."

"I have to agree with your sister," Jacqueline stated and pointed at her goosebumps. "These are goosebumps, caused by temperatures below my comfort level. I usually wear something a little warmer when I skate."

Brian held up his hands in defeat. "All right, ladies. We are going up."

With that statement, they turned toward the elevators. Within minutes they were at the top level. They were able to take in the view from this height and it was indeed spectacular. The city stretched along the sea on one side. On its other side was the vast and never ceasing desert.

Grace pointed to an area along the sea. "That is where we live."

Jacqueline could feel the weariness return but she didn't want to disappoint the twins, who were so excited to show her around. All she wanted to do was sit by the water, swim, and soak up the sun. Her friends laughed and teased each other, while she walked alongside quietly. They made their way back to the elevators. Grace bounded along with such energy it almost sapped all of hers. She felt the headache returning and hid her eyes behind her shades.

"Are you all right?" Brian asked quietly when they got back into the vehicle.

"Just a little weary," she answered tiredly.

When they got back to the house she welcomed their suggestion that they spend the rest of the day at the beach. The sun was sinking into the water, painting it with vibrant shades of red. Jacqueline splashed through the cool water, when she heard Grace shout a warning to her.

"You may want to stay close to shore, Jacqueline. In the recent months there have been rumors of shark attacks right around here."

Jacqueline made her way extremely rapidly back onto shore, glaring at the twins, who laughed at her.

"Your face," Brian sputtered. "Priceless! I have seen you sprint, but you got out of the water in record time."

She kicked up some water at him and he held his hand up in surrender, laughing. Dinner was served that night by the pool and Grace and Brian shared the day with their parents, who listened to them attentively. Again a stab of regret, almost jealously went through Jacqueline's heart. Her new friends had such an easy relationship with their parents. Her own parents were warming up, but she could still feel the distance that was between them. She sighed and tried to imagine having a close relationship with her parents. With a stab in her heart, she realized that she couldn't imagine it.

When it was time to retire, she fell headlong into her soft bed. Grace put on a movie and Brian joined them, throwing his long form onto the floor by his sister. Jacqueline couldn't follow the movie. Her thoughts were disturbed. She didn't like them at all. She was troubled about her relationship with her parents. She felt the distance between them all the time. In the past it didn't bother her, but now it did. Now, she wanted what the twins had. Theirs was a strong relationship. Their bond with their parents was genuine and loving. They could joke around with them. When was the last time she had joked with her parents? With these thoughts in mind, she slipped into an uneasy sleep.

187

Chapter 26

Jacqueline woke again bright and early the next morning and proceeded outside. The sun was just rising above the horizon. The beach was cool and the water refreshing as she waded through it. Her thoughts turned inward again. She realized that she was feeling the effects of the strain of the past months. Her crazy schedule was finally bringing her to her knees. At least with all her mind numbing activities, it saved her from dwelling on the lack of relationship in her family or in her life.

Why had she never seen it before? Where had she been all her life? The crashing of the waves along the beach had a soothing effect. Jacqueline realized that she was stuck with the family she had. There was nothing she could do to change them! She couldn't even change herself, so how was she to change them? She realized that she needed to accept that her family members merely coexisted.

Brian and Grace had already packed this day full of more adventures. They showed her the indoor ski slope. Jacqueline couldn't believe that she was skiing in the desert. She laughed her way down the slope thinking of it. Her mood lifted even more when she took a jump and landed on her face, sputtering. Later on, Jacqueline gathered her skates and made her way to the rink to take a practice spin. Fiona met her there. Being on the ice again, she felt the strain lift the moment her music started. Her friends had promised they would wait for her and watch her while she skated.

"I enjoyed watching you," Brian said lazily, lounging in the bleachers. Grace nodded her head enthusiastically.

"Well, I aim to please. It's actually kind of nice not to have the pressure of competition hanging over me all the time. Of course, on the other hand, there is always the thrill of that," she said as she sat down next to her friends and emptied her water bottle.

"I think we will bring down the house on Saturday," Fiona grinned at her, when she joined them. The manager came down to thank them and to speak with Fiona. Jacqueline, Grace, and Brian were free to go back to the house and they enjoyed the rest of the day at the beach and at the pool.

The sun was baking her again and she was just about to slip back into the water, when Brian thought it would be a good idea to help cool her off. She shrieked as he dumped ice water on her head. The cold water ran down her back. Both her and Grace had the same though at the same time, grabbed Brian, which had to be done at lightning speed, and threw him into the deep end of the pool. He came up coughing but grinning from ear to ear. He reached up to grab his twin's hand and she tentatively gave it to him. A mischievous smile flashed into his eyes and he pulled hard. Grace tried to resist and Jacqueline jumped to grab her arm, but it was too late. Grace fell, arms flailing, into the pool.

"I will avenge you, Grace!" Jacqueline shouted and did a cannon ball into the pool, splashing her friends.

There was laughter as the three splashed each other and tried to dunk each other. After a few minutes they stopped, each of them breathing heavily. Jacqueline climbed out of the pool still laughing. So much for her frayed nerves! They were untangled for the moment. Spending time with these two was the best medicine she could have asked for. Not even a long session with a psychiatrist could have helped her as well as laughing and carrying on with them.

The rest of the evening was spent pleasantly with their parents by the pool. Out of the corner of her eyes she watched her hosts' interactions and once again felt that loneliness creep in. She just couldn't get enough of their easy banter with each other or their total acceptance of one another. Her own parents sat a bit stiffly, talking quietly with each other. Sometimes they would turn to her and ask her a question to which she would have to come up with a brilliant answer. That alone almost sapped Jacqueline's remaining strength.

She woke early and quietly made her way out of the room. She bumped into Brian, who was fixing himself a fruit smoothie in the kitchen.

"Hey there, you want some?" he offered and ran his hands through his disheveled black hair.

"You're up early again."

"Not any earlier than you," he joked and poured her a glass. "So, you ready for a run along the beach?"

"Sure, why not," she answered.

Jacqueline followed him out past the pool and onto the beach, where they set off at a brisk pace along the beautiful crystal blue water. This morning there was a strong breeze blowing against them and Jacqueline was tired by the time they had run a few hundred yards.

"Listen," she puffed. "I'm not used to this running in the sand. I think I've had enough."

"Already?" Brian puffed and grinned at her. "You don't want to keep going?"

"No, I shouldn't. I only run as long as I don't overtax myself."

"All right," he conceded and they walked back. "Since we have nothing to do until my sleeping beauty twin and the rest of the family rise in another," he looked at his watch, "two hours, why don't I show you where my grandparents live. You up for an adventure again?" he smirked.

"Another one?" she groaned not quite trusting him. "Does this one include driving through the desert?"

"Nah, all roads lead to their house," he chuckled. "You like horses, right?"

Yes," she replied a little bit hesitantly. Brian's adventures were a little too intense for her.

"Ever ridden a pure bred Arabian?"

She shook her head. He nudged her shoulder.

"Let's go then. My grandparents have a stable and they don't mind if I take their horses out for a run."

"I'm not sure I should attempt anything dangerous before the show,"" Jacqueline replied hesitantly as they walked up to the house.

"These guys are old horses. No danger there," he said with mischief in his eyes.

Jacqueline finally allowed him to convince her. They hopped into his four-wheel drive vehicle and sped through the town. Jacqueline had to admit that driving here was a little unorthodox. In certain areas speed limit signs were strictly observed but in others it seemed there were no speed limits at all and everyone was free to dart in and out of traffic at high speeds. She squirmed a couple of times when a battered taxi almost sideswiped them as they changed lanes.

Chapter 27

They pulled into an older neighborhood where the large houses were protected by tall walls, with plenty of vegetation within the grounds. They stopped just outside such a neighborhood at a gate. Brian got out and opened the iron cast grate. When he hopped back into the vehicle he smirked.

"Welcome to the farm."

Jacqueline saw several houses within this walled in compound. A main house, old and stately, was set apart from two smaller houses. In the front of these houses grew different flowers, vegetables, and fruits. The far left corner was occupied by a curious looking structure, shaded by tall palm trees as well as various other trees. Within this structure, which was open to the air from all four sides but covered with a tin roof, she could see four separate pens. Each stall was fourteen feet square, containing a dozing horse. Two of the individual pens were separated by a brick wall.

"Wow, the horses are right there!" Jacqueline said surprised. "They don't really have a proper stable," she continued rather severely.

"These are desert horses. They like living out in the sand. This is a typical Arabian barn. There aren't any walls so that the breeze can go through the structure. We make sure our horses have plenty of shade, but they were bred for the heat. They can tolerate it quite well," Brian informed her and walked up to a dapple-gray mare, nibbling on some hay.

"This is Insha'Allah. She is thirteen years old and fast as the wind. She is the matriarch here."

He patted the velvety nose. The mare nuzzled him quizzically as though she expected him to be hiding a treat for her. He chuckled and patted her head.

"This over here," he walked over to a gray stallion, "is one of her sons. His name is Shamal and he is nine years old. He still thinks he is a colt, so he is a bit of a handful. Next to him is his sister, Impshi, who is the diva of the bunch. If she is having a bad day, watch out. She will bite your fingers as she takes the treat from your hand," he laughed softly and patted the steel gray mare gingerly on the neck. "She is actually my favorite of the bunch. You never know what you are going to get with her."

He walked over to the last horse, a chestnut, standing almost sixteen hands tall. The horse raised his regal head and regarded him with his liquid brown eyes.

"This is Sheik, the father of the bunch. He is quite the fireball, and I have not ridden him much. He only is ridden on special occasions. He had quite a racing past, and now he is retired here on my grandfather's farm."

"I am amazed that this is right here in the middle of the desert."

194

"One thing you must know is that we Arabs are quite industrious. We try anything," he grinned proudly. "Come and meet my grandfather. I see him coming out of the house."

He pointed to a wise old man walking toward them with a cane. His beard was pure gray and quite long. His black eyes sparkled as he slowly approached them, hobbling as he made his way.

"Grandfather. *Salaam Alaykum*," Brian kissed the old man on both cheeks. "This is Her Royal Highness Jacqueline Chevalier of Lichtenbourgh, a friend of the family."

"*Wa'alaikum Asalam, habibi*," the old man looked at his grandson, his intelligent eyes shining. "I am pleased to meet you, Your Highness."

He bowed his head to Jacqueline and asked her how she liked his country. Jacqueline replied respectfully that she had never experienced such an interesting place. The old man chuckled and leaned heavily on his cane as he crouched.

"Grandfather, please sit." Brian helped the old man reverently over to a little outbuilding. He sat heavily on a stone bench.

"So, *habibi*, you have come to take my little children for a ride?" the old man asked when he finally caught his breath.

"Yes, grandfather. I thought it has been quite some time and they look in need of some exercise. Old Impshi is looking rather rotund, Grandfather. What have you been feeding her?"

"Yes, well, the last stable boy left with only one hand," he joked and looked proudly over his horses.

Jacqueline took a step backward, looked at the mare with respect and said with a tinge or sarcasm, "She sounds downright pleasant."

Grandfather and grandson laughed and assured her that the stable boy was fine.

"She is just a bit touchy," the wise man explained.

The old man softly spoke to the chestnut, who had turned his intelligent eyes and large ears toward him.

"That is my best stallion," he explained and got up to caress his velvety nose. "We have had some excitement the two of us," he mused and his eyes took on a faraway look.

"Well Grandfather, we just thought we would come and take Impshi and Insha'Allah out for a quick ride."

"By all means, *habibi,*" the old man nodded and painfully hobbled toward the garden. Brian passed out the brushes and lead ropes to tie the horses to their stalls.

"I'm still amazed that they are just out here in the elements. Our horses are brushed every day, pastured, and stabled. They are sheltered from any rain or wind and especially snow."

"That would not do for our horses. They need to be in the desert," Brian said and put a beautifully decorated saddle on Impshi's back, staying well away from her teeth. "She is in a mood today," he grumbled.

Insha'Allah was the most gentle horse Jacqueline had ever handled. She inspected Jacqueline carefully with her velvety nose. Once she was brushed and saddled, the mare perked up and her eyes became alert and full of anticipation. Her ears twitched this way and that.

"Ready?" Brian swung onto his mare's back. She pinned her ears and kicked as he tried to settle into the elaborate saddle. "You are beautiful but finicky," he scolded and tried to get his foot into the stirrup.

He finally succeeded and the mare settled down. Insha'Allah waited patiently for Jacqueline to mount. She walked quietly along the path and soon they were outside the enclosed compound. Brian picked up a trot and Jacqueline followed, eager not to be left behind. They soon were galloping along with Jacqueline marveling at the softness and smoothness of her horse. When they slowed the horses to a walk, they were quite a distance from the house. Jacqueline stopped her horse and looked around.

"I really envy you your home," she told Brian quietly, gazing around. "There is such a wild beauty about this place." They started walking back allowing their horses to cool down. "So, your mother is Arabic and your father is American. How did that come about?"

"My mom's parents were ambassadors to France. She met my dad there, whose father was also a diplomat. Long story short, they married and decided to live here. My father got involved in the oil business through my grandfather," he answered patting his mare's neck.

"Growing up with two distinctly different nationalities must have been pretty interesting."

"Yeah, I guess so, but not more than you. I mean, it is not every day that one is born of royalty, even if your country is teensy weensy," he replied, taunting her. "What languages do you speak?"

"We all speak French, Italian, and German. Of course we all went to school in England so we speak English as well. At home we mostly speak French except when we have company. And you?"

"Arabic, some French and of course English."

"So, your father is a Christian and your mother is a Muslim. Grace is a Christian, what are you?"

"I haven't made up my mind," he stated and scrunched up his eyes. "I am not quite sure I believe either of their religions. I mean, it's nice to have something to lean on, you know, but I am more of a realist. I make my own future. I mean neither of my parents really practice their religion. Grace is a different story. But we try not to think about it. She has thrown our family for a loop when she became a Christian," he stated wryly. "How about you guys?"

"I mean we don't really talk about God. We sometimes go to church. But it is not a usual occurrence. I guess God exists. I haven't really thought about it much, except lately, starting with our near plane crash after the Olympics. Trust me, I did call out to God. I'm still here, so He must exist," Jacqueline said slowly, pensively.

"I don't know. There are coincidences and chances. I don't hold much to the existence of a god," Brian replied. "Look around you. This is the result of millions of years of erosion."

"I don't know, Brian. Sometimes I think that we are not here by chance, that there is a purpose for us."

198

"Oh sure. There is a purpose for us. We are here to live a good life, make as much money as we can, and spend this life helping others, less fortunate. I guess Jesus was a great teacher because He pointed that out to people."

"I suppose so, but can a sandcastle build itself up by chance or does it tend to fall apart unattended?" she asked softly, as she pondered aloud. She wasn't sure his point of view was correct. "Anyway, I don't think about it too much, really. Just Grace is different, you know. There is a kindness about her I have not seen much before."

"You are right about that," he said and huffed. "Grace used to be such a brat. Oh man, she would throw temper tantrums and be really snooty. And then she went to this camp a year ago and came back different. She didn't have a date every weekend. She stopped sneaking out of the house and she is actually nice to people. So, yeah, she has changed for the better," he conceded as they entered the walled compound again.

"So what if she is right?" Jacqueline asked quietly. Brian looked at her and shrugged his shoulders.

"Then I guess I know where I'm headed," he chuckled wryly.

She nodded. She still wasn't sure on this whole God-thing. She was willing to concede that God did exist, because He had helped her out on a few occasions. She just wasn't sure what Grace had said made total sense to her.

They reached the stable and got busy grooming their mounts. Insha'Allah looked quite content and dozed while Jacqueline brushed her soft coat.

"This was a lot more pleasant than digging your old vehicle out of the desert," Jacqueline teased as she checked the mare's hooves.

"Well, thank you. I am obliged to be of service," Brian said in a gravelly tone and bowed in the saddle. "Let's get back home. The others are probably just getting up."

They bid his grandfather a good day and Jacqueline thanked him for allowing her to ride his beautiful horse. He seemed very pleased by that and wished her a nice stay. They sped back to the house, narrowly avoiding a collision into a large black sports car. The driver honked wildly and Brian yelled something back in Arabic. Then he smiled when he recognized the driver and waved cheerfully.

"That crazy Daniel! He is a menace behind the wheel. He must have just gotten that. Last I knew he was driving an old beat up junker. His parents must be glad he is done with school."

He just avoided a taxi pulling right in front of him. Jacqueline was glad when they made their way out of the populated area, hence no more traffic to contend with. She let out a deep breath, one that she had been holding for a very long time.

They entered the house and everyone was already up and about.

"Jacqueline, where have you been?" her father scolded. "You left no note, you just disappeared."

"I am so sorry, Your Majesty," Brian apologized sincerely, and bowed his head. "It was my fault entirely. Her Royal Highness had no idea where we were going. We went to my grandparent's farm to ride

200

the horses. Next time I kidnap your daughter I will let you know. It was very irresponsible of me."

"It was, young man," her father frowned. "Thank you for owning up to it, though. Apology accepted." He shook Brian's hand and slapped him on the shoulder.

As they walked back to the pool, her conscience started to nag at her. She had known where she was going. How could she have allowed Brian to take the blame for something that was not entirely his fault? She stared moodily out to sea.

Chapter 28

After spending another day at the beach and the pool, Jacqueline felt like she had gotten way too much sun. She showered and fell onto her bed, exhausted. She must have fallen asleep again, because when she woke, Grace was half way through a movie.

"Welcome back," she chuckled when Jacqueline stretched her tired muscles and pushed her hair out of her face.

She touched her face gingerly. "My face is really hurting," Jacqueline croaked and reached for a bottle of water next to the bed.

Grace giggled hardily. "It was really hot out there today. Hey, your face is totally red. You should put something on it."

"Great!" She moaned pitifully after she checked her face in the mirror. It was bright red! She groaned and gingerly touched her cheeks, wincing at the pain.

"Don't worry about it," Grace tried to reassure her. "Let's put some aloe on it. That should help with the sting and keep it moist. Otherwise you are going to start peeling."

Jacqueline groaned again and collapsed onto her bed .

After a light dinner on the terrace by the pool, Brian tried to get the girls interested in going out. Both refused vehemently.

"C'mon!" Brian cajoled, pouting at their unwillingness..

"What is the matter with you, Brian?" his mother finally asked exasperated.

"I want to go out and the girls don't want to come," he whined.

His mother looked at him and laughed out loud. "How old are you, dear boy?" She clapped his face between delicate hands covered with intricate designs of henna, shaking it gently back and forth. "Go if you want. The girls don't have to come with you."

"It won't be as much fun without them," he complained.

"Really, Brian? Grow up!" Grace told her brother. "We are tired. Hey, you dragged poor Jacqueline out to ride bright and early."

"Fine, you girls stay here. I am going out," Brian grumbled and rose from the table.

That night Jacqueline's parents joined as they played a board game. Jacqueline felt warmth run through her.

"I had a really great time tonight, Mother," she said when they were heading to bed. Her mother smiled.

"It was a very unusual evening for us, wasn't it?"

"Do you think we could do something like this again? Perhaps once a month with everyone together... and play games and, I don't know... just spend time together?" Jacqueline asked.

Her father was thoughtful. "I enjoyed myself very much, and I think it would be a wonderful idea to implement it at home. We will have to see. But I like the idea."

She fell asleep the moment her head hit the pillow.

When she rose bright and early the next morning, she was filled with a warm fuzzy feeling. She remembered the night before, and sighed contentedly. Then she hurried to get ready for her morning session at the rink. She couldn't believe that she *had* to be up at such an early hour, on her vacation, no less! A driver would take her and Fiona to the rink at six. She was waiting for Fiona, sitting in the car, when her coach finally entered the vehicle. She yawned as she buckled up.

"I hope you are more awake than I am," Fiona grumbled, holding a cup of coffee in her hand. She took a sip and closed her eyes.

"Are you going to be awake by the time we get to the rink?" Jacqueline teased Fiona. Fiona closed her eyes, ignoring her sass.

"Why do you think we schedule training time in the afternoon?" she grumbled sarcastically. "You know I am not a morning person. I mean, I can't believe they had us come this early to practice. Who wants to be up at this time of the day?" she grumbled.

"And on our well-earned vacation, no less," Jacqueline added, shooting her coach a disgusted look.

The building was quiet when they got there, entering through a side door. They could barely see in the dimly lit arena. Jacqueline slipped on her skates and glided onto the ice within moments. Her heart skipped a few beats, when she felt the ice under her feet. By the time she had warmed up, Fiona called her over, ready to talk civilly. Jacqueline didn't feel as sluggish as she had a few days ago... mornings were the best time for her anyway. And she loved to skate! After practicing for an hour, both coach and student were well pleased with the program. Jacqueline felt absolutely no pressure to win anything. She was just going out there to have fun.

As they were leaving, the manager arrived and he talked to them about the show. Because of her last minute addition to the show, the arena had been completely sold out, he told them excitedly. He hoped that she might join them that evening for a run-down of the whole program. Inwardly Jacqueline wanted to refuse but she smiled brightly, something that didn't go unnoticed by Fiona, who raised her eyebrows ever so slightly. Jacqueline assured the manager that she would be happy to come.

Brian and Grace were up when she returned.

"You are up early, aren't you Grace?" she teased and was rewarded by a pillow being tossed at her. The day was spent leisurely between the beach and the pool. She felt as though this was about as much as she was able to do. Even though she was careful, she managed to burn on top of her burn. She groaned at her bright red face in the mirror and touched her sore shoulders.

When it was time to leave for the rink again, the twins volunteered to take her and Fiona.

"Thanks guys," Jacqueline said as they squeezed into the vehicle and Brian sped down the driveway. "Or perhaps we should rethink this since Brian is driving," she chuckled as Fiona flinched when they sped through the gate and swerved onto the main road.

"What's wrong with my driving?" he asked a little too innocently as she smiled crookedly and honked at the car in front of him.

"Brian, are we going to get there in one piece?" Fiona squealed as they got rather close to the car next to them. "You are carrying precious cargo, remember that Brian," she scolded.

"What is the precious cargo?" he laughed.

Fiona growled at him and said that it was not every day that he transported royalty and an Olympic and World Champion. He laughed and slowed down just a little.

They arrived with plenty of time to spare and in one piece. Jacqueline jumped out of the back and stretched her limbs. It was good to be alive!

"I don't think your parents would look kindly upon your driving with that young man again," Fiona told her quietly as they walked into the building.

Grace slipped her arm through Jacqueline's. Jacqueline felt warmth rush over her. She looked at the twins walking next to her. She felt the comfort of Grace's arm in hers, and took pleasure in Brian's lopsided grin on the other side of his sister. They were her friends! They considered her one of them and not a person to be put upon a pedestal. They joked with her. She felt at home with them. They didn't expect her to perform for them. They didn't expect anything from her!

"I think I'll check out who is at the pool. Sarah may be here tonight," Grace smiled. "I hope you don't mind that I don't watch the practice."

"Why would you want to do that?" Jacqueline mused and waved as Grace hurried toward the pool.

"I for one think I'm going to get some fries and watch the practice," Brian said. "Want some?"

"No thanks," she smiled as Fiona frowned at him.

"Brian! Jacqueline can't eat fries," her coach scolded.

"Right, I forgot. So no fries for you. How about a burger?" he asked and scurried away quickly, laughing loudly over his shoulder.

Jacqueline shook her head. She would get even for that one! Her stomach growled at the thought of a burger with fries. It had been some time since she had enjoyed a warm, juicy hamburger with salty fries. She shoved the thought out of her mind, but as she approached the rink, unfortunately the smell of burgers hung in the air, coming from the snack bar.

"That young man is a bad influence on you, Jacqueline," Fiona huffed.

Chapter 29

They entered the arena to find a tangle of confusion. Little girls in skating dresses rushed to and fro on the ice, their parents yelling at them. The manager stood in the middle of the ice trying to get everyone to assemble in some sort of orderly fashion. Jacqueline quietly got her skates on while Fiona approached the manager to offer her help.

"Everyone, may I have your attention please," he shouted above the chaos and a few of the skaters turned to him. The little ones slowed down and their parents stopped shouting long enough to hear what he had to say.

"This is Fiona Morris, the coach of Olympic Champion Jacqueline Chevalier, who has graciously agreed to be part of tonight's practice. I would ask you all to please settle down. I know we are all excited. If the little ones could just stop and come over here for a moment, I will be able to explain what is going to happen tonight."

Apparently this did the trick, because the little children stopped racing about and came to listen to him. Jacqueline quietly made her way through the parents onto the ice, so she could hear his instructions.

"Please let us welcome Her Royal Highness, Jacqueline Chevalier, to our Spring Show," he said and clapped his hands.

She felt quite self-conscious and blushed brightly. But because of the sun she had gotten that day nobody seemed to notice. She was glad for that. Jacqueline smiled and shook the manager's outstretched hand.

He explained the order of the practice. Each older skater was responsible for a younger skater for the show. The youngest skaters went first. They practiced an adorable program and everyone clapped with delight. Each group featured the most advanced skater who had a one-minute solo skate. The youngest solo skater was about four years old and she performed some simple turns and a two-footed spin. It was quite charming.

"There is your future competition," Fiona whispered to her as they watched the little girl glide on the ice, totally unafraid.

Jacqueline's eyebrows shot up and she took a deep breath. Who knew how long she would be competing at top level, as she had this last season, with this on the way up the ranks?

The little ones were now running around the arena like little rockets set on fire since their practice time was over. Jacqueline watched them and laughed to herself. Some of the older skaters were quite good and they were aware of it. One soloist was extremely talented and Jacqueline kept a close eye on her. She skated like she owned the ice. She had the confidence to tackle some of the more advanced jumps and she did quite well. She had managed a single axle and landed the jump quite eloquently. Fiona and Jacqueline exchanged knowing glances. If she ever got into competing, this was going to be a skater to watch closely. As this group came off the ice, Jacqueline smiled at her, and she smiled back confidently.

"May I say that it is an honor to share the ice with you," the young girl spoke to Jacqueline as she passed her. Jacqueline guessed that this charming girl was about a year younger than she was.

"Thank you, that is too kind," Jacqueline replied. "How long have you been skating?"

"I started when I moved here three years ago. I was twelve. I love doing it," she replied. "My name is Monica, by the way." Jacqueline shook her hand.

"Nice to meet you Monica. I can tell you like doing this. You skate well," she replied. She wanted to encourage the girl but also not inflate her ego.

"Thank you. I skate every night after school. With school out I get to spend the day here. This is where I belong, you know. I am hoping to become a coach here."

"That is a great goal to have. I hope you get there," Jacqueline told her. Inwardly she let out a relieved sigh.

As Monica left their company, Jacqueline smirked and elbowed her coach gently.

"Hey, it looks like you may have some competition."

Fiona replied back with a tight smile. "I told you *he* is a bad influence. The smirk you just made looked just like his."

"What!?" she said surprised.

Finally it was time for her to take the ice. The crowd hushed expectantly as she took her position. She waited for the music to take her through her moves and once again, she found that it was just plain fun to be out there. She landed her jumps, completed her spins, and combination spins with a lot of speed, and reminded herself to slow down just a little. Huge applause resounded through the arena when she finally came to a standstill. Jacqueline smiled, satisfied with her performance and skated off the ice. Fiona was quite pleased with her student.

"Well done, dear girl."

"Thanks, so what are my marks?" she joked.

"I would give you all 6.0's, but I am partial," Fiona laughed back. After her performance they all assembled on the ice.

Jacqueline was to lead the whole assembly off in a simple ensemble, which turned out not to be so simple after all.

She was exhausted by the time the rehearsal was over.

As she was taking her skates off, the manager came over to her.

"I just want to thank you for being such a good sport. I know this was a long procedure and somewhat tedious. But I think it really encouraged our skaters by having you here. I don't want you to come as early as the other skaters. If you are here at 7:00 o'clock it will be just fine."

"Is there any time to practice tomorrow?" she asked.

"Of course, we can set aside some time for you tomorrow. When would it be most convenient for you?" he answered looking at Fiona.

"How about we come down right before six? That way we don't have the drive back and forth," she grimaced. Jacqueline chuckled at the memory of Fiona squealing in the vehicle.

"Yes, Fiona is quite put off by the driving in this country," she said and didn't move a muscle in her face. Fiona shot her a glance.

They agreed to the time, and Jacqueline looked around the arena for the twins. She spotted Brian munching on a bag of popcorn. Jacqueline's mouth watered, as the smell wafted toward her. Grace was talking to a fair-skinned girl in the stands next to her. As she climbed through the lingering crowd, Grace spotted her and beckoned her up.

Grace introduced her friend. Jacqueline was bone tired and wanted nothing more than to get back to the house.

"Well, you ready to go, girls?" Brian asked as he popped the last of his popcorn into his mouth. "Sorry, Jacqueline, did you want some?" he teased.

She shot him a glance that would have melted a piece of iron, but he only laughed and finished his can of soda.

"I'm sorry, but my brother has no manners. None whatsoever," Grace grumbled as Brian let out a belch.

Jacqueline would miss the twins once her time here was over. Chances were pretty slim that their paths would cross again, once they were in the States. They made their way to the vehicle, while Fiona implored Brian to drive carefully. He gave an evil laugh and cautioned everyone to buckle up as he revved the engine. They made it home in one piece.

Chapter 30

Jacqueline woke with a slight lingering headache but after taking two pills to stop the headache, she was good to go. She actually had slept in late, awaking at eight o'clock. To her surprise, Grace was already dressed in a beautiful long, flowery dress. She was fixing her hair, when Jacqueline stretched and yawned.

"Good morning," Grace smiled.

"You're up early."

"Today is Sunday. I am going to church. Do you want to come?"

"Church? I haven't seen any churches around," she replied groggily.

"We don't have a building," Grace explained. "We have to be careful because this is a Muslim country and Christian gatherings are strictly monitored. So we meet at each other's houses. I don't even tell my parents where I'm going."

"Really? Why ever not?"

"Muslims and Christians don't jibe. My parents are an exception to the rule, but they didn't like it that I have started going to these house meetings. I can't help it. I just need to go once a week to hear the songs and to hear the message spoken out loud," she murmured and tears shimmered in her eyes.

"Sure, I guess I'll come with you. Is your brother driving?"

"Are you kidding me? He wouldn't be found dead at a meeting like that. Unless," she paused. "No, that is unkind to say, so I won't." She turned to her friend.

"I'll meet you downstairs in twenty minutes."

Jacqueline jumped out of bed and quickly got ready. Her stomach growled and she needed something to eat. She brushed her hair and wondered whether to put it up in a ponytail, like her friend. She decided on that. She sprinted downstairs in a flash and had time to eat a quick bite.

Grace was a much more careful driver than her brother and they made it to the meeting without irate honking and the screeching of tires. They stopped in front of a large modern-looking adobe and brick home. A solid, six foot wall surrounded it, blocking the view from the street, like most of the homes in this country. Inside the lusciously green grounds, they found four other cars in the driveway. The door opened and a young woman about their age waved to them with a welcoming smile.

"Petra, meet my friend Jacqueline," Grace told her after giving her a friendly hug.

"Welcome. We are so glad to have a new face come. Praise the Lord," she beamed, as she enveloped Jacqueline in a warm hug.

"Yes," Jacqueline said hesitantly, beginning to wonder what she had let herself in for. They were led to a bright living room, which led out to a terrace with a round pool in the middle. There were about twenty people present, talking quietly amongst themselves when they walked in. They all stopped and glanced at Jacqueline. She was introduced to a gray-haired man in a suit and tie.

"Glad you could join us," the older man's eyes shone and twinkled. Jacqueline felt an overwhelming sense of peace radiating from the man.

"My name is Mr. Van Der Hooven," he introduced himself. He introduced her to his wife, a tiny woman with light brown hair, speckled with gray. Her eyes also twinkled when she hugged Jacqueline. Grace introduced her to the people around the room. Jacqueline found herself at loss of what to do. Everyone was still chatting quietly and there was no sign of an altar or crucifix or organ was playing in the background. Instead, a CD played very quietly.

"Well, I think it is time to start," Petra's father announced. Everyone pulled up chairs. Several people gathered around the piano and someone started playing soft music.

"Welcome on this wonderful day the Lord has made," Petra's father said gently, smiling around the room. "We have a guest, and we want to welcome you. May the Lord be with you," he smiled just at her. He scanned the room again.

"I can see that the Flanagan family are not here today. We will be in prayer for them as they travel back to Ireland to spend the summer there. Please also pray for Peter, as he will be alone for the next two months. I am sure we will be setting up some time to encourage him during the week. Toby, are you planning on being his buddy while he is alone?" he looked at a young man with bright red hair, who nodded his head quickly.

"Great, any other prayers?"

Grace raised her hand and spoke up, "Yes, as usual prayers for my family, especially for my brother. And a prayer of thanksgiving that Jacqueline, our guest, agreed to join us." Grace smiled and squeezed her hand. Everyone murmured and nodded, smiling at Jacqueline. This was not going to be a usual church service and she became just a little apprehensive.

"For my friend Mohammed, who is really seeking the one true God and a relationship with Him. We have been meeting in the souq once a week and he is asking deep questions. But he is quite hesitant, of course," John, one of the young people, said and everyone nodded knowingly.

"Would you please pray for the good and honest people of this country? My heart is breaking for them to know Christ," someone whispered. More nodding followed.

"We need to pray for strength to be a witness to these wonderful people."

After a few moments no one else spoke. Mr. Van Der Hooven bowed his head, along with everyone else. Jacqueline felt compelled to bow with them.

"Heavenly Father," he said softly, his face shining with love, "we gather here today in Your name, because you have called us by Your name. We thank you that we are here and we know that you are with the families who cannot be here. I know that you would guide my words, that they would be a balm for our hungry hearts. I pray for the Flanagans and for Peter as he is going to be without his family for a while, that you would watch and guide them as they visit their loved ones in Ireland. Let Your light shine through their lives and our lives as we acknowledge You in everything.

"I pray for the Spencers and especially Brian, Grace's twin. Show them that you are the answer. Thank you that Jacqueline is here today. Lord, nothing is an accident and we know that you have a reason for her to be here. Please show her who You are. I pray for John's friend Mohamed. He is seeking You, Lord, and You promise that if we seek we shall find. I pray for our Muslim friends, the people of this wonderful, beautiful country. Thank You for putting us here, right now, and please open the hearts of these generous, kind people. Lord, give us the strength and the wisdom to show these people the one true God and our Savior Jesus Christ. In His name we pray, Amen."

Jacqueline's head popped up and she felt as though she was in the middle of the rink with the spotlight on her. She had never heard a prayer like that before. Mr. Van Der Hooven sat down and the musicians started to play. The instruments were quiet, almost muted, and the singing of all those gathered was quiet, hauntingly reverent. Their voices were no louder than normal conversation. The music they played were no lofty hymns, but the songs touched her deeply. The words of the songs were calling to her that things were not at all right with her life. They were telling her that life had far more, that there was a peace that she had never felt. They told her of people going to the cross, she assumed it was the one Christ was crucified on, and laying down their lives. The words made her sad but also hopeful. When the last song was sung, Mr. Van Der Hooven stood again.

"My dear brothers and sisters, I want to talk about John 3:16. I know, we have all heard it before. *For God so loved the world that He gave His only begotten Son, that whosoever believeth in Him shall not perish, but have everlasting life.* What a statement! All we have to do is believe? In what? Well, it is clear that we must believe in Christ, the One who died for us. The one God sent to us and for us. What does this belief require? We must do it with our heart. For some of us, we have that belief in our head. We know that Christ is our Savior, but we don't live it as He was. We still curse at the driver who cuts us off. We get frustrated when we don't pass our test. We get angry with family members when they don't measure up to our standards or meet our needs. Christ asks us to believe in Him. To fully trust, rely, and follow Him.

"That means that we first have to come to grips with the fact that we are not our own Saviors, we cannot be... we cannot save our selves. Nothing in the world will save us except for Christ. We can't get rid of our own sins. The Bible tells us that our righteousness is as filthy as rags. We are sinners through and through. Thus, we can't change our hearts on our own. Only He can, and when He does, the change is wonderful. We are new creatures, in Christ, given power to defy the works of the devil. That means that when someone does something we don't like, we can move on and not seek revenge. We can forgive them and ask God to forgive them. We can love that person by obeying God, the way Christ did. We can lay down our hurt feelings for that person by giving it to Him, who is the only begotten Son of God and who promises everlasting life. This is when you can say, it is well with my soul. He will take care of us so intimately, that our thoughts and His become one."

Jacqueline was fascinated. When he spoke them, she was even more aware of something lacking in her life. She was struck by the importance of what he had said. They were not merely phrases he had written on a sheet of paper. They meant something to him. Something from the bottom of his heart. His expression showed that he was deeply serious about this. He meant every word of it.

"Lord," he bowed his head, "please help us to put You first this week. Help us to lay down our earthly desires before You and follow what You have for us, without doubt. In Your name, Amen."

Everyone sat for a moment, and let the words wash over them. Then one by one, the families got up, stretched, and looked around as if they had just become aware of their surroundings again. For Jacqueline it was the clearest, most interesting sermon she had ever heard. She sat still after people around her started chatting.

"Are you all right?" Grace asked concerned when she didn't stand up.

"Mm, I'm fine. I just have never heard anyone speak like that before. I guess I have not had the occasion to think about what you told me back home. Because once you were gone, I stopped thinking about God. I guess it is time to have some serious thoughts."

"It will not be enough just to think about God. He wants us. Think of the Bible as a love letter. If you received a love letter, wouldn't you want to read it?"

"I guess so," she said and blushed. "I have never gotten a love letter before."

"Oh yes you have. God wrote it to you," Grace smiled gently.

"Hmm, I guess so."

"I tell you what. We can sit down and read together before we go to bed. How does that sound?"

Jacqueline was reluctant.

"All right, think about it, then. But for now let's go and eat. We always share a meal together after the service. Then we hang out together a little bit. But we can get going after, since you have to prepare for tonight."

There was plenty to eat for everyone. The young people sat by the pool and chatted.

"So, Jacqueline, did you just move here with your family?" Petra asked as she sipped some punch.

"No, we are visiting the Spencer family for a week. We will be leaving on Tuesday," she replied, realizing with a start that the end of her stay was so close. "I really like it here," she admitted and everyone nodded.

"It's all right," John told her, "when you get past the heat and humidity in the summer." Jane, another girl about their age, nodded fiercely.

"Where are you from?" she asked.

"I'm from Lichtenbourgh, located between Switzerland and France," she stated.

"That's neat. How long have you been a Christian?" someone asked.

Jacqueline blushed and stammered. "I… I'm not really. I just came because Grace asked me to. But I somehow feel it was right to come," she said quietly.

"God knows, doesn't He?"

Everyone nodded and mumbled their assent.

Jacqueline was surprised that she was reluctant to leave. Mr. Van Der Hooven looked her deep in the eyes and smiled as he shook her hand.

"It was good to meet you, Jacqueline. I hope you will allow Christ to become real to you," he said.

She didn't know what to make of that. His eyes held hers and he put a hand on her shoulder.

"Jacqueline, my wife and I will continue to pray for you."

Chapter 31

Jacqueline was quiet on the drive home. Needing to take a walk along the beach to collect her thoughts, she quickly put on her shorts and made her way outside. She passed her parents on the way, sunning themselves by the pool. Jacqueline waved to them. Her mother squinted over her sun glasses.

The breeze was wonderful along the beach and the rhythmic pounding of the surf stirred something inside her. Brian was paddling out on his surfboard. He waved to her and she waved back. Her thoughts drifted back to the morning. She did not think she was a bad person, but the songs convinced her differently. They convinced her that she was a sinner. She was an upstanding moral person, a princess, a successful Olympic and World Champion, a leader in her community... But a sinner? Yes, there was something missing in her life.

She had always thought that what was missing, was a relationship with her family. She gasped when she realized that it was not all that was missing. Was it that she did not know this God, the One who had come and died for her?

Was that what the crux of the matter was? This missing relationship that could only be fixed through knowing Christ?

Jacqueline hugged herself tightly as the soft breeze tugged at her hair, wrestling it free from her pony tail. Suddenly the breeze became soft and almost playful, as it continued to tug at her. She giggled softly.

Then she gasped when the weight of her sin came crashing down at her. It wasn't that she had done things, such as spoken harshly to her parents, manipulated to get her way, looked down upon people, who weren't her. Those things hit her hard as well. The enormity of not knowing God, of not wanting... to know God. It caused her stomach to tighten unpleasantly. She had thought herself above it all!

Tears sprang to her eyes as this sank in. All her life, she hadn't given one thought to God. Oh sure, there had been occasions when she had bowed her head. The time in her bedroom sprang to her mind. But she had never give God the time of day, not really. And she had strayed as far away from Jesus as she possibly could, bringing Him out at Christmas and Easter.

A loud sob escaped her throat, and the tears started running down her cheeks.

"Okay, Jesus, how do I get to know You? I guess since You are God, would You show me how to do that?" she said as she looked out over the waves.

She felt a certain assurance that her words were heard. It was a daunting thought that the God of the universe had heard her yet again. She walked farther on down the beach, still thinking about what she had heard only hours ago. What was she supposed to do now?

She kicked at a wave that came crashing over her feet. The water was warm and she allowed herself to walk in a little deeper. The next wave almost knocked her over. Jacqueline felt the undercurrent pulling away the sand beneath her feet. She made her way a little further out savoring the warm water and the wave slapped into her back. She laughed as it picked her up and carried her yet further. Her feet touched the bottom and she turned around just in time to see a slightly bigger wave come barreling down on her. It engulfed her and her feet were pulled out from under her. She gasped in surprise as she tried to get her feet back on solid ground. There was none! Her mouth filled with sea water.

She was being swept out to sea with alarming speed, as the next wave crashed over her head. She panicked and struggled against the current. She glimpsed the pool in the near distance as the next wave arrived. Brian was on his surfboard, painfully unaware of her dilemma. Then she felt it! It was unmistakably clear. There was a Presence with her in the water. It was whispering to her to keep her hand raised above the water's surface. She gulped down what air she could and tried to take a slow breath to stop panicking, but her position did not improve. She was far too quickly being pulled away from the safety of the shore.

Jacqueline felt a strong urge to raise her hand as high as she could. As her head bobbed back up above the surface of the water, she saw that the distance to the beach had increased. A lot! The current was strong. She thought she saw Grace running along the beach toward the water, her hands waving in the air. It was hard to make out whether it was actually she. Jacqueline forced her thoughts back to her own situation. She was getting tired. The constant kicking against the current was draining all her strength, and yet she could feel her body slipping underneath the warm water. She didn't see much point in keeping her arm raised. It was almost a comfort to let herself get dragged under and farther away from shore. Her thoughts turned to God and Jesus. *I would have liked to have gotten to know them better here on earth. Would You please take care of my family?*

Her lungs burned from the lack of air and she once again gave a mighty kick. It would be her last kick, she knew. Her head popped out of the water and she greedily gulped down the air. Just as quickly as she shot out of the water, she slid back in. She was comforted by the warmth that engulfed her as she slid farther and farther from the surface. Her tired brain and the Presence with her implored her not to give up, to kick one last time, but the surface was so far away and her muscles were so tired. She had done well. She felt she hadn't disgraced her family in this last fight. Tiredly she gave it one last effort. The need for air took over her thoughts.

One kick propelled her closer to the surface. She felt her finger tips break through the water's surface. Only mere inches separated her from a chance to live. She couldn't. Her muscles were not obeying her anymore. Desperately she hoped to breathe air in, to alleviate that burn in her lungs. Oh, to fill her lungs one last time with life-giving air.

Pain shot through her, as her shoulder smashed into something hard and unforgiving. She gulped in sea water as she cried out in pain. Something grabbed her hand, and she responded by clinging to that with all the strength that was left within her. Her body was being yanked from the water fast. The back of her head connected with a hard

225

surface. Suddenly, the calm, quiet of the sea was replaced by harsh sunlight and... Her music?

She rolled into a tiny ball, her muscles trembling all over. *Breathe, in through your nose and out through your mouth. This is your moment.* Her music was starting. She could hear it. They were expecting her on the ice! She would not win the Olympics, if she was just trying to breathe!

The music began to fade and was replaced by a soft voice.

"Come on, lassie. Breathe!"

Her body convulsed and she vomited. Water spewed out of her mouth and she took a deep breath. Life! She coughed up more water as gentle hands rubbed her back, imploring her to take another breath. She drew in another labored breath.

"That's it, lass. You're all right now."

She took a great big gulp of air. Jesus had been with her and He knew what He was doing. She was absolutely certain of this.

Grace ran up and down the beach, yelling at her brother and gesticulating wildly.

"Jacqueline is in trouble, Brian! Do something!"

Brian scanned the surface of the water desperately looking for Jacqueline. He couldn't see her. She was gone! He shaded his eyes and propped himself up higher on his surfboard, to get a better angle. She had been dragged out! Out of his reach! There was panic in his eyes as he looked back at Grace, who had collapsed onto the sand, her eyes filled with terror. He let his twin down, he let Jacqueline down. He

226

noticed Jacqueline's parents standing behind Grace, eyes trained on the vast body of water. His breath caught in his throat.

He had been unable to protect someone who had become so important to him, in such a short amount of time. He dove into the water, letting out a blood curdling scream! Water filled his mouth. His lungs burned as he searched below the surface of the water, knowing full well that it was a fruitless effort. Was this what she felt like? His head exploded through the surface of the water and he heaved himself back onto the surfboard.

He paddled slowly back to shore, spent. Grace was still sitting at the edge of the water with Jacqueline's parents behind her. Jacqueline's mother put her hand on Grace's shoulder, tears in her eyes. Then, she sank down next to Grace, grief shaking her body. Jacqueline's father looked like he was going to faint, dead away. He clung onto hope that his daughter might yet be alive. His tear-filled eyes scanned the horizon for any evidence of his youngest daughter.

Brian dragged himself onto shore and collapsed on the other side of his twin, gulping in another breath. He moaned when he thought of how Jacqueline would never take another breath of fresh air. And he ached that he hadn't had a chance to reach her. He roughed his hands over his face.

Brian heard his sister's mumbled prayer. He lifted his head.

"Come on, Grace. Cut it out! This is not the place for prayer! Especially prayers to that guy!"

His sister ignored him, and continued her soft prayer.

Jacqueline's father continued scanning the horizon. His daughter! His precious daughter! Taken from him! He shook his head and blinked his eyes, clearing the tears. The surroundings became a blur for a brief second, as more tears flooded his eyes. As he cleared them again, a sob escaped him. He would never be able to debate with her again! Ripped from him, when they were just beginning to have a relationship. Sometimes life wasn't fair.

His eyes cleared and he focused his attention out to sea again. A speed boat approached them from the right. His breath caught and for a moment he held on to the hope that maybe, just maybe, Jacqueline could still be alive. He straightened himself, his heart beating in his throat. The boat slowed as it approached their position and the engines were cut. It bobbed on the surf while the two men moved about the small cabin, bending over. No! He wouldn't believe that they had recovered the body of his daughter out at sea. He gritted his teeth. She had to be alive!

"All right, lassie. Put your arms around me, now. I got you. I am a burly Scotsman who can carry a wee little girl like you."

Jacqueline almost laughed at the skinny man, heaving her up from the surface of the boat. She was still trembling, her muscles weren't responding to anything she told them to do. Except to breathe. Every breath she took in, was like a celebration.

"Mick, are you sure you haf her?" the older, more burly German asked, as he jumped out of the boat to keep it from floating away.

Mick growled at him and gently lowered himself into the water. Jacqueline winced as the wave covered her and she clung to him.

He chuckled. "Don't you worry, now. I won't let you go."

She saw them standing at the water's edge, Grace on her knees, eyes widening in relief. Brian pushed himself off the sand, his face unreadable. Her mother dabbed daintily at her eyes. It was her father, who rushed forward to take her from Mick, as a wave propelled them forward, onto the shore.

She felt herself enveloped in her father's comforting arms.

"My precious daughter," he whispered.

She closed her eyes and allowed herself to enjoy this rare moment. Her father gently put her down on the beach.

Her mother was now standing up, brushing the sand off her shorts. She cleared her throat and walked toward the men, her head held high.

"I want to thank you for rescuing my daughter, my good boat people. Do you have any immediate needs?"

The men looked at each other and rubbed their faces.

"Eh, sure," the Scotsman said, chuckling. "This here boat is a might expensive."

A smile played on the Queen's lips. She pulled out a business card and handed it to him. "Call this number and tell them who you are. They will take care of you."

Mick gaped at the embossed crown on the card. He winked at her. "All right, lass. I might just do that."

Jacqueline's mother bristled and frowned. "I am not a lass. I am a Queen!"

"All right then, Queen lass!" he laughed as he made his way back to the boat. After they had both climbed back on board they turned toward Jacqueline, who had been watching this scene, a smile on her face. They both bowed sincerely, and Jacqueline could feel the first tears prick her eyes.

She blinked and turned to her parents.

"Mother, may I have some hot chocolate, and Father may I have a blanket. I am a bit cold," her voice sounded like a little child's. Both parents nodded quickly with smiles and glistening eyes.

Jacqueline heard her mother say to her father that she had a proper name, and had never been called lassie, as they hurried off to the house. He responded by putting his arm around her. "You are my lassie."

Chapter 32

"Are you all right?" Grace asked as she flopped onto the sand next to her. Jacqueline nodded weakly as Grace put her arm around her protectively.

"I should have warned you that the undertow is really strong on days like this," Brian said.

"Thank you for your prayers," Jacqueline finally managed to whisper. "How did you know that I was in danger, Grace?"

"I just had a feeling that things weren't right. So I came out here to see what was going on and I saw you struggling," her voice faded. She bowed her head, tears running down her cheeks.

"Hey, Gracie, it's all right." Brian patted his sister's hand. "It's over," he said gently. He put his arm protectively around his sister's shoulder.

"I think Christ protected me," Jacqueline whispered so quietly that nobody heard her at first.

Then Grace's eyes widened in surprise. She turned to her friend and hugged her tightly. "I think you are right."

Brian snorted loudly. "Girls, that is a bunch of hogwash," he grunted and heaved himself off the sand. "Jesus was a good prophet, a good man," Brian growled. "Not God! And by the way, you came out," he pointed at his sister, "saw that Jacqueline was in trouble, and started praying. But you didn't save her! Neither did I!" His face contorted in anger. "It's got nothing to do with God, all right?" he growled as his face contorted in anger. Then he huffed and started stomping across the beach sending sand every which way, back to the house.

"He is wrong," Jacqueline stated softly. "I felt a Presence, something willing me to kick one more time to get my hand above the water. That last thurst of strength did not come from me."

Grace nodded and squeezed her shoulder. Jacqueline could feel the strength creeping back into her legs. Soon she was able to get up and together they walked back to the house.

They met her parents as they came out of the house with the hot chocolate and blanket. Jacqueline sank into the lounge chair. Walking had drained her strength again.

"I hope you'll be all right for tonight," Grace said quietly and looked concerned.

"Indeed," her father said and sat down next to her. "I think we will be canceling the event."

"No," both Jacqueline and her mother shouted. They looked at each other for a moment, an understanding passing between them. "I'll be fine. Besides." Jacqueline pulled herself to her full sitting height. "It is what we do!"

She showered and dressed quickly, and then spent some time on her hair. She tied it into a bun and pinned it tight. She then sprinkled it glitter. As she looked at herself, a comment Grace had made came back to her. Her costume was indeed quite short. She was shocked that she had never thought about this. All of a sudden she felt embarrassed. Grace entered the room as she was looking at herself.

"Hey, great. You look like you are ready," she enthused.

Jacqueline smiled at her.

"What do you think of this costume?"

"Well, you know that I would not be comfortable in it. But you have to do what you feel is right."

"That is the problem. I feel wrong in this." Jacqueline frowned. "What should I do?"

Grace's eyebrow shot up. She cleared her throat.

"Wow, hmm, I don't know. It's amazing that you should feel God's directing you like that so soon."

"What do you mean, God's directing me? This is just me, feeling a little naked in this dress."

Grace took her hand and looked earnestly into her eyes. "When the Holy Spirit gives us a nudge, sometimes we feel uncomfortable. It's God's way of telling us that He wants us to make a change in our life. It is usually a good idea to listen to His suggestions right away. You are learning that you have choices. You can either listen and take His nudges to heart, or you can ignore it, and do whatever you want. I suggest you listen. But it's entirely up to you. He will provide you with what you need, even though you may not like the choice."

Jacqueline got up and paced the room. She wasn't sure of what to do in this instance.

"What do I do?"

Grace smirked. "I have found that if I don't know what to do, I ask for direction."

Jacqueline frowned. "There is no one to ask direction from."

Grace threw her head back and laughed. "Of course there is. He is always available."

Now Jacqueline was thoroughly confused. "Who?" Had the events of her day gotten to her friend?

"God, silly!"

Jacqueline's mouth formed a perfect O. Grace bowed her head and closed her eyes. Jacqueline felt awkward. She swallowed hard.

"Father God, thank You for making Your wish known to Jacqueline. Would You guide us to make the right decision as to what costume she should wear? We thank You for keeping her safe today. In Your name, Amen."

Jacqueline looked expectantly at Grace. She looked around the room as though she expected a dress to appear in front of her. Nothing happened, but a sense of right entered into her heart. It was totally strange and yet exhilarating.

"Come on," Grace walked to her large closet. "It is my turn to lend you something you can wear."

They arrived at the rink in time and Fiona was waiting for her in the arena.

"It's time to get on the ice and warm up," she patted her on the back.

Jacqueline forced herself to feel good. To feel normal. She was back in her world, in which everything was normal.

"Jacqueline, are you all right?" Fiona yelled to her as she skated by. "You look a little tense. You are not competing, remember?"

She remembered, all right. She stretched her tense shoulder, surprised that her sore shoulder didn't bother her much. She felt tense, but as she skated she started to relax. Fiona was right. Jacqueline willed her trouble out of her mind.

"All right, I think you are warmed up," Fiona called. She handed her the skate guards.

"I need to change," she told her coach quietly.

"Aren't you wearing your costume?" Fiona asked, confusion on her face.

"Don't ask. I can't explain it myself."

She went into the changing room and pulled out the baby blue dress, Grace and she had found. Because she was slightly taller than Grace, the skirt came down to just below the knee. The cotton dress was light and flowing. The sleeves hung down to her elbows, with a gentle scooping neckline. A white belt wrapped gently around the waist. She hoped that her skates would not get caught in the flowing hem.

The arena started filling up with spectators. Everyone was ushered back into the changing rooms, which grew crowded and extremely noisy. The older girls got busy with the younger ones' hair. Jacqueline tried to find a quiet corner but it was impossible to escape the din in the room. She needed to get into her shell, and she put her earplugs into her ears, to try to drown out the commotion. She closed her eyes and instantly, she was back in the water, the current taking her out to sea. That didn't help her at all!

Soon the program started and the little kids were shepherded to the rink. They stood by the doors giggling, waving to an enchanted audience. Jacqueline glanced around trying to see her parents. She spotted them at the top of the bleachers, talking quietly to the Spencers. She spotted Grace and Brian sitting with some friends, eating popcorn and drinking soda. She thought she spotted one of the young people from the house church sitting next to Grace. They all seemed to be having a good time.

The program went smoothly with some falls, which were expected. As the skaters became more proficient, the falls became fewer and fewer. Jacqueline waited expectantly for her time. She was ready. She took a deep breath and made her way to the door. She handed her skate guards to Fiona, who gave her an encouraging squeeze. The manager announced her and the arena burst into excited applause.

She waved and smiled at the excited audience, skating to her spot on the ice. The arena quieted down and her music started. Again, her body responded to her song and she flowed across the ice in fluid motions. At one point she panicked when her skate did catch on her hem for a split second. She breathed out a sigh of relief when it came loose right away. The music ended and again the applause was enthusiastic and energetic. She smiled and curtseyed to the audience.

She grinned as she got off the ice, taking her guards from Fiona, who beamed at her.

"That was very nice. Although, I don't think that dress helped you much." Fiona shot her a knowing look.

"Yes, well," she smiled and slipped her guards onto her blades. She had a couple of moments before the finale and grabbed a drink from her water bottle.

"How was the ice?"

"It was nice. Hey, that rhymes," she chuckled. Fiona gave her a blank look, then raised an eyebrow, slowly. Jacqueline laughed. The lights were dimmed, her cue to get ready again. She gave her guards and water bottle back to Fiona.

"I guess I have just become the holder of the guards," her coach chuckled ruefully and grabbed Jacqueline's water. "I feel like a mother hen."

The finale was well received. The audience gave a standing ovation. It pleased Jacqueline to have been part of something like this. She hoped she could come again in the future. Fiona motioned that she was leaving her on her own. Jacqueline mouthed a sarcastic thanks to her coach. After changing back into her warm up pants and jacket, she tried to make her way through the crowd. The manager stopped her and asked if she could come the next day for a little celebration. She told him that she would try.

It proved to be hard to leave because so many of the audience stopped her for an autograph. At this point she was bone weary but smiled at yet another fan. She looked up and recognized Mr. Van Der Hooven and his family.

"Did you enjoy the performance?" she asked and signed her name on their program.

"We were quite surprised to recognize our demure visitor from this morning as the main attraction," his wife laughed. "It was quite beautiful. You have a real gift there."

"Thank you so much. And I really enjoyed meeting with you this morning. Your talk really changed my perspective," she told them honestly and was surprised at the hug she received from Mrs. Van Der Hooven.

Grace and two of the young people she had met in the morning found her. John looked at her with an approving look.

"You know, I actually enjoyed your performance the most. Not because you are clearly a professional, but it was refreshing to see that you had the foresight to wear such an unassuming dress. I don't like seeing the immodest dresses on these young girls." His face turned a slight shade of red. "It just makes me uncomfortable, if you know what I mean."

Jacqueline looked at him. "It does?"

"Sure. If the girls wear something clingy and short, what do you think it does to us guys?" Now his face was bright red. He had clearly stepped out of his comfort zone. He muttered a good night to them and followed his family out the door.

Chapter 33

Jacqueline watched them leave, thinking about what John had said. Distractedly, she signed more autographs, posed for pictures, and shook hands with members of the audience. It seemed to take forever before she could extract herself from the melee. She found Brian reading a magazine and sipping a milkshake, leaning against the wall near the front entrance. He looked up and a smile spread over his face.

"There you are, finally. Grace went home with the parents. She was pretty beat."

"Thanks for waiting," Jacqueline yawned. "Getting out almost took longer than the show itself," she sighed as she slowly swung herself into the front seat of the vehicle.

"You are a popular person right now," Brian said and started the engine. He drove swiftly through the evening traffic, carefully avoiding the other cars.

"It was really nice tonight, Jacqueline. I really like watching you skate. It was as though you were just out there on your own, having a great time," he said.

"Thanks, I did have a great time. I only get a little uptight right beforehand."

"I can imagine. There must be a lot of pressure on you when you compete."

"I put a lot of pressure on myself, because I am the one who wants to do well. But yes, there is a lot of pressure, especially once you start winning. People expect you to continue to win. I told myself that if I get to the point that winning is my only motive to compete, I'll give it up."

"That's probably a good plan. So how long do you think you are going to keep going?"

"I'd like to make another Olympics. And beyond that, we will see," she told him honestly.

They drove in silence. Jacqueline could feel her eyes slowly closing as she leaned her head against the window. The rumbling of the pavement against the glass had a calming effect.

"So, you okay? You know, with what happened this afternoon?" he suddenly asked a little huskily and she shook herself awake. "I can't get over what might have...," he paused and swallowed. "You know, I thought you were gone. That undercurrent can be really deadly. I feel responsible for not telling you about it."

"I'm okay, really." She was just really, really tired. "I won't lie to you. I was scared. Not something I want to repeat too soon. But really, I kind of knew I would be all right. I am not kidding you, Brian. I felt really calm even though the situation was terrifying. I don't make light of these things," she explained seriously. She turned to face him. "And you don't have to feel bad, Brian. There was nothing you could have done. God was the One who protected me."

"Okay, okay. I just don't get it," he grumbled darting a quick glance at her.

"I don't either, but He was there, no question about it. So now we come to ask ourselves if we can believe in a God who is interested in each of us personally," she mused. "I don't have any answers for you."

They continued in silence until they had almost reached the house. The desert was dark as the stars shone extremely bright. She looked up and marveled at the beauty. Brian pulled the car over to the side and turned to her, his face bathed in darkness so she couldn't quite see his features.

"I just can't see how it is possible. You know, I studied the Koran as a kid. I went to religious school right here and all I heard was that god is not your friend. He is the judge and we will burn in hell if we don't get things right. There is a balance. In the end, you better hope that you have more stuff on your good side than on your bad. I heard over and over again that any unbelievers are to be converted or gotten rid of. That included my father! How can I believe in a god who expects me to hate my father? To make an enemy out of him? For a long time my father became an enemy! I hated him! There was too much anger within me when I tried to follow what the Mullah was telling me to do. I don't want to believe in a god at all. I find it easier to believe that I can make my own future if I work hard enough!"

Jacqueline was quiet for a long time. She didn't know what to think. She felt Brian's anger and hurt.

"I know one thing," she whispered. "When I went to the meeting with Grace this morning, I didn't expect to come away with more questions than answers. I didn't expect the preacher to almost radiate peace. His talk touched something deep inside of me, something dislodged in my heart. It struck the deepest part of my heart. It was convicting but comforting at the same time. I had the feeling that God knew my deepest secrets and yet was asking me to come and explore Him more. As the preacher spoke, I felt that what he was saying was directed to me personally. I can't explain it any more, but I know that there is something out there for me to discover. I want that glow, Brian," her voice came out in spurts, as if it was hard to breathe.

"He radiated?" he asked sarcastically. "Maybe he was just outside in the sun too long."

"Funny, very funny. No, there was something that man knows, and I want to know what it is. I am telling you, I felt something in the water with me. There was peace, even though I thought I was going to die. I can't explain it," she said, pursing her lips in frustration.

"All right, I give," he grumbled and put the car back into gear. They drove the rest of the way home in silence.

"Hey, good night, Your Highness. You did great tonight," he smiled and held the garage door open for her.

She thanked him and made her way to her room. Grace was already in bed, a movie playing on the TV. She was fast asleep. Jacqueline was too keyed up to sleep now. The catnap in the car seemed to have given her energy. She slipped into shorts and a T-shirt and made her way quietly outside.

The sea was active but nothing like it had been during the day. The full moon sat low above the horizon. It was beautiful how the light of the moon glistened off the top of the waves. The whole world seemed spread out before her, but there were so many mysteries lay hidden beneath the surface. She almost stepped onto a jellyfish but managed to avoid its slimy, iridescent body. Little sticky black spots littered the normally pristine beach. They stuck to the bottom of her feet. The wind took her loose hair and tousled it about. In the distance she spotted the lights from different vessels. Above were the lights of heaven. The lights from heaven! She pondered. What had changed? She didn't have the answers. She needed answers. She leaned back onto her elbows, felt the sand prick her skin and contemplated the events of the day.

So, where do I begin? She thought. *What is truth? Where does this truth come from? Here is Brian, who has a totally different outlook on deity. What is the truth?* She sat up, hugging her knees. The wind picked at her hair again and she stuck it over her earlobe, out of the way. *If you believe in the Son of God.* The Son of God. What did she know about this Son of God? She knew that every Christmas they celebrated His birth and every Easter His death. *Oh no, there is more to it. He rose from being dead. And apparently if we believe this is true we can live forever too. So I have to believe. What is this believing? I just say that I believe and we are done? All right,* she reasoned with herself, *I believe in the Son of God.*

There, it was done. She took a deep breath, listening to her heart beating. It still beat, she was still alive. She hadn't been struck with lightning. Over the sea she noticed a falling star, a meteor, as she reasoned. She laughed at her one sided conversation. If anyone in her family had heard her tonight, they would have thought she was crazy. She got up brushing herself off and turned to the house, trying to avoid the sticky black pieces of goo.

Quietly, she let herself the door. She tiptoed upstairs and went to get into bed, when she noticed her feet were covered in the sticky black yuck. She went to the bathroom and attempted to wash it off but it stuck to her stubbornly. She yawned, suddenly drained of all energy and dragged herself to her bed.

Chapter 34

When Jacqueline woke late the next morning, to find Grace sitting in shorts and T-shirt by the window, reading. Jacqueline stretched and yawned.

"Good morning," she squeaked and stretched luxuriously again. Grace glanced up from her reading and smiled.

"Hey, you're awake. How did you sleep?"

"Like a rock," she mumbled. "What are you doing?" Grace held up her thick book. *Ah,* Jacqueline thought and took a deep breath. *God's love letter.*

"May I read to you?" Grace bounced up and sat on Jacqueline's bed jostling her a bit. Jacqueline stretched and puffed up her pillow for Grace to lean against.

"Hmm. So for someone like you and me at the beginning, many would suggest we start in John. But we should ask God and see where He would like us to start." She closed her eyes and bowed her head. "Lord direct us right now as to where You want us to read in Your word, Amen."

Grace opened her eyes and pursed her lips, contemplating the book in front of her. Her dark eyes were soft and unfocused, as though she were listening to an inner voice. She shrugged her shoulders and opened her Bible. "I'm reading John now, so we might as well start there for today," she mused and turned back to the beginning of the gospel of John. Jacqueline read along as Grace read the first chapter.

She held up her hand. "I am already confused," she said. "What is going on here? There is a guy who is crying out and he baptizes. That all is no problem. But who is the guy? And what is this about a Lamb? I assume he is talking about Jesus."

Grace laughed and turned to her friend.

"Relax. Take it in and just let it sit there. Think about what you have just heard. It will sound really strange, to be sure. But just think on it, okay?" Jacqueline nodded, squinting her eyes.

"Did he baptize in the rain or just in the middle of the summer heat? Which counts more? Getting wet in the rain or in the water? Can't you just get baptized in the rain? Why are people going so far into the wilderness when there is water in the town? How important is it to be baptized? What does it mean?" she asked excitedly

Grace held up her hand. "Hold on a minute! Just *think* about what we just read. It is important to not let it go out of your mind. See if, once you think about it, things start making sense. You should also pray and ask God to help you figure out what you are reading. After all, the Holy Spirit inspired the authors to write the Bible," Grace explained patiently.

"Did you ever go to the Muslim school?" Jacqueline asked after a little while.

"Yes, it was not something I would like to go back to," Grace answered quietly. "Both Brian and I went. I only went for a year. He was forced to go longer, and the affects of it really stuck with him. It affected him more than it did me. He used to walk out of the room as soon as our father walked in. It was terrible and almost split the family apart. When I heard about Jesus, I struggled to come before Christ because of the teachings that I learned all my life. It took a long time for me to work through the conflict that was in my heart. But then He convinced me to come so sweetly, that I had no choice because Christ offered me that peace I had been longing for. Once I accepted Him, there was comfort and... love. I pray for my brother every night."

Jacqueline nodded and stared out the window.

"I told God that I believe in His Son last night. I don't know what to do next."

"That is so awesome!" Grace hugged her friend tightly. "Now, you have to start building on that. God asks us to seek Him first. Oh, Jacqueline, when we do that everything falls into place." She grabbed her hands, her eyes shining brightly. "The result of that is that we have the ability to live a full life, a life led by Christ first and foremost. There is the peace, Jacqueline, the love that we all long for. When we follow Him in everything we do, we can rest. Because all of a sudden it's not only us who is in control. We have given Christ the control of our life. It makes a huge difference. We may not understand where He is leading us, and it may be a really scary place, but He won't leave us in that scary place. He works everything out as long as we follow Him. When we come to that place where we allow Him to lead us through everything, our life in Christ begins. We call that being born again, because we are dependent on Christ like a newborn baby. It is something that Christ works out in us, we can't force it to happen. The Bible tells us that the Lord is our Salvation and we are to search for that like the most important riches. But don't look at me so terrified," Grace said with compassion and put her hand on her arm. "It's been difficult for me too. But Christ will show you what to do. It is not going to be easy. But it's all part of God's plan. So, to begin with, start reading His word. I know, it makes no sense, but it will start making sense."

Jacqueline took a shuddering breath and hooked a strand of chestnut hair over her ear. "All right." She swallowed hard. "There is a lot to think about."

Moments later, Jacqueline sluggishly crept out of bed and spotted the gooey spots on her feet.

"Grace, what are these?" she asked pointing.

"Yuck, you stepped in oil residue. Whenever it is really rough out there, we get the nasty gunk from oil spills. Come on, let's take care of it."

It took her half an hour to scrape the nasty stuff off her feet.

"So much for my beautiful beach," she grumbled and looked at her feet that were now goo free but full of faded black spots. Grace laughed at her but told her that if she walked along the beach a couple of times, carefully, she would soon be rid of the spots.

"Fine, but first I am starving," Jacqueline confessed.

They made their way down into the dining room, where everyone had gathered. Brian was out on his board again, since the surf was high. She shuddered and decided to stay out of the water today.

248

"Jacqueline, we had such a wonderful time last night," Mrs. Spencer beamed at her, her dark eyes shining brightly. Jacqueline thanked her hostess.

"It was certainly very entertaining," her mother nodded and gingerly buttered her perfectly toasted bread. Jacqueline quenched her thirst with a huge glass of freshly squeezed orange juice, followed by another. She quickly glanced at her mother and gently dabbed the corner of her mouth with her napkin. She gobbled down scrambled eggs, no cheese, and a fruit salad. It felt as though there was a hole in her stomach. She finished with another tall glass of juice.

Brian walked in, grabbed a piece of toast, and flipped his sister's ponytail. She made a face at him, and his mother frowned in his direction.

"Do you have any manners, young man, to just saunter in and grab and not sit? I don't think I taught you that," she scowled and pointed to an empty seat.

"Sorry Mother," he flashed a bright smile her way and sat, dripping on the marble floor.

"Son, for heaven's sake, get dried up. You are going to give Pamela a heart attack!"

"Why do you think I didn't sit down?" he asked sarcastically. His mother glared at him.

"I think Brian's in a mood, Mother. Best leave him alone," Grace cautioned.

The adults decided to go to dinner together, leaving the young people free to make their plans.

Jacqueline excused herself after breakfast for a stroll along the beach. She trudged haltingly through the sand, littered with pieces of old wood, seaweed, and other trash. Carefully she stepped around the black goo that dotted the beach, but there was so much of it, it covered her feet.

She pondered what she had read with Grace. Could it be possible that this stuff was real, and not just some old story? Grace mentioned after the reading that the Kingdom of God was hidden, impossible to reach without the help of the Holy Spirit and being born again. She stared out to sea and wondered how it would feel to be born again. A baby definitely knew it! It came from the warmth of the womb to the harsh surrounding of the world. Was that what it would be like? She shuddered. It didn't sound like such a pleasant experience. It frightened her!

She had a choice. The experience of a painful birth was overwhelming. She lifted her chin as the waves crashed onto her feet. There was something about this. She had felt God with her as she had struggled for her life in the water the day before. He cared! Would He care enough to see her through this rebirth? She frowned. She decided that she would continue on this path.

This meant that the story she was reading in John was true and not some made up thing; it meant something. First of all, she was struck that Christ was referred to as the Lamb of God who took away the sin of the world. Then she pondered about the opening statement. She couldn't understand it. God was before the beginning, and Christ was right there with Him and was Him? Christ, so it seemed, had created the world. So every drop of water in the sea was created? No, that was way too far-fetched! She knew that scientifically water was formed in the upper atmosphere.

"Hmm, where is heaven anyway?" she asked and gathered up a piece of sharp metal.

Brian lounged at the pool, his surfboard propped against the low back wall, when she strolled by.

"Hey, you want to learn how to surf?" he asked, as she flung herself into the seat next to him.

She grimaced. "I don't think I want to brave that water today." She pointed to the waves. They were still impressive and she was not going in!

"Come on! The undertow is nothing like it was yesterday. I'll stay right by your side," he suggested, looking at her expectantly. She really wasn't ready to brave the surf today, or tomorrow for that matter, and tempt another repeat of yesterday.

"Are you sure it is safe?"

"As safe as possible," Brian replied. "Come on. You know you want to."

"No, I really don't," she said. Determination seeped through her. "I don't mind admitting that I am scared."

"Nothing to it, Jacqueline. Trust me." His eyes shone with assurance and he took her hand, leading her from the pool to the water. The waves crashed into her legs sending her a step back.

"Come on, it's fine. I've got you." His hand gripped hers tightly as he led her past the breaking waves.

"Wait, Brian. I'm not so sure about this anymore!" She swallowed the fear that was worming its way through her.

As the waves crashed into her, tried to tell herself that she was okay.

"It's nothing, Jacqueline. And look," he nodded toward her hand in his. "I still got you. I'm not going to let go."

A large wave approached them and Jacqueline watched in increasing fear.

She shook her head.

"No, wait." Terror gripped her and wouldn't let go. "I really can't do this, Brian! Please. Let me go!" Tears stung her eyes. "You can't guarantee that I won't get swept out to sea again. You can't keep me safe! You can't play god! I... need to get out of here!" she gasped as her throat threatened to close up on her.

She yanked her hand out of his, suddenly angry that Brian was so recklessly playing with her life, tempting fate after she had barely escaped with her life. The force of the large wave helped extract herself from his grip. She allowed the wave to carry her back to the beach and headed toward the pool. She didn't notice that Brian was pulled under by the wave.

A few seconds later it drove him into the beach, where he managed to sit up, spitting out the salt water and sand. He turned onto his back, panting as the waves pushed him farther up onto the sand. Once he washed up on dry ground he rolled over and groaned softly.

The sand had left chafe marks all over his chest and arms. It burned in the salt water. As painful as that was, it wasn't as painful as Jacqueline's last remark.

Chapter 35

They got to the arena just in time. Brian and Grace wandered off to the bar to get sodas. Jacqueline entered the arena and there they all were. The little ones flitting about on the ice, the older ones were standing around, talking. Fiona motioned to her.

"Just go out on the ice and mingle," Fiona suggested.

"What?" Jacqueline asked. Fiona groaned and repeated her instructions.

"So I don't do anything other than mingle?" she asked again.

"Precisely, dear Jacqueline, precisely." Fiona chuckled at Jacqueline's surprised look. She donned her skates and stepped onto the ice.

"Ah, there you are," the manager said and clapped her hands in both of his. "I just want to tell you again, that I am so thankful that you came."

"Well, it was my pleasure, believe me. I have really enjoyed being here," she told him. Everyone gathered on the ice and a photographer was on hand to take pictures.

"May I have a moment of your time," he asked Jacqueline.

She sighed inwardly but told him she was happy to be available to him after. He beamed and stayed close at hand. The little girls gathered around her and asked a million questions.

"Can you show us how to do a sit spin?" one shy little one asked.

Jacqueline smiled and slowly showed them how she had been taught. They squeaked in delight and when one of them fell on her butt, Jacqueline helped her up. Tears started to form in the little one's eyes.

"Are you hurt?" Jacqueline asked as she helped brush off the ice. The girl shook her head and now the tears were falling.

"Don't cry. Do you know how many times I have fallen on my bum? Hey, listen, I still fall sometimes. And it hurts even more now," she whispered into the little one's ears. "Let's try it again, slowly," she suggested and for sure the little one was able to rotate once or twice.

Jacqueline clapped in delight.

By the time she was done on the ice, it was almost six o'clock. She hoped that the shops would still be open after they were done. Brian and Grace leaned against the wall and waved. They were waiting for her to finish.

She changed into a light summer dress, which she had brought with her and was glad for it, for when she walked out the building she walked smack dab into a wall of humidity. Just walking toward the vehicle, caused her to sweat. She had brought along a light white cardigan, which she discarded immediately.

"How can you stand this humidity?" she puffed. The twins grinned and teased her mercilessly. Grace chuckled in the back.

"Why do you think we leave at the end of the month? Montana is really nice this time of year."

"You go to Montana in the summer?"

"Yep, our grandparents have a ranch up there. We love it. Mom drops us off for a month and we hang out with the horses and the cows," Brian said merrily.

"Sounds really nice," she replied wistfully.

"Hey, why don't you come?"

"I can't come, because we are still on holiday! And that means a lot of shopping, fancy hotels, and many social gatherings."

She tried to look excited. After this week, the remainder of their holiday looked bleak and dismal.

They made it to the restaurant in one piece. Jacqueline was glad to get out of the vehicle. That was one thing she would not miss about Dubai: the traffic. Dinner was wonderful. Not only was the food delicious, but the whole atmosphere was elegant. The skyline was beautiful. After dinner they strolled around the gold souq again, drawn by the precious metal. The last shop they stopped in was the same gold shop from her first visit. The shopkeeper brightened when he saw them enter. She cringed but was still drawn to the beautiful rose ring. She did not pick it up but the shopkeeper eyed her closely.

"Young miss, would like to try it?" he asked, and opened the display case. She was very reluctant to, but did try it on. It was a perfect fit. The gold was so soft. She had never worn anything like it. But she still couldn't persuade herself to buy it. Regrettably, she put it back.

"I'm sorry, but I really don't need another ring," she told the shopkeeper.

His bright smile faded and he closed the case. He bowed his head and turned to Grace, who was looking at a pair of earrings. She did buy them, brightening the man's face considerably.

"Jacqueline, you have to learn to spend some money," Brian laughed at her when they finally pulled into the drive at the house. "You didn't spend any, again. I think you broke that poor gold shop owner's heart. He saw you coming and his whole face lit up. It was funny to see, actually."

"I guess I'm cheap," she said. "I just don't like extra things around. I couldn't justify the purchase."

It was past midnight but nobody wanted to go to bed. They sat out on the terrace, enjoying the night breeze, which had lessened the humidity. Jacqueline thanked the twins. She didn't want the night to end. Tomorrow would mean leaving. Jacqueline dreaded it.

"This has been such a wonderful week," she sighed. "I have seen so much. I really don't want to leave."

"You just have to come back when we are here," Grace said and smiled at her friend. "And you need to come to the ranch. It would be such a blast!"

"I don't know if I would be allowed to come," Jacqueline said as the wind picked up her hair and blew it across her face. "I also want to visit a skater friend in Colorado."

"Well, that would be perfect. Colorado is only a couple of states away from Montana," Grace giggled. "You can come over right after. Oh, Jacqueline, you would love it!"

"She is right, you know," Brian whispered.

Jacqueline sighed. She would love to take the twins up on their plan. She just didn't know how to do this.

As they got into their beds, Grace coughed under her breath, looked at her friend and said, "Do you think we could pray together tonight?"

Grace looked at her with pleading eyes. Jacqueline was taken aback.

"Huh, you mean right now, you and me?"

"Yeah, I think it would be something really good for the both of us. Would you join me?"

Jacqueline hesitated for a moment, but looking at Grace's face aglow in the bright moonlight, she swallowed and nodded. Grace took her hand and closed her eyes.

"But wait, I don't know how to do that?" she protested. She wasn't sure she could pray with someone else in the room.

"You know how to close your eyes, right?" Grace grinned.

Jacqueline reluctantly closed her eyes.

"Father, thank You so much for my new friend, who has become like a sister to me. I pray that You would grow her in Your faith, help her to seek Your kingdom, and Your righteousness, and above all else, bring us back together in Your time. Show her how much You love her. Thank You so much for this extraordinary time we have had together. Allow our friendship to grow, in Your name," Grace peeked at her with one eye open and nodded her head. "It's your turn," she whispered.

"I really don't know what to say but I have to agree with Grace that this week has been wonderful. I guess I can thank You for the new friends You have brought me, when I was just thinking of how lonely I was." A tear ran down her cheek when she thought about her loneliness. She pushed the thought aside. "I really hope they have a good first year of college and that we can get together this summer in Montana. Okay, Amen," she mumbled quietly.

Grace hugged her. "See that wasn't so hard," she grinned and hugged her tightly.

She woke earlier than Grace the next morning, and the clock told her that Grace would probably not be up for a couple of hours. She tried to nestle back into her pillow, but she was too wide awake. Looking out the window, she noticed the sea was calm and quiet. She quickly donned a bathing suit under her shorts and dashed downstairs. The water was perfect: cool and refreshing. Little gray and brown fish darted back and forth as she approached. Suddenly, a large flat fish got under-foot, and she almost stepped on it. It scooted away from her with its long tail dragging behind.

"If I know anything about fish, and I don't know much, that was a stingray," she said to herself, and decided to retreat back to the beach. It was safer there. She sat down and surveyed the scene.

Since her arrival she had suffered a nervous breakdown that had left her weak and shaking. A lot had happened. Now, she was leaving with a lot of things to think about. She bit her bottom lip and thought of the experiences she had: from getting stuck in the desert to almost drowning. In her heart she knew it had been a life-changing experience.

"Hey, my favorite morning person," a cheerful voice woke her out of her musings. She turned toward Brian, who sat down next to her.

"It's beautiful, isn't it?" he asked quietly. She nodded. They sat there in silence for a while, just surveying the scene.

"Hey, listen. I'm sorry for the other night."

"The other night?" she thought not knowing what he was talking about. "Oh, you mean when you tried to get me to go surfboarding? You know, after I nearly drowned?"

Brian cleared his throat nervously. "Uh, no. Oh, man! I did that too, didn't I? Well, okay you got me. I'm so sorry for that. No, what I was thinking about was when we talked about the time I spent in Muslim school. I came out a bit strong."

She suddenly remembered. She shoved her shoulder into his.

"Thank you for sharing with me what was on your mind. I really appreciate it. It must have been a painful time."

"Well, it was not my favorite time in my life."

"Don't worry about it. You spoke about a painful experience. I can't imagine hating my father. It must have been hard."

For a long time neither one spoke. They both were busy with their own thoughts. Jacqueline's revolved around having to leave. She dreaded leaving her new friends. She was fearful of forgetting her experiences this week. Knowing that once she returned to her life, there would not be much time for thinking, for looking for more. She knew that she didn't want to go back to her old life.

"How about we hit the desert one last time and see if we can't really get stuck this time?" she heard Brian snicker.

"Somehow, I think I should say no, but I really want to go. Sure," she replied. "Do you have more boards ready?"

"Where do you think all the scrap wood went?" he chuckled.

And yes, they did get stuck; really stuck. It took them two hours to get the vehicle out of the sand dune. By this time, Jacqueline was again drenched in sweat and dusty, but she laughed and laughed, picking on Brian for getting them stuck. She loved teasing that she had been the one who dug them out, when he was the one who got them stuck. He didn't seem to mind and laughed right along with her.

Grace laughed at her when she walked through the door of their shared room. Her hair was covered in sand, as was her face.

"So I guess he convinced you to go out again, didn't he? And you guys got stuck. Aren't you going to learn?"

Jacqueline laughed and pulled her fingers through her tangled hair. "Nope, I guess not. It was so much fun. And so hot! I thought I was going to melt if we didn't get out of there when we did. Boy, oh boy. I haven't laughed this hard in a long time."

She rushed into the shower, which by this time only spouted hot water. She winced as the hot liquid touched her skin, but after a few moments it had cooled down.

"I want to talk to you, Jacqueline," Grace said very seriously when she came out of the shower. They sat facing each other on the couch. Jacqueline waited for her friend to begin.

"I want you to know that when you leave here you are going to start to see things you have never seen before." Grace held on to her gaze.

Jacqueline's eyes opened wide. "What sort of things, Grace?"

"Be prepared to be amazed. God will show Himself to you in ways you couldn't believe.

Jacqueline gasped. She couldn't see that happening.

Grace smiled at her softly and continued, "And then, it's important to surround yourself with people who can encourage you and help you when you are in need."

"I wouldn't even know where to find them. And then there is my time. I usually don't have time to make friends. My life revolves around skating, studying, and public appearances. There is not much time for anything else." Jacqueline leaned back against the soft cool couch cushion. Her life sounded absolutely dismal! It was downright empty of humanity.

Grace pushed her dark hair behind her ear. "I think we need to send you off with prayer. You are going to need it, my friend. God loves it when we talk to Him. So, we can ask for guidance, help and just talk to Him. You see, prayer is very important in every believer's life. So start praying to God to give you a good solid believer to turn to, who can help to guide you. He hears all. In fact, He is always with us."

Jacqueline shivered. It was not a comforting thought. A God, who was always with her!

"He reads our thoughts, knows our fears, and knows what is in the deep recesses of our hearts. There is nothing He doesn't know."

Jacqueline felt very uncomfortable now. She swallowed the urge to look around to find God looking over her shoulder. What would He be thinking of her right now?

Grace reached for her hands and closed her eyes. She took in a deep breath.

"Heavenly Father, we ask You, in Your Son's name, to be with Jacqueline, who has taken the first step toward You. She has knocked on the door and You have opened it. We pray that she will find a group, an individual, who will walk alongside her, who will instruct her in Your righteousness, in Your Kingdom. Help her to withstand and to fight the good fight. Love her into Your heavenly arms, in Your name."

Jacqueline sat, waiting for something to happen. The room was silent, but for the humming of the air conditioner.

Chapter 36

The afternoon seemed to drag along. A heaviness had settled over her. She was sad to leave. The time had arrived for Jacqueline to get ready for their flight. She donned the traveling suit that had been laid out for her.

"I hope you can come and visit with us in Montana. The summer would be so lonely without you, Jacqueline. You have no idea what you have done to my heart." Grace tried to smile through her tears.

"Please don't cry, Grace," she sniffed. "I'm having a hard time leaving as it is. I was wondering if you could keep praying for me."

"Of course I will. Oh, Jacqueline I will miss you so much. Why can't we go to the same college and be roommates. I think my heart is breaking," Grace sobbed.

Jacqueline put her arms around her. It was amazing what a dear friend Grace had become in such a short amount of time. They finally let go of each other and smiled through their tears.

"Well, we are connected through Christ," Grace whispered and wiped her tears.

"That is a little weird," Jacqueline laughed trying to lighten the mood. Grace smiled.

"Are you girls having a party without me?" Brian asked as he knocked on their door. "Argh, I see tears. All right, I'm gone," he grumbled and turned to go.

"No, stay Brian. We are done," Grace implored her brother and wiped her eyes with the back of her hand. He sat on the arm of the plush chair across from the sofa and kept his hands busy by continually throwing a baseball up and catching it.

"Jacqueline, it has been a lot of fun. Next time we have to go into the real desert. Just you wait," he chuckled and his eyes twinkled mischievously. "You haven't gotten stuck yet."

"Are you kidding me? What was today? Ah, I get it. You just need someone to help dig you out of your mess, is that it?" she teased back and shoved him a little harder than she expected. He slipped off of his seat and sat gaping up at her from the floor. Grace threw a couch pillow at him, hitting him right in the face. Soon the mood in the room was lifted as they waged a massive pillow fight.

When it was time to leave for the airport, Brian transported the girls. They hopped into the vehicle one last time, and Brian sped off down the road before the grownups could get out of the drive. The girls were laughing and teasing him. Jacqueline grimaced as he came close to the car in front of him.

They made it to the airport in one piece. Jacqueline could see their private little plane waiting for them on the tarmac. It looked dwarfed compared to the huge commercial airlines. Even at this time of the evening, the heat shimmered off the desert. She wished she could stay. She bit her lip and tried to suppress her tears. She didn't dare look at Grace who was swallowing hard. As they opened the car door Brian stopped her.

"Hey Gracie, wait for us inside, will you?" he asked his sister and she looked at him as though she wanted to argue. "Just humor me, all right?" he said quietly.

Grace shrugged her shoulders and made her way through the mass of people to the terminal.

"Listen, I hope you don't mind, but I want to tell you that I had a blast with you. You are such a great sport. And I wanted to give you something to remember this visit by. So, here," he shoved a small package at her. "I wrapped it myself," he said proudly, as she tried to undo the massive scotch tape that was holding the poorly folded paper together.

"I think you need help in that department, Brian," she laughed but her face turned rather serious when she finally got it open to reveal a small jewelry box.

"You didn't," she whispered as she opened to reveal the rose ring.

"I felt bad for the guy. You should have seen his face when I bought the ring. And I got such a deal on the thing. I think he really wanted you to have it too."

"You really shouldn't have," she scolded. She slipped the ring on her finger. A perfect fit, as though it was made for her. She swallowed hard. She didn't know what to say.

"Thanks, Brian," she whispered.

Her weak response seemed so inadequate to her.

Grace was waiting at the entrance and glanced at them, a deep furrow between her brows. She gave her brother a look of concern. He chose to ignore her. The parents arrived and ushered them toward the passport control area.

"It is time, dear friends," her father gestured to the waiting officers. "I have to say that this was a wonderful visit," he told the family, and there were hugs all around. Grace's eyes spilled over again and she hid her face. Jacqueline kept her face without emotion, but her heart was breaking. She hugged her friend one last time.

"I will see you later," she whispered as her voice cracked. There was a deep ache in her heart. Grace nodded and sniffled.

"Gracie, Gracie," her brother murmured and put his arm around her. He heartily shook Jacqueline's hand. She smiled and thanked him for everything. He winked at her mischievously.

Her father ushered them through passport control and to the waiting attendant. Jacqueline let the tears fall down her cheeks. Her mother took her hand and squeezed it tightly for a split second. She smiled at her through her tears. Her mother felt her new ring and looked at it.

"That is a beautiful piece of jewelry. When did you get this?"

"It was a gift to remember our trip here. Oh, Mother, I had such a great time here," she whispered. Her mother squeezed her shoulder tightly.

"We will be back," she assured her. "I also had a wonderful time. The Spencers are a very nice family."

Their trip to Spain and on to Miami was uneventful. She was able to call Grace from the plane to tell her that she would see them in Montana at the end of the month. Her parents had given their consent after she had used her power of persuasion on them during the long flight. Grace's excited shrieks could be heard all over the plane. Her parents chuckled. Fiona left them in Spain to spend some time with her family in England. She reminded Jacqueline to stay in shape.

Chapter 37

Miami! Jacqueline rested her hands on the porch railing. The beach was pristine and clean with blue water shimmering in the fading sun light. People were promenading on the sand, kites were flying in the light breeze, and Jacqueline was standing on the outside again, watching! Since she had arrived here a few days ago, her parents had shuffled her to this tea and that social event. Gone was the leisurely pace of the week before. Gone was the peace she felt. Instead, she was left with an overwhelming sense of loneliness. Being presented to various groups of admirers, who didn't care for her one way or the other, made her stomach roll.

She quietly cried herself to sleep every night since they had arrived. Jacqueline brushed a stubborn tear from her eye and tried to gather her thoughts to focus on something else, but was unable to. Not only had peace deserted her, replaced by loneliness, but also her nerves strained into tight chords again, ready to snap. She missed the closeness of her friends. She missed the genuine friendship she had experienced with them. She missed the intimacy of family. Jacqueline had yet to sit down with her parents even if only to chat. They were out when she arose and she saw them only at social gatherings. Another tear stung her eyes. It irritated her to feel like this.

In fact, she had never really dwelt on her feelings before last week. She never let the loneliness bother her all that much. Since she met her new friends, this feeling of loneliness was almost too much for her to endure. She had always been able to control her feelings! She had thrown herself into her busy schedule, maybe so she wouldn't have to think about this hole in her life. Until the last week, she hadn't known what it was really like to live; she had only been existing.

She was thoroughly unhappy!

Jacqueline pushed herself away from her perch and threw herself onto her bed. She turned and stared at the ceiling. The ring on her finger felt almost like a reassurance, a promise of something she didn't quite allowed herself to understand. Jacqueline sighed when she thought of how different she was after last week. She picked up her new Bible, something she had picked up when she wandered into a book store between appointments. She wanted to understand the words of Jesus, but understanding seemed a long way off. When she read, she felt peace returned, albeit temporarily. She wanted to dwell on it, savor it.

A knock on her door interrupted her.

"Jacqueline," her mother said as she peeked her head around the door. "We will be leaving in fifteen minutes. Are you ready, dear?"

Jacqueline suppressed a groan and rose from her bed to join her parents for another lonely night of social interactions with strangers she would never see again.

Next morning, she was surprised when, after her run along the beach, she found her parents present for breakfast. They made small talk while buttering their toast. They then turned toward her and looked at her seriously.

"We can see that you are not enjoying yourself here," her father told her. "How can we improve this part of the holiday?"

Jacqueline steadied her breathing. Now was her chance to voice her opinion.

"I am tired of running from one social event to the next, spending my time with people who don't know me, and who really don't care for me. I would rather spend an evening here, talking just like we did last week," Jacqueline said.

Her mother looked at her with deep affection. She took a sip of her tea.

"My dear daughter," she sighed. "You have always been so different in that respect. There is a reason for the many social events. We are the royal family! There is no time for just us. You have to accept it!"

"So I can't expect to spend an evening alone with just my parents?" she said quietly. "While we are on vacation?"

"It can't be done. Too many activities are already set up. You can look forward to tonight, however. We are going to go cruising on a yacht," her mother said cheerily.

"Jacqueline. Why not take the time now?" her father advised her. "We are all together and we can talk. There is no reason to waste our time with complaining. Let us have a nice breakfast together. Why do you think your mother and I have joined you this morning? Let us enjoy what time we are given."

Jacqueline tried to smile but the hole in her heart just widened. She nodded bravely and sipped her delicious orange juice.

"There will be quite a few young people on board tonight I have heard." Her mother stirred her tea.

"That sounds just absolutely dreadful," she whispered into her cup.

"What was that, dear?" her mother was busy shaking out her newspaper and looking at her daughter over her glasses. "I didn't hear you mumble there."

"That sounds perfectly," she paused for a moment to gather her thoughts, "wonderful. Thank you for thinking of me."

Jacqueline felt like pulling her hair out and screaming.

But instead she smiled and tried to work up some interest in her parents' conversation. Soon she was bored. She had another question to ask. It pertained to schooling. She hoped to visit the school she had become interested in. It happened to be in Boston, and they accepted long distance students. Jacqueline hoped she could entice her parents into going there too. Her father sighed and shook his head.

"With all your flitting about the country, I don't know how we can arrange it."

"Very true, Jacqueline. Remember we are off to Bermuda next. Just how we are going to get you to Colorado first and then Montana and now Boston? It is going to be quite difficult, dear," her mother said, pushing her reading glasses up her nose and leafing through one of the newspapers stacked before her and her husband.

"I could take a commercial plane," she suggested. Her parents both looked at her as though she had taken leave of her senses.

"A commercial plane," her mother gasped. "That is unheard of!"

"Mother, people fly on commercial planes all the time," she said blowing a strand of hair out of her face. She always did that when she became frustrated with her parents.

"You are not people, Jacqueline, you are not people!" her mother sighed. "How long until you realize that?" She put the newspaper down and glared at her daughter. "The populace expects a certain standard to which we have to adhere. How long are you going to strive against this standard?"

"Mother, I sometimes just want to be a normal teenager. I don't want the state dinners, the accolades, which accompany the populace's expectations. I know that there are some things that are really great about who we are, but there are a lot of things I am just not cut out for," she sighed.

Her parents sat in silence, staring at their newspapers. Her father looked sad and her mother looked concerned.

"Dear, we are who we are," she said quietly. "We can't change it."

"I know."

Breakfast was over for her. They sat in silence until the stacks of papers were read through. Jacqueline had her devotional with her and read slowly. She really needed some inspiration. She closed her eyes and tried to imagine her family as a normal family, like the Spencers. It didn't work. They were always going to be who they were. And Jacqueline just didn't fit into their neat little package.

Her parents were getting ready to start their day. Jacqueline frowned.

"Take this day for yourself, Jacqueline," her father beamed at her. "We don't need you until tonight."

"Thank you," she sighed. "I can use some down time, Father."

"Well dear." Her parents finally pushed their seats back. "We are off. How about you go shopping? Or take a day at the beach. Enjoy yourself, dear."

Her mother smiled and pecked her youngest on the cheek. Her father gave her arm a squeeze and looked at his youngest with tender eyes.

She wished them a good day. Jacqueline knew the loneliness would not go away any time soon. The beach sounded like a good idea, she thought to herself. She grabbed her beach things and decided to take her parents up on their suggestion.

She spent the day in the sun reading. The book she had picked up when she was at the bookstore was interesting. She read about different people and their stories of coming to Christ. She loved reading about their lives before they believed and the difference their belief made. A young woman talked about her marriage and how lonely she was in it before she knew Christ. Jacqueline understood. She was not in a marriage, but within her family, she was lonely. She felt a spark of hope.

Chapter 38

The Frisbee hit her in the head with a *thunk*. Pain temporarily stunned her.

"Ouch, that hurt," she grumbled, and touched her forehead. A young woman in shorts and T-shirt ran toward her, followed by a couple of young people.

"Are you all right?" one of them asked and squatted in front of her.

"Let me see, I am almost a doctor." An older guy pushed his way through and his friends laughed.

"No permanent damage," he assessed as he looked at her head. "We really are sorry. The wind just took the Frisbee away from us," he chuckled ruefully and held out his hand. "I'm Dan. This here are Meara, Tanya, Jack, David, and Hannah," he introduced his friends. "Seriously, are you all right?"

Jacqueline was taken aback by his friendliness. For a moment she couldn't answer.

"Certainly, I'll be fine. Just a little dazed, that's all," she assured them and put down her book, which she was still holding.

Dan glanced at it and shot a surprised look to his friends.

"Good book you are reading. Have you ever heard other testimonies?" he asked and the group lingered around. They squatted down around her, looking at her expectantly.

"What?" she asked. "I don't know much about this stuff," she stammered.

"Interesting!" Tanya and Hannah exchanged a knowing glance.

Jacqueline now was a little confused and cautious. What did these people want? She felt her stomach tighten and swallowed hard. She looked around to see if there were other people around. The beach was crowded, but nobody was taking notice of her and the group that surrounded her. Her breath came in spurts.

"Yeah, listen, there is a big meeting this evening. A ton of people are going to give their testimony. It is so popular, that they have to hold it at the football stadium here in Miami," Jack said and looked at her expectantly.

"Jack, we are scaring her, I think," Meara said. "We are not freaks or robbers or anything like that. Well, maybe we are Jesus Freaks but that is different."

"Oh, you mean you guys are Christians?" she asked, letting out her breath.

"Yes, we are," answered Hannah, "and the author of the book you are reading, Dr. Rich Gray, is here in town tonight holding a big meeting. We're actually part of his crew and just popped over to the beach for a little R&R before the big event."

"What are you talking about?" Jacqueline asked.

"Guys, guys, she is not from here!" David looked at the group. "Can't you tell she is from England? The accent?"

The others nodded their assent and went on to explain that Dr. Gray held what was called revival meetings, where thousands came to hear the gospel and to accept Christ as their Lord and Savior. The event was to be held at the Miami stadium because thousands would be gathering together.

"Listen, we have some tickets we could leave for you at the booth if you are interested," Dan said. "Are you interested?"

Jacqueline thought for a moment. She was very interested. But she also knew she couldn't go. Her parents were expecting her to go on a cruise with them.

"I am very interested, but I have a previous engagement tonight," she told them and their faces fell.

"Well, how about I leave a ticket for you anyway," Dan said.

"I don't think so," she said sadly. "I really would like to go, but I have an obligation."

"With God all things are possible. His plan is already set in motion, whatever that happens to be," Hannah whispered. The others nodded and smiled at Jacqueline encouragingly.

"What is your name," Dan asked. "I will leave you a ticket. Perhaps you have a friend who would like to attend?"

"No, I don't have a friend here," she answered sadly. "My name is Jacqueline." She shook everyone's hands.

"Well, Jacqueline, we hope to see you tonight. The event is at seven o'clock at the football stadium. You know where that is?"

"No, but if I can come I will find it," she assured them.

"Want to join us for a game of Frisbee?" Jack asked. "It might be safer for you," he chuckled.

She agreed but had to admit that she had no clue how to play. They were kind enough to show her and she got the hang of things quickly. After an hour they gathered together.

"We have to get going," Dan said, he seemed to be the eldest and the one in charge. "Can we pray before we leave?"

Everyone gathered around in a circle, holding hands, and took turns praying. They prayed that she might come to the revival that night, that the people who were coming would hear and be touched by what they heard, and for their leader's strength and clarity of words. She was amazed at their prayers but did not offer anything. She was too new at this.

"We'll see you tonight," Hannah winked at her.

Jacqueline was sad to see them go, but she realized that one of her prayers had been answered. She had met a group of believers, even if only for an afternoon, and recognized that this was indeed something she would need. She had felt very encouraged by their meeting though. She doubted she would see them again.

"Jacqueline, do you have a last name?" Dan shouted as they left.

"Sorry, it's Jacqueline Chevalier," she shouted back, and almost regretted it as some people glanced over at her. Some continued to stare at her, and she became self-conscious. It was time for her to leave and she walked toward her driver, who had been waiting for her.

"Thank you for waiting here all afternoon," she told him as she got in.

"No problem, Your Royal Highness."

They made their way back to the hotel, a quarter of a block away. Why her mother didn't allow her to walk to the beach was beyond her! A note was waiting for her from her parents.

Dear daughter,
Due to an unfortunate accident, the
cruise is canceled. It seems that you will
have the evening free. Hope you enjoy yourself.

Love, Father

She stared at the note for a while. The suite was quiet and deserted. She was free to go and do whatever she wanted! This was unbelievable. She was free to go to the meeting. Quickly she glanced at the time. She had enough time to grab a bite to eat on her way out and to make it to the stadium with time to spare. A note was left for her parents stating that she had met some young people at the beach and was going to spend the evening with them.

Chapter 39

By the time she got to the stadium, the parking lot was crammed full of people. Her driver dropped her off at the front entrance and promised to pick her up at the exact spot after the event, whenever she was ready. He pulled out a well-thumbed-through paperback novel and reclined his seat to begin reading. She thanked him and stood in the long line for the ticket booth. She noticed a sign that indicated that they were all sold out.

A man walked up behind her.

"Here you go, Your Highness." She startled at his voice and stared at her limo driver. He held a ticket in hand. "You shouldn't have to wait in line like this."

"W-where did you get that? I thought this was the line for tickets."

He pointed to the front entrance. "I explained the situation to the manager and he went and got me the ticket. I'm sorry you had to stand in that line."

Jacqueline walked away, a little dazed. She forgot to thank him and when she turned around, realizing her mistake, he was already back at the limo, engrossed in his book. She would have to thank him later!

There were people sitting outside the stadium with their beach chairs and coolers. It looked like they were having a great time. They were laughing and singing together. There was music blaring out of several boom boxes.

She walked into the packed stadium. People were greeting each other, laughing, hugging. The party atmosphere outside seemed the same as on the inside. She hoped she had not gotten herself into some sort of crazy cult meeting. But from what she had read in the book, Dr. Gray was a well-known speaker.

She showed the well-dressed attendant her ticket, and he motioned her to follow him. They walked all the way up front to where an area was cordoned off. She thanked him as he motioned her to her seat.

"God bless, Miss," he smiled as he walked away. She noticed people moving around on the stage and getting last minute things in order. At one point she thought she saw Hannah, and she was right. Hannah was dressed in choir clothes, getting ready to come on stage.

The spotlights increased the heat in the stadium and Jacqueline felt sweat dripping down her back. She wished she had a bottle of water with her, and saw a vendor walking between rows, selling drinks. She quickly purchased a large bottle of water and finished half of it in one draught. The atmosphere in the arena was charged with something she had not experienced before. There was a joy about the place.

When the choir came on stage, everyone took their seats, an expectant hush settled over the audience. Jacqueline spotted both

Hannah and Meara in the choir. Soon the arena rang with their beautiful voices. People joined in, some standing up, others remaining seated, raising their hands to heaven. She could not help but get to her feet and although the songs were unfamiliar to her, she soon attempted to sing along. Other singers followed and in between the different singers, men and women came up to share their stories.

Dan was one of them. He told them how he had grown up in the gang-infested area of Chicago, his father a member of the local mob, his mother an alcoholic. He had joined a gang at an early age, much to his father's dismay, who wanted him to join him in crime, and had been kicked out of his house. He soon got involved with drugs and alcohol, at first selling drugs but soon using whatever he could get his hands on. It was not until he had met Rich Gray, who was visiting the shelter he was holed up in, that he saw his mistakes. He committed his life to Christ right then and there, but it took him some time to change his life and to get out of the gang he was in. There was a lot of struggle but finally Christ had won. He laughed when he told everyone that it was pretty useless to fight against Him. A ripple of laughter ran through the stadium as well, along with a couple of hoots and hollers. After he returned home to come to terms with his parents, he made the decision to join the revival team and to attend medical school.

His story touched her. Here was a guy who honestly had left his past behind. He also didn't sound as though he was angry at all. In fact, he told them that his father had recently "accepted Christ" and was now working in the inner city, helping victims of mob and gang violence. When he told them that, Jacqueline could feel tears falling down her face. Or perhaps it was just the heat?

The evening went from good to better when Rich Gray walked to the podium to speak. She was impressed by his strong voice, laced with a deep compassion. He spoke from the heart, and Jacqueline could feel a shift in her heart. He made her see the condition of her heart, that she was dead without the saving grace of Christ. He pointed out that all were sinners before meeting their Savior and that the only way to be saved was through Christ's sacrifice on the cross and His blood. He shared that through Christ everyone has the opportunity to be free from sin and to live a life as sons and daughters of God. To be as royalty. With all her heart she wanted this! She and thousands of others were given a chance to come up front, to be prayed over, and to commit their lives to the Son, the only begotten Son of God, for Him to lead their lives.

Jacqueline was glad to be jostled and pushed along as she made her way up front. She was just one of many! She was nothing different from everyone in front of her who needed to be covered by the blood of Christ. When she spotted Tanya, who locked eyes with her, she smiled.

"You made it," she laughed. "See, everything is possible with God. How can I help you tonight?"

"I want to commit my life to Christ," she said barely audible, her voice laced with emotion. "I feel it in my heart!"

"Welcome sister, welcome. Are you willing to admit that you are a sinner, in need of a Savior? The only One, who can save you from everlasting damnation in hell?"

284

"Yes," she whispered as tears flowed freely.

"Pray with me, Jacqueline," Tanya placed her hand on her shoulder. "Confessing with your mouth is important as is believing in your heart that He was raised from the dead."

Tanya hugged her tightly and both wept with joy after they had finished the prayer. She noticed that many people were doing the same thing. Tanya gave her a Bible, and a small handbook.

She felt almost giddy when she made her way back to her seat. The music from the choir was coursing through her veins. She felt a peace about her she had not felt before. She laughed and cried at the same time, reaching for another water bottle. She was completely drenched.

By the time she exited the stadium, she knew it was late. She wondered why none of these people had come up to her, demanding an autograph. For the first time in her life, she had been treated the same as everyone else in this huge crowd. It made her thankful. Her driver had indeed waited patiently for her, but he was asleep, with the finger in his closed book, and she carefully jostled him awake as she closed the door. It was one in the morning! Jacqueline looked at the clock in alarm. Her parents must be worried beyond belief.

Every light was on in the living room of the suite when she tried to quietly open the door. She swallowed when she saw her father pacing back and forth, speaking in rapid French to his wife who was sitting very upright on the couch. She cringed. She knew they were furious with her. When he spotted her, his face was set in anger.

285

"Sit," he pointed to one of the chairs.

She sat herself down, waiting patiently for the dressing down. She knew she deserved what was coming her way! It was way past her curfew. She lowered her eyes and prayed to God for strength and help.

"Where have you been?" he asked, barely keeping his temper in control. Her mother looked at her with great concern. Before Jacqueline could answer her mother erupted.

"We didn't know what happened to you! We called the police, which are searching for you this very minute! How could you do this!? Be so irresponsible! My dear Francoise." She covered her face with her shaking hand. "Have the public relations people contact the police immediately to tell them that Jacqueline has not been kidnapped after all. We were worried sick for you and now you seem all right! This is a terrible situation! We need to have someone run interference with the media. Young girl, where have you been?"

"I was at a revival meeting," she said quietly.

"What!" her father shouted.

Jacqueline explained in halting tones the evening. "There was no foul play involved, nothing illegal going on, I can assure you," she ended her long account. Her parents stared at her, not knowing what to say.

"You went to a cult meeting?" her mother finally found her voice.

"No Mother. It was not a cult. It was a church meeting."

"Oh," her father growled. He shook his head once, as if clearing his thoughts. "We didn't know where you were, and we certainly do not approve of your activities. You, Jacqueline, are now grounded. You will not be able to go off by yourself. Someone will be with you at all times when you are not with us. While we are in Miami you will be confined to only the social activities we have arranged for you. Is that clear?" Her father's face became a deeper red the more he spoke.

She swallowed hard thinking of the peace that had so filled her heart. Was it still there? She sat for a moment. It was and she honestly could not blame her parents. In fact, she was thankful that they loved her enough to care.

"I am really sorry that I was late tonight. The time just got away from me. I didn't know what time it was until I got into the car. I won't let it happen again," she told them and gave both a hug and a kiss good night. "I am terribly sorry for the public relations nightmare I caused. If only the limo driver had been contacted before the police. I will take all the blame."

They stared at her more than a little confused as she left the room. She knew that they expected her to try to convince them that they needed to reconsider. Jacqueline knew that the fault was entirely hers and her parent's actions were warranted. She was not going to fight them. When she finally fell asleep, she imagined herself falling into the arms of Christ and resting there.

Chapter 40

The remainder of the week dragged. Everywhere Jacqueline went, when she was allowed to leave the hotel, she was shadowed by a man in a black suit and dark shades. It really made her laugh because the man had not said a word, other than that he was there to keep an eye on her. He was the stereotypical bodyguard. His muscles were bulging under his shirt and his neck looked way too thick for his head.

She had changed. She not only didn't mind that her parents had restricted her, she felt peace in it. She didn't feel as lonely as she had before. When she read the scriptures, they had personal meaning for her. She still hated the social events her parents dragged her to, reviling the shallow conversation between people she would never see again. But she acknowledged that her parents needed her.

On the day before they were due to leave for Bermuda, they received notice that a storm was heading toward the island and threatened to make land just about when they were supposed to arrive. This storm was then heading over to Florida and would blanket it in rain and wind. It was not a hurricane but the weather was promising to be nasty.

"Jacqueline, what do you think we should do instead?" her mother asked when they had a rare lunch together on the balcony located just off their living room. Jacqueline raised her head and looked at her mother in surprise. She figured her name was still mud. "We appreciate your behavior this past week. We were very afraid that something had happened to you, because being so late is so uncharacteristic for you. So, we are willing to go to Boston for a few days, take a tour of this university you mentioned, and then drop you off in Colorado. We will then return to Lichtenbourgh, send the plane back for you to take you to Montana. We don't want you on a commercial airplane. Would that be agreeable to you?"

Jacqueline smiled at her parents. "Thank you so much. I... I don't really deserve this after what I have done. I really appreciate it. That sounds really good."

"Excellent, we are leaving this afternoon. Tomorrow we are expected at Powder University. We have a tour at three in the afternoon," her father explained. Jacqueline felt quite satisfied. Her parents were nothing, if not efficient!

Excitement surged through her when she watched Boston's historical district pass by her car. She was amazed at how European the city felt and looked. Her parents reluctantly allowed her and her bodyguard to take some time to visit the many outdoor cafés. She loved the feel of the small town atmosphere she felt in this city.

She was impressed with the school. Although it was a large school it didn't feel like it. The dean of students practically fell over himself to show them around. He wore a perpetual smile as they walked through the well-stocked labs. The veterinary wing was impressive and Jacqueline would have loved to have listened to lectures. Her parents, however, expressed their desire to continue and she reluctantly moved on. It was almost too good to be true.

The dean was sitting on a bomb, which he released when they retreated to his office.

"Our long distance students usually do not complete their four years as long distance students. You must understand that, especially with your interest in the sciences and veterinary science in particular, the lab time is extremely important as is the hands-on experience we can offer our upper class students. The maximum time we allow for long distance is four semesters.

"We also feel that students benefit from personally attending their classes and getting involved in campus activities. We highly recommend you think about this if you are planning on enrolling with us. We would be happy to work around your competition schedule," the dean told them seriously, "and we would probably give you credit for your time on the ice. But as a pre-veterinary student, we highly recommend you come here after your first two years."

"We really would prefer our daughter to stay with us for the duration of her undergraduate program. She is part of the royal family and has obligations at home that she cannot fulfill overseas," her father said seriously but graciously.

"Of course, yes, I see. May I suggest you give me some time to discuss this with some of the professors and the head of the department," the dean answered thoughtfully. "As Dean of students, I think it goes without saying that we would love to have your daughter attend our university. Once we review her transcript and examination results, I am sure we will be only too happy to offer her a place among our students."

They were also informed that because of the Internet, all classes were recorded so that the long distance students only had to log into their account and pull up the audio of the lecture they needed to hear. It made distance learning possible, the dean informed them.

Jacqueline knew that her parents would never allow her to attend the school away from home. She felt sadness engulf her when they returned to the hotel and she excused herself to her room. There she tried to do what she had been reading in the Bible. Talk to God about it!

Chapter 41

Her quick trip to Colorado was finished and she was on her way to Montana. She and Linda had done the sight-seeing thing. Jacqueline had been introduced officially to Alex, playing hockey in Colorado, as Linda's boyfriend. Jacqueline felt an unexpected disconnect between her and her friend. She wanted to share her latest experience with Linda, but whenever she tried to talk about God, she got a cold shoulder, so she left it alone. It made for a difficult and long couple of days. *But*, she thought, *at least there are no social engagements.*

Jacqueline's stomach twisted and churned when the airport in Billings, Montana, came into view. On approach Jacqueline saw the white-topped mountains in the distance. The view took her breath away. The air was cool and crisp. As she gathered her bag, she noticed a battered old truck on the other side of the fence, its rusted tailgate down. She waved enthusiastically when she spotted the twins waiting for her, seated in the bed of the truck.

Grace gave Brian a push and they jumped out, racing for the gate. Grace threw her arms around her friend first.

"You are here! I can't believe you are here. It seems like ages since I last saw you." She shouted as she jumped up and down enthusiastically clapping her hands like a child.

"It's been a life time," Jacqueline hugged her back and chucked her heavy suitcase at Brian.

He laughed and caught the suitcase out of the air. "Yes I can play butler."

Both Brian and Grace wore faded and torn jeans and long sleeved T-shirts. Jacqueline grinned and pointed to the battered Cowboy hats they both sported.

"I'm afraid I feel overdressed. I left my hat at home," she drawled. The twins grinned at each other.

"We all know just the place where we can remedy that, Miss," Brian drawled back, amusement spreading on his face. The twins hooked arms with Jacqueline, on on each side of her.

He threw her suitcase into the truck bed. "What is in here anyway? Rocks? You girls always pack way too much stuff."

"I don't think so! I have been living out of that suitcase for over a month or so now, if I might remind you," Jacqueline teased right back.

She sure had missed them.

They stopped at an outlet store. The twins quickly showed her to the section with appropriate attire: namely boots, jeans, and not to forget, the ever important Cowboy hat. Half an hour later, Jacqueline was the proud owner of three pairs of jeans, comfortable boots, and a very nice black Cowboy hat, that would shade her face and help her blend in. She looked pretty good in it, even if she did say so herself.

"All right, ladies," Brian announced as they squeezed back into the truck. "Dinner is next. And Jacqueline, sorry to tell you but you are going to be eating a lot of burgers this week, with fries!" he shouted over the squealing engine. "And real sorry about the noise, but Grand's new truck was in the shop for repairs. So we got stuck with this old workhorse. It's fine for farm work, but it is not so great on long distance rides," he chuckled as they squealed out of the parking spot, black smoke trailing ominously. The truck fishtailed into the road.

"Especially with Brian behind the wheel," Grace said softly.

Jacqueline snorted very un-princess like.

They stopped at the nearest gas station where Brian filled up the truck and two extra gas cans.

"Uh, how far is your grandparent's ranch?" she asked.

"We're about three hours north of here. Just a drop in the hat, really if you consider the size of this state."

At the diner Jacqueline could just imagine her mother sitting in one of the worn plastic seats, with stuffing showing through rips. She could just about see her pass out at the loud country music blaring from a jukebox in the corner. The food, however, was surprisingly good. Delicious! Jacqueline devoured a *loaded* burger with *loaded* fries. She loved it! And then she regretted it, as she shoved the last fry in her mouth and downed her coke. She would have to run ten miles tomorrow, at least.

"Don't worry about exercising," Brian grinned, as though he read her mind. "You just eat. You're going to need all the energy you can get. We have a packed week ahead at the ranch. We have to round up some steers and brand them. Then the vet is coming," he winked at her, "to vaccinate the heifers, which need to be brought back to the herd after. We need all the hands we can get. It will mean a couple of hours in the saddle each day."

"Seriously?" she felt her whole body quiver with excitement.

"Sure and tomorrow you are going to learn how to work around the cattle, on horseback."

She felt like jumping up and down with excitement.

A couple hours later they pulled off the main road. Ahead lay vast and beautiful meadows, filled with an assortment of wildflowers. The sun's last rays were just gleaming off the tops of the mountains.

"So how much longer," Jacqueline asked Brian, who was finishing up the last of the thermos the waitress at the diner had filled with coffee.

Grace had fallen asleep an hour ago. Neither Brian nor Jacqueline had talked much. Jacqueline had been too excited and enchanted by the beauty around her. They could never outrun the majestic white-capped mountains in the distance, that seemed to follow them. She was amazed at the scenery around her. There were deep green meadows overflowing with wildflowers. They had just passed a huge lake with several cabins scattered around it. She found the log cabins charming, and was looking forward to seeing the ranch house, which was also a log cabin from what the twins had told her.

"Well, all around us is my Grandparent's land. We will be there in about ten minutes."

"Wow, that is a lot of land," she whispered and peered into the near dusk. "Your grandfather is king of his own dominion."

Brian looked at her and pulled a face.

The truck coughed and sputtered its way around the winding roads, and up and down the hills, of which there were many. Jacqueline found out that it was a good thing that Brian had stopped for extra gas, because they had only passed one gas station. And it looked like it had seen its last customer during the Depression era. At last Brian slowed the truck on the last hill.

"There it is," he said proudly and pointed out the driver's side window. "'Peaceful Haven'."

Jacqueline sat bolt upright. Below her was a large spread of outbuildings, large stables, and silos. In the middle sat a sprawling log cabin style ranch house. To the left of it was a large lake, that snaked in and out of the tree-lined shores and seemed to stretch on forever. It was fed by a bubbling river, coming down from the north and snaked its way past the house and some of the pastures.

"This is beautiful," she gasped.

Brian smirked and said, once again with a drawl, "Wait 'till you start working. It ain't gonna be that beautiful anymore."

"I beg to differ," she replied with confidence. "I can't wait."

"So you going to be ready in the morning to do five stall, feed, water, and brush five horses?" he asked a little skeptically.

"Bring it on," she replied, thinking her mother would be appalled by her language. Grace woke up and rubbed the sleep out of her eyes.

"Are we there yet?" she mumbled and yawned.

"Go back to sleep, baby," her brother teased.

But she woke up completely when the truck pulled up in front of the cabin. Immediately the front door opened and a tall, wiry woman darted out through the bright light.

"I thought you were stuck on the road with that old truck," she gleamed as she hugged her grandchildren tightly. When Jacqueline held out her hand to be shaken, the woman embraced her in a tight bear hug.

"We ain't so formal here in the back woods," she laughed hardily. "And my grandkids have not stopped talking about you since they got here. So I feel like I already know you."

She wore her age well. Jacqueline guessed she was in her early seventies and stood ramrod straight. Her gray hair was tidily gathered in a bun at the nape of her neck. Although she wore a pair of worn jeans and a blouse, she had a gracefulness about her.

The house had a well-worn, comfortable feel to it. The short hallway led to the grand room with a fireplace and dining room, and a very roomy and large kitchen with brand new appliances, cabinets, and counter. There were hand woven throw rugs over the well-worn wooden floor in the grand room, and a worn couch stood near the tall windows overlooking the lake. There was a fire crackling in the

297

fireplace, since the evening had a bite to it. This cabin was not grand but it was ever so comfortable.

"How'd the truck hold out?" asked a booming voice from the kitchen. A tall, hefty man with a neatly trimmed white beard and hair stepped out from behind the island counter. Brian grinned and admitted that it had been a rough ride.

"It is nice to meet you, Jacqueline," he also greeted her with a bear hug and added with a wink, "finally."

He chuckled and offered them all a cup of hot chocolate, with tiny marshmallows. "These grandkids of mine have not stopped talking about you since they got here," he glanced over to where Brian and Grace were sipping from their cups.

Jacqueline blew on the hot liquid. It smelled wonderful and she was glad for something to warm her aching bones. Sitting in that bouncing, rattling truck for hours had not been the most comfortable way to go.

"Please call us Grand and Grammy. We are not formal at all here, like I said. And I hope you don't mind sharing a room with Grace." Grammy smiled when she saw Jacqueline's face light up. "The other guest room is being remodeled and it is a mess." She motioned for Jacqueline to follow her to the comfortable couch.

"Brian will bring in your luggage, dear," she told her and shot her grandson a warning look that made him shuffle out the door to the truck.

"That truck has got to be put out of its misery," Grace complained as she plopped down next to her friend. "My achy bones. And with Brian driving it is twice as bad," she grumbled.

Jacqueline was fighting to keep her eyes open and after her luggage was inside, Grammy suggested that they all head up to bed after having a bowl of corn chowder. Jacqueline moaned softly when the thick, rich soup warmed her up. It was delicious.

"Tomorrow comes early around here," Grand laughed as he wished them all a good night.

After pulling out pajamas and toiletries, Grace and Jacqueline chatted for quite some time about her experience at the revival meeting.

"It's like a light went on upstairs," Jacqueline told her.

Grace nodded and yawned.

"Good night, Jacqueline. I am so glad you are here," she closed her eyes.

Chapter 42

Morning did start early at the ranch. With the sun not yet peeking over the horizon, a knock at the door awoke them. For a moment Jacqueline did not know where she was but when she saw Grace rub her sleepy eyes, it all came back into focus. After a hearty breakfast of bacon, eggs, sausage, and toast, Grand informed them of their duties. Grace mostly stayed with Grammy to help around the house. She was not really an animal person, she admitted wryly.

Jacqueline offered her help with the barn duties. Brian lifted his eyebrows. By the time she had mucked her second stall, her muscles were complaining. She looked at Brian, who was busy spreading wood shavings in his clean stall and straightened up.

"I thought I was in really good shape," she moaned as she massaged her tender shoulders, "but this is not good. If I come home sore and aching Fiona is going to lynch me!"

Brian laughed and continued his chores. "You'll get used to it soon enough."

"I sincerely doubt it," she mumbled. By the fourth stall, she wanted to curl up in a tight ball and cry. On top of her muscles revolting, her hands were now sore and sported blisters. She showed them to Brian, who immediately chastised her for not wearing the gloves he had handed her.

"Greenhorn," he grumbled as he led her to the utility bathroom off the stable and ran warm water over her hands. She winced in pain. He carefully applied antibiotic cream over the open sores. Then he took soft gauze and wrapped it gently, all the time grumbling to himself.

"You did this to get out of cleaning stalls for the rest of the week, didn't you?" he smirked as he finished.

She had to laugh. "I really thought I could handle this, but I guess my lily soft hands are not used to this kind of work."

"What do I do with you now?" he mused and rubbed the back of his neck. "Ah, take old Rusty here and walk her around slowly. As you can see she got a little banged up and has to be hand walked. That would help me out a lot. She's my charge but really, I don't have time for her. But while you are here, you can take over her care. Sound all right to you?"

It was more than all right. She stared at the old liver-spotted Appaloosa. It was the first time in her life that Jacqueline had dealt with such a breed. She walked toward the stall, and slipped the halter over over her head.

"Oh, by the way, watch out. She is a little ornery," Brian yelled as they made their way out into the bright sunlight.

"How ornery can you be?" she asked softly, as she patted Rusty's velvety neck. "I'm sure we'll get along just fine."

The mare soon showed her the ornery side of the Appaloosa breed. No sooner had they left the barn than she dragged Jacqueline over to some tufts of grass. Jacqueline was not to be outdone by this 1500 pound animal and yanked on her lead rope. Jacqueline winced but otherwise ignored the pain shooting through her hands, arms, and shoulders. She was determined not to let the horse get the best of her. The mare pinned her ears back and glared at her.

"Oh no you don't," she muttered. "We are walking, not eating."

She yanked the mare's head up again and proceeded to drag the grumpy horse down the dirt road. They stopped every few feet because Jacqueline had to continually pull her along! She was glad Brian had bandaged her hands and she had put the heavy work gloves over the gauze. Her hands still hurt but the gloves offered protection. After twenty minutes of pulling the stubborn mare on the dirt road, Jacqueline felt all her strength give out.

"All right, you win," she grumbled and allowed Rusty to move over to a grassy area.

Jacqueline blew several strands of hair out of her face, and wiped her forehead on the sleeves of her jean jacket. She took a deep gulp of the fresh air and marveled again at the beauty all around. The rolling meadows before her were alive with summer activity. Butterflies, bees, and other flying critters were busily flittering around.

When she heard the lunch bell chime from the house she realized just how hungry she was. As quickly as she could she pulled the mare along back to her stall.

"Hope you enjoy your hay," she said and checked her water pail. She would have to fill it after lunch.

Everyone seemed to have been waiting for the signal to stop working. About ten people had gathered around the large dining room table when she arrived, out of breath. She was introduced to all of them.

"So," Grand laughed, with kindness in his eyes, when he saw her bandaged hand. "How is your first day going?"

She reluctantly confessed her oversight on the gloves but quickly stated that she had learned her lesson.

"For heaven's sake, child," Grammy said softly and muttered to herself as she put the platters filled with thick steaks on the table. "You come with me after lunch and we'll fix you right up. I can't believe you didn't make her put on those gloves," she glared at her grandson, who was busy filling his plate with mashed potatoes and steak.

"It was entirely my fault," Jacqueline said.

"It sure was!" Brian shouted back at her and glared toward his grandmother.

Jacqueline helped herself to the smallest piece of meat. She could only imagine what Fiona would say if she saw her eating all this food. She would have her skating for seven hours straight. Speed skating, no less!

"Honey, you need to put some meat on those bones," Grand said and reached to put another large spoonful of potatoes on her plate. He then lathered her steak with thick gravy. She winced, but thanked him. Brain hid behind his tall glass of iced tea and didn't dare to glance at her. Everyone waited for all the plates to be filled. Then they bowed their heads, and Grand blessed the food. Jacqueline was taken by surprise.

"So, most of the morning chores are done," Grand stated. "Brian, you and Jacqueline go and ride the fence on the southern side starting by the old stone wall. That should take you the rest of the afternoon. I expect it to be in good shape. The rest of us have to get ready for the round up. Dr. John is coming to vaccinate the heifers, so y'all be ready for a busy day then. Young lady, you will have to take a crash course on cow wrangling. Paul, over here," he pointed to a slightly older man with skin as tough as leather, "is my resident expert. You seek him out for a lesson, you hear?"

"Yes sir," she heard herself saying and both Grace and Brian tried to hide their laughter behind their hands.

"Lunch was delicious, Mother," the old man gave his wife a peck on the cheek and rose from the table, picking up his battered Cowboy hat. He gave a curt nod and all around chairs were shoved from the table, and murmured thanks were said. Grace helped her grandmother bring the dishes into the kitchen where an industrial sized dishwasher stood waiting.

"Come with me, young lady." Grammy motioned, and Jacqueline followed her. For the next couple of minutes her hands were soaked in aloe. Then Grammy gently spread a salve on the worst sores and re-bandaged her hands.

"Make sure you wear gloves, dear," Grammy said gently. "If it hurts too badly you tell those boys you are staying inside to help me."

"I'm all right, but thanks, Grammy," she said shyly.

304

Grammy gave her a genuine smile and sent her off with a backpack filled with water and muffins, just for the road, she had told her with a secretive wink. Jacqueline thanked her and rushed outside.

Even though it was midday, it was quite pleasant outside. Her horse, a gentle looking strawberry roan, was already saddled and ready for her. Brian sat on his gray mare, his leg draped over the saddle horn, chewing on a piece of hay. His hat was pushed over his eyes, making it impossible to see them.

"Took you long enough," he teased.

"Funny, I didn't see *you* secure an afternoon snack," she smiled cheekily and pointed at her pack.

"You didn't!? Wow, Grammy must have taken a liking to you, I can tell you that. Are those her muffins that I smell?" he asked sniffing the pack greedily.

"That is for me to know and you to wonder," she teased as she put her foot in the stirrup. The worn leather creaked as she jumped up and settled in.

"Quick lesson. Jimbo here is used to neck reining. Very simple really. All you do is hold the reins really loosely, yep just like that. If you want to go left you just move the reins to the left. That's right. The same to the right. Just remember to keep the reins loose and you will have a happy horse. Ready?"

He gave his mare a nudge and they meandered off behind the house, following the fence line. Brian soon reached a gate and he leaned forward in the saddle to open it for them to ride into the huge pasture that stretched for miles.

"How are your hands?" he asked as they made their way over the first hill.

She could barely tell she had blisters under the leather gloves she was wearing. From time to time she felt a twinge of pain, but she assured him that they were fine and that she had endured worse injuries in the past.

"Yeah, but I should have taken better care of you. I forgot about your lily white hands," he said softly. "But I know that the leather gloves help a lot, especially when you are riding. I don't ride without gloves anymore. Actually I have learned that I need those gloves for all the chores around the ranch," he said and reached for the backpack bouncing on her back.

"Oh no you don't," she scolded but Brian laughed and told her he wanted to secure it behind her saddle.

"I won't touch the goods inside," he promised with a cheeky smile.

"Thanks," she smirked. Then she eyed him sideways. "So, you got lily white hands too?"

Brian grinned at her, lopsided. "Only at the beginning of the summer."

It was a lot easier to ride without the burden on her back. He replied by squeezing his mare into a canter and soon they were flying across the pasture. It took them about an hour to find the southern border. By this time, they had a beautiful view of the gigantic mountains sticking out right before them.

"At night we get bears that wander through. An occasional wolf pack will try to get into the chickens and that makes Grand real cranky. He will sit out there with his rifle and wait for them. He doesn't shoot them but he scares them away. They are really cool to watch. I hope a pack comes while you are here."

Jacqueline felt shivers run up her spine and hoped they would stay away. They rode in companionable silence for a while. The afternoon sun beat gently on her back.

"It's really good to see you again. Grace is really happy about you staying here. I guess it's fine with me too." He looked at her sheepishly.

"I want to thank you again for the ring, Brian," she said as they made their way up a steep hill.

"Don't mention it. I told you it was made just for you," he mumbled, glanced at the barbed fence and frowned. "Looks like we have a bit of repair to do here." He dismounted and spent twenty minutes splicing and stretching the broken barbed wire fencing.

They stopped to let their horses rest and ate the most delicious muffins Jacqueline had ever tasted. She was munching on her second muffin when she thought of Fiona.

She groaned and swallowed the bits of muffin in her mouth, guilt setting into her like a lump. "I am going to be in so much trouble!"

Brian looked at her and frowned. "Why?"

307

"Oh, you know. Fiona is really strict with what I can eat and what I can't, as you know. This would be a definite no-no," she said seriously, and brushed the crumbs off of her shirt. Brian laughed.

"Send Fiona over here and we will see how long she can count calories. I am always amazed at the amount of food I pack away while we are here. But I work sun-up to sun-down. And I get hungry! Just wait, I bet you'll lose some weight, not that you should. You are skinny as it is. Well, no..." He shoved his hand through his hair, bumping his hat in the process, making it fall into the dirt in front of him.

She turned to look at him and cocked her eyebrow.

"What I meant to say is, that you are well proportioned," he said and looked down at his boots, embarrassment coloring his cheeks. "Not that I've noticed or anything like that." He groaned. He was digging a deep hole for himself. How was he going to get out? "What I meant to say is that you are not fat but well-muscled!"

That should do it! He snatched up his hat and dusted it off on his faded jeans.

"What are you trying to get at, Brian? Am I fat or am I not?"

Brian grumbled to himself. He knew he was indeed digging his hole deeper and deeper. He glanced at Jacqueline, who wore a half smirk on her face.

"You are not fat. You are just right!" His face turned bright red.

Jacqueline turned her head because her face had turned just as red as his.

It took the rest of the afternoon to check the fence. She had wondered why they didn't take the truck, but by the end of the afternoon they were climbing some uncomfortably steep hills. They finally got back to the ranch just as the sun sank below the mountains.

"Did I call that or what?" Brian asked, hunching his shoulders in exhaustion.

They took care of their tired horses, who were happy to have their feed and water. After rubbing them down with liniment, they were ready to clean up themselves. By this time, Jacqueline had to admit that her stomach had a great big hole in it and she badly needed to fill it.

That night at dinner, she was surprised that the farmhands did not assemble around the table.

"They head home to their houses and families after quittin' time," Grace told her as she handed her a bowl of fresh steamed green beans. Tonight's menu was green beans, rice, and chicken; Jacqueline was sure it had squawked its last that morning. Again, before digging in, Grand prayed for the meal, thanking God for His provision. Jacqueline couldn't help but glance at Brian, who wore a stony face. As soon as Grand said amen, he dug into his pile of food. He reported that all went well along the fence and that it was in pretty good shape. Grand seemed pleased.

"And how did you like your first day?" the old man asked Jacqueline with twinkling eyes. She informed him shyly, that things had gone pretty smoothly, considering. A few eyebrows raised around the table.

"Jacqueline, we have something called arnica on hand for such a day as this. It will help with the aches and pains to your muscles." Grammy started clearing the dishes.

After dinner Jacqueline awkwardly attempted to help in the kitchen. She laughed softly to herself and examined herself in the mirror in the hall. She expected to be bow legged, with all the riding she had done for the day. Her muscles were tight and she realized that after a month of holiday, she would be in trouble when she returned to serious training. She decided that maybe putting some salve on tonight would not be a bad move.

Grand watched her out of the corner of his eye as she stiffly walked into the kitchen.

"I know just how you feel," he murmured. He grabbed a cup of coffee and headed out onto the porch.

Jacqueline joined the rest of the family. They all settled on the wicker furniture on the wraparound porch. Fireflies were starting to sparkle against the darkening sky and Brian chuckled.

"Hey Gracie, remember we used to catch them and put 'em into jars. They were so much fun to stick into jars. Then we would pretend they were flashlights."

"Yeah, and you would take a few of the unfortunate ones and pull their legs off," Grace growled and glared at her brother. He shrugged his shoulders innocently.

Grand and Grammy settled on the love seat and Grand sighed contentedly and draped an arm over his wife's shoulder. "I am so glad I got out of the rat race when I did. Can you imagine what I would be like now if I had stayed in the corporate world?"

"Oh dear, I think you would have had a heart attack a long time ago. It was a good choice to move up here permanently." Grammy patted her husband's knee and smiled at him with bright eyes. He returned her glance. "Well, that is after the Lord got a hold of us."

His wife nodded fondly. Brian scowled and sighed. "I guess this is where I head to bed."

"Son, stay. We are just talking," Grammy pleaded with her grandson, who was almost to the door.

"Nah, I'm beat. It's going to be a long day tomorrow. G'night, everyone," he murmured and walked through the door.

"I wish he would open his heart to Christ," Grace whispered. "I worry about him so." Tears glistened in her eyes.

"Don't fret, dear. We will continue to pray for him. Eventually he will know. I know it." Grand patted her shoulder. "So, I understand from my granddaughter, that you became a believer very recently. That's wonderful. I had a feeling about you when you got out of the truck. Good things will come from you," he nodded and faced his wife.

Then he opened a large Bible and began to read from Acts. Jacqueline had not heard of these stories and she was very attentive. When the girls made their way to their room, Jacqueline , limping a little, thought that it was an interesting coincidence that Grace's grandparents were Christians.

"I really enjoyed today. I thank you for inviting me. This is going to be such a great week," Jacqueline told her friend.

Grace handed her a tube and instructed her to rub the ointment on the sorest spots. Once that was finished, Jacqueline sighed as the soft sheets covered her. She wanted to pray with Grace but her eyes wouldn't open anymore and her mouth refused to move. She had never been so tired in her life!

Chapter 43

Jacqueline had to admit that getting out of bed was difficult the next day. The lingering tiredness soon disappeared once she had made her way downstairs. The coffee smelled great and she grabbed a cup before slowly making her way to the table, where everyone was chatting. Another hearty breakfast followed and Paul told her to meet him out back after finishing the barn chores.

"Eh, Brian," Jacqueline whispered as they entered the barn.

"Yeah?"

"You were right about being hungry," she confessed.

"I saw you dig in this morning," he asked, laughing, and leaned against the barn door, watching her. "Are you sore from yesterday?"

"I have to confess that I am more than a little sore. That cream helped a lot, but there is a lingering stiffness."

"Tell you what. After feeding these guys, you take old Rusty out for her walk again and I'll let you off the hook today. That and you gotta feed the chickens for me, all right?"

She beamed at him and helped feed.

"I will try to walk Rusty, but she pulled me all over the place yesterday. I can't guarantee that I will do any better today," Jacqueline confessed.

313

Brian grunted and shoved his his hat to the back of his neck. "Listen, I'm sorry I didn't stick around last night, and I didn't mean to disrespect my grandparents but you know how I feel about this God stuff."

"Yeah, I understand. You ought to give God another chance. He really is not too bad."

"Are you serious? You have succumbed too? And I was beginning to like you," he growled and shoved a scoop of feed into Rusty's food trough.

"I haven't *succumbed*," she laughed. "But yes, I did make a decision to be a Christian."

Brian groaned and continued working in silence. He kept glancing at her, grumbling.

"Why would you subject yourself to a dictator in the sky who has no interest in you at all? You are an intelligent girl. You can make your own decisions. I wouldn't want to let someone take that away from me!"

"God does care, Brian. I felt it in the water, I felt it later. He wants to be part of my life."

He huffed and threw a hay bale into the cart. "Right!"

By the time they were done with the feeding, Jacqueline's muscles were starting to relax again and she was able to move quicker and without so much pain. She haltered Rusty and pulled the mare out onto the dirt road.

"Today, more walking and less snacking," she warned the old horse, who eyed the patch of grass in the middle of the road.

After an hour of intermittently pulling and being pulled, Jacqueline had had enough. She practically threw her back into the stall and slammed the door with a little more force than she had intended. Brian raised his eyebrows.

"Don't ask," she barked and stomped to the chicken coop, whose inhabitants were eagerly awaiting their food and water.

Her wrangling lessons with Paul took up the rest of the morning. She would have liked to have become an expert wrangler by the end, but she could barely throw the lasso. The whole thing was harder than she had expected. She managed to hook the lasso around the target once and Paul kindly pretended that was a great achievement.

Jacqueline scooted into her seat at the table and waited expectantly with the rest of the group for Grand to finish praying a blessing over their food. She had to admit she was famished. For the last half hour, her stomach had told her so.

"Brian, you and Jacqueline head over and check on the pregnant cows this afternoon. It's a little easier on the behind than going all the way to where the steers are. Paul and I will take that," Grand informed them at lunch. They ate hamburgers and homemade fries. He then asked how her lessons went and she blushed in response.

"It's not as easy as it looks, is it? They make it look so easy in the movies but when you are the one throwing the lasso it is a different story," he grunted and playfully pulled on her pony tail.

315

"No, no, boss," Paul piped up. "She did all right. She's got the technique down, but now she just needs some practice. Hey, practice when you go out, all right?"

Jacqueline did not say anything but concentrated on her last fry. It was so good. She doubted that she would ever eat as much as she was eating this week.

Before they set out, Grammy had given her some food and water for their trek. Her seat hurt for the first two minutes in the saddle, but it soon got used to the motion of the horse again. Though they started out at a leisurely pace, Brian soon decided they should pick it up. A surprise was waiting for them when they got to the pregnant cows. A calf was just struggling to get up on its feet as they arrived at their destination. Within moments the little one was busily drinking its mother's milk

"You know," Brian said softly as he watched mother and daughter. "I don't think this ever gets old. I could watch this kind of stuff all day long. I kind of envy you. You picked a pretty cool career."

Excitement surged through her and she leaned softly against Jimbo, who was unaffected by what was playing out in front of them.

"I know," she whispered.

Brian snagged the calf and quickly gave her a once-over. It seemed that both mother and child were in good health and the mother complained loudly as he let her go again. Jacqueline was stiff when she dismounted and made her way to the barn, where she untacked her horse and brushed him. It had been a pretty great day.

After soaking in a hot tub of scented water, she felt human again; a clean human. It was amazing how much dust she was attracting. When she joined everyone gathered around the dinner table, Brian sniffed the air as she walked by. His eyes were full of mischief, but he held his tongue. The evening proceeded quietly as the young generation took out Monopoly and settled in for a long game. By nine, Jacqueline was winning but Grace had just given her all her properties. Jacqueline decided to finish it.

"I will put two more hotels on Boardwalk and Park Place as well as on all the green and yellow properties."

Brian groaned as he had just passed the free parking space on the board and was just waiting to land on her most expensive holdings. He had already mortgaged most of his belongings. She smiled sweetly and extended her hand to collect his payment for landing on Atlantic Ave. She then passed GO and whistled as Brian landed on Boardwalk. He feigned weeping dramatically as he handed over his last remaining money.

"I may be a princess, but I sure beat you tonight!" she boasted and made it a point to count her money aloud.

"Gloating over someone is not something we, as Christians, ought to do," Grand told her quietly.

"Brian teases me all the time," she explained.

He smiled at her and said gently, "You should repay him by heaping coals of kindness on his head. That means that you be nice to him."

"Oh, I see," she mused and got up from the table.

She went to the kitchen and put ice and water into a large cup and placed it in front of Brian. He laughed and thanked her. Grand once again picked up his large Bible and proceeded to read the next chapter in Acts. Brian quietly left the room just as before.

Chapter 44

As Grace and Jacqueline made their way downstairs the next morning, something special hung in the air. The hands were talking quietly, but there was an extra energy about them. They paced about in excitement.

"Remember? Today is a really busy day. The vet is coming this afternoon and so everyone has to be on his horse by seven," Grace explained to her.

"Let's saddle up," Grand told everyone and there was a general scraping of chair legs as everyone scrambled to the barn.

Jacqueline looked reluctantly at her horse, Jimbo. "You know, you are a sweet horse, but if I don't have to sit on you for a day or so I would not complain."

"Mount up," came the call not ten minutes later.

The horses sensed that something was going on. They were snorting and whinnying and dancing around as the ranch hands tried to mount. Even gentle Jimbo was snorting and tossing his head. He jogged out with Brian's mare, who was pricking her ears. The mob made its way out to the pasture and as it opened up, the horses were eager to go. As a group, they picked up their pace and soon were flying over the meadow and hills. Jacqueline felt totally exhilarated. The pace was breathtaking. Soon they came upon the herd. The heifers, grazing quietly, picked up their heads as the horses approached.

"We play it like normal," Grand explained. "Jacqueline, you hang back. If you think you need to take a young 'un down and it looks like a sure shot, go ahead. But don't get into a situation where you are in over your head. The herd is to be driven back to the ranch - that is the goal. Any stragglers, get 'em, boys."

Everyone wore sober expressions on their faces. Jacqueline could feel the adrenaline spiking through her, making her jumpy and nervous, ready for action.

Jimbo pranced around, tossing his head anticipating her nervousness. Jacqueline had to hold on to the old horse's reins a little more securely or he would have taken off. Everyone fanned out and the herd was slowly but steadily moving.

"Watch that black and white one on the left, Paul," she heard Brian yell and Paul spurred his horse on to catch up to the straggler. Jimbo seemed to know what to do. They were jogging along, when Jimbo stopped. He turned away from the herd and headed to an area of bushes. She saw the heifer, who was stuck in a bush. She got down and with her hand cutters started cutting the young cow out of her prison. When the heifer was free she gave a great big bellow and tottered down to meet the herd. Jacqueline patted her horse's neck.

"Well done, Jimbo."

She spurred him on to follow the heifer, who after her initial joy at gaining freedom, had started to wander away again.

"Oh boy, oh boy," she muttered as she was getting her lariat ready. "I can do this," she encouraged herself.

She approached the heifer, who by now was grazing at a new patch of grass, and threw her lariat. It missed the cow by inches. She gathered it up and threw it again. This time it struck the haunch and the cow moved away a few steps. Sweat started to trickle down Jacqueline's nose. She concentrated on the next throw, wanting to make it count. This time it slipped right over the cow's head and she snapped it into place. She sat on Jimbo, panting and grinning at her achievement.

Without warning, the heifer decided that she was not going to put up with Jacqueline anymore. She barreled toward the herd, bellowing at the top of her lungs. Once the heifer had reached the end of the rope she continued going and Jacqueline felt herself being ripped out of her saddle. She held on to the end of the rope and was soon eating grass and dust. Her body bounced along the rough and rocky ground. Suddenly her head hit the ground hard and she saw stars and tasted blood. By this time the heifer had reached the edge of the herd and Jacqueline heard people shouting.

Her heifer must have stopped because the bouncing and jarring and ingesting grass and dirt stopped. She lay facing the sky. *Oh look, more stars*, she thought as her head spun. She touched the sore spot on her head and her fingers came back bloody. *Oh no!*

"No, don't get up!" Grand was right next to her. "Brian get Jimbo! Everyone watch the herd! Get them to the ranch. We don't need a stampede on our hand."

321

He examined her head. As he touched a particular spot on her forehead, she winced and almost passed out.

"Jacqueline, you Greenhorn. You should have let go!"

Her whole body was screaming out in pain. Her pants were shredded and she had dirt and rocks all over her. Brian appeared with Jimbo, who seemed to look down at his rider in confusion.

"Are you all right?" she heard concern in Brian's voice.

She attempted slowly to sit up but her muscles didn't want to respond. She groaned and thought of how she was going to explain this to her parents. Grand examined her and asked her questions. No, she didn't feel any numbness. Yes she was hurting all over. Yes she knew what her name was.

"We need to get back to the ranch," he said and slowly helped her stand up.

She was dizzy, but after a moment or so that went away. The cut on her head was still bleeding and the blood was mixing with dirt and sweat, making a terrible mess.

"Here, have my jacket," Brian took his jacket off and carefully helped her into his denim jacket. She thanked him. Suddenly a realization hit her. Here they were and the herd was nowhere in sight. Where was that ornery heifer she had chased down?

"I am so sorry to have caused so much trouble," she stammered and slowly walked toward a patiently waiting Jimbo.

"Don't worry about it. As long as nothing is broken we are fine. The boys know what they are doing. Let's get you back on the horse and get you home," Grand said, as he gently lifted her onto Jimbo's back. She grimaced and tried to hide her pain but both saw it.

"Grand, I'll catch up with the herd. You stay with Jacqueline." Brian suggested, spurring his mare on.

"No son, this is your friend. I'll catch up to the herd. You see that she gets home safely. "

Grand squeezed his gelding into a ground-covering gallop and soon disappeared over the hill. Brian set a slow pace. Jacqueline felt every move her horse made and the was excruciatingly painful. She bit her lip and tried to concentrate on the birds flying about.

"How you doin'?" Brian asked, as they slowly made their way down the hill. She grimaced but told him she was holding up.

"Hey, why didn't you let go?" he asked trying not to laugh. "And that is going to be one huge shiner you are going to sport by tomorrow."

She winced as she touched her eye. She wiped the blood off of her face with the back of her arm.

"Don't worry, Grammy will put a steak on that and take the swelling down nicely. But, why didn't you let go?" he repeated.

"It didn't occur to me to let go. I... I was in shock!" she answered slowly. He muttered something about a greenhorn and shook his head.

"I guess you won't be coming back here again," he grumbled.

She looked at him and shook her head. Her head swam and she was about to fall off her horse, but Brian reached out a hand to steady her. "I have had so much fun this week that it would take a little more

323

than being dragged by a crazy heifer to stop me from coming back here."

Brian grinned and then let out a bellow of a laugh.

"You really should see yourself," he chuckled and reached over to take a clump of grass and dirt out of her hair. He laughed when he gave it to her. "You should keep that as a souvenir."

"Gee, thanks," she smirked and felt the dirt on her face crack, or was it dried blood? She dared not to think about it. "How does my face look?"

"Like you have gone a round with a heavy weight champ. That will be one nasty shiner," he looked at her and chuckled.

"There is the road. It will cut off at the corner and we will get to the ranch in twenty minutes rather than an hour."

Brian opened the gate and they were on the dusty dirt road. She was thankful when they finally pulled up to the main house, forty minutes later. She felt as though she could not stay on the gently plodding along Jimbo much longer.

Chapter 45

"Grammy! Grace! The greenhorn tried to be a hero," Brian shouted as he helped her onto the sofa. Grace came running into the room and gasped when she saw her friend. Grammy mumbled something and went off to find gauze and other helpful medicines.

"I've got to get back to the herd," Brian explained and shot out the door.

"What happened?!" Grace asked as she helped Jacqueline take off the jacket.

Her body was covered with abrasions and cuts. Her head was throbbing. Grace and Grammy carefully washed out the worst of her wounds and had her soak in another hot bath, admonishing her to scrub at the abrasions. It was a painful procedure and she wasn't sure what was worse, being dragged behind a cow, or patching up her body afterward.

She looked at herself in the mirror and had to admit she looked like Frankenstein. Her cheeks were cut and raw and her left eye was almost shut from the swelling. She looked and felt battered. Her parents could never learn that this had happened. She would have to stay until she was completely healed. When she made her way back downstairs, slowly and gingerly, she heard the commotion of the heifers arriving at the ranch. As Brian had predicted, Grammy took a huge steak out of the freezer and gently plopped it onto her battered eye. She sighed as the cold steak numbed the area. Grand stomped into the living room to check on her. He was covered with dust and sweat.

"You doing all right?" he asked, and sat down on a straight chair next to the sofa.

"I'll be fine," she mumbled and tried to smile. It hurt to do even that.

"Well, Greenhorn, you did well. Welcome to cattle herding. Next time, let go of the rope, all right? Or better yet, tie it around the horn. That's what it's there for."

"I bet this hasn't happened to you, has it?" she asked, chagrined. He laughed out loud and slapped his hat on his leg. Dirt flew everywhere.

"It hasn't happened to me? No, I did let go of the rope when the steer dragged me twenty feet. You are going to hold the record for that one. But we all mess up at one point or another. It is a part of life," he grinned and leaned closer. "That is why we need a Savior, hmm?" Grand ran a gentle finger down her cheek. Jacqueline contemplated that statement, when Brian crashed through the door.

"Hey, that steak looks mighty fine on you," he drawled, laughed, and plopped down in the overstuffed chair.

"Okay honey," Grammy walked up to her. "Time to flip the steak. Don't worry, I have seen worse. The boys always come in from wrangling with some sort of cut or bruise. Cattle ranching is not for wildflowers. That is why Grace prefers to stay with me. Maybe you should too?"

Jacqueline shook her head. "I'll be fine by tomorrow," she said and Grammy looked at her seriously. "Okay, maybe the next day. I probably should not ride tomorrow, should I?"

Both Grand and Grammy shook their head.

"But you can come out since the vet is coming. Brian tells me you want to be a vet. Well, you are more than welcome to watch. But I think we will let you watch from the back of the porch," Grand said seriously as he made his way to the kitchen to get a cookie, which had just been taken out of the oven. He burned his fingers. Grand dunked his cookie into a glass of fresh milk. He brought one over for his grandson and they enjoyed their snack.

After about twenty minutes they made their way back outside. The vet was just arriving.

"Grammy, I would like to watch the vet," Jacqueline told her host. Grace glanced at her and took the steak off her eye and shook her head.

Jacqueline slowly made her way outside and was introduced as the "greenhorn" who wouldn't let go of the rope. Everyone laughed and explained to the vet, a young man about thirty, that she had beaten Grand's record. He grinned and gently shook her hand. From the back of the porch, Jacqueline was amazed at the speed with which he could vaccinate each animal once they had their heads immobilized.

The dust and noise was horrendous and by the end of the afternoon everyone was covered in dust, sweat, and cow spit as the heifers shook their heads in defiance. Jacqueline breathed a sigh of relief when the last of the complaining cows was let out to pasture. The herd slowly made its way down the pasture, away from the annoyance.

"Well, Doc. How about a nice glass of iced tea and cookies? They are mighty good, I can tell you 'cause I snagged one before I came out here." Grand slapped the exhausted veterinarian on the back, sending dust everywhere. "Let's wash on up in the barn. You know how women folk are about bringing the dust and dirt into their house," he laughed, and they disappeared through the barn door.

Brian and the rest of the farm hands were busy getting the horses unsaddled and rubbed down. They put them out into several paddocks to enjoy the rest of what was left of the day. Finally, he made his way to the barn to wash up, too. Jacqueline heard the men laughing in the kitchen and wanted to make her way in there for a drink but she just couldn't get up.

Grace appeared and set a plate of cookies and a tall glass of iced tea on the table.

"How are you doing?" she asked concerned.

Jacqueline laughed ruefully. "If I sit still, I am just fine. As soon as I move, I'm in trouble. I think I have more cuts and bruises on my body than skin."

"You have to tell your parents."

"Are you kidding me? They would send the Royal Guard and declare war on this state if they knew. I can't do that."

"It is only right, Jacqueline. You can't keep this from your parents. When you decided to follow Jesus, and as such, you need to let them know what happened. It would be disrespectful and the Bible has a thing or two to say about that. It would be kind of like lying to them. Besides... They will find out anyway when you go home."

"Grace, you don't know my parents well. They would send the plane for me today, with a group of nurses and doctors on board to make sure I am all right. No, I don't think I should tell them."

"But you gave your life to Christ? He doesn't like lies. You have to tell them."

"I can't!" Jacqueline shot back.

She was getting a little bit annoyed at Grace. Her body hurt and now Grace was trying to get her to tell her parents? Not a chance! She looked at her friend, whose eyes were closed and her head bowed. Was she praying? Jacqueline felt a wave of discomfort sweep through her.

"I'm sorry Grace. I didn't mean to snap at you."

"It's all right. But you still need to do the right thing. I can't make you do it. It is your decision. We can't have two masters. We can't serve God and our own self at the same time. You choose."

They sat for a long time not speaking. Jacqueline felt heat rising in her face. Shame swept through her body. She sighed.

"How do I do this?" she asked her friend. Grace took her hand and looked into her eyes.

"You ask, seek, and knock. Wait patiently for Him to answer. He answers by saying 'yes', 'no', or 'wait'."

They bowed their heads and prayed together. Jacqueline knew Grace was right... letting them was the right decision after all. Brian stomped onto the porch, looking a lot less dusty. He sighed as he saw them pray, and flung himself into the wicker chair. He grabbed a cookie from the plate.

"Hey, get your own. These are Jacqueline's," Grace scolded. "Do you mind? We are praying!"

Brian groaned as he was about to get up.

"All right, all right. We are just about finished," she consented. "You sit and I'll get you a plate. You look about done in too." She patted his shoulder as she made her way inside. Brian closed his eyes.

"I guess I can't complain about the choice of sisters, can I?" he asked.

Jacqueline grunted in reply and took a sip of her refreshing tea. The cookies were delicious indeed. But her jaw hurt when she bit into them and chewed. Doctor Toby and Grand joined them on the porch and of course everyone had a good laugh at her. She didn't mind. But she was glad that the vet talked to her with ease about his job and the ups and downs of veterinary practice.

"You may not want to go into large animal practice. It really is tough and very physically demanding. You have time to think, though, and they will give you a chance to test both out in school."

Jacqueline took the phone with her to the porch. The sun had set, her stomach was full, and she had to make this phone call. She could feel butterflies in her stomach. She dialed her parent's private number. It would be early in the morning in Lichtenbourgh.

"Hello," her father's sleepy voice cracked.

"Good morning Father, it's Jacqueline," she tried to sound cheery.

"Are you all right?" He was wide-awake now and she could hear him whispering to his wife.

"Well, I am having a great time here," she said tentatively.

"What is wrong?"

"Nothing really," she replied, marveling at her father's ability to know when something was wrong. "I had a little bit of excitement today, but I am just fine."

She slowly proceeded to tell her parents about her fall. She could hear them whispering.

"I think it would be best if you came home, Jacqueline," her mother said.

"Mother, I'm fine. Just a couple of bruises and a black eye. But Grammy put a steak on it and it looks a lot better," she assured her parents.

She could hear sharp intakes of breath on the other end of the phone.

"A steak, as in from a cow?" her mother finally asked.

"Jacqueline," her father commanded. "We are sending the plane today to pick you up. Please be ready tomorrow afternoon."

"Please don't do this," she pleaded. "I am having so much fun here on the ranch. I am learning so much. The vet was here today and it was fascinating to watch him work. I promise I won't do anything dangerous for the rest of the week. Please let me stay!"

"You didn't intend to do anything dangerous today but it turned out that way. You are coming home." her father demanded.

"Father, before you send the plane, would you please speak with Grace and Brian's grandparents? And whatever you decide I will obey." She added a diplomatic sniffle at the end.

"Yes, please let me speak with the host," her father requested.

She slowly made her way into the house, where she found Grammy in the kitchen pouring herself a cup of tea.

"Would you mind speaking with my parents?" Jacqueline asked, tears in her eyes.

Grammy put an arm around her and nodded. Jacqueline was too upset to stay for the whole conversation. She joined Grace on the sofa. Grace gave her a knowing look.

"Whatever happens, Jacqueline, it is for the best."

She sighed and leaned her head against her friend's shoulder.

"I don't want to go home," she whispered.

"I know."

"I feel like I am a part of a family with you both. I guess that is why I like being around you two. At home it is me, myself, and I. I get a little lonely."

"I'm sorry, Jacqueline," Grace mumbled.

Brian's snoring interrupted them and Jacqueline couldn't stop giggling. His head was bobbing on his chest as he sat in the chair he had fallen asleep in.

"Do you see why?" Jacqueline asked and pointed to Brian when she was able to speak again.

Grace smirked and nodded. "We are the comic relief team."

"Well, Jacqueline," Grammy said to her. "Your parents have allowed you to stay the remainder of the agreed upon time." Jacqueline let out a yell, waking up Brian, and hugged Grammy and then winced.

"Thank you. Thank you. How did you manage to convince them?"

"I told them that you would be staying away from cows. They seemed fine with it. Now, let's get together and pray."

She called her husband and together they thanked God that Jacqueline was all right. They thanked Him that she would be able to stay and most importantly they thanked Him that Jacqueline wasn't seriously hurt. After the prayer Jacqueline opened her eyes. She was thankful that God saw her through the difficult phone call to her parents. She glanced over toward Brian to give him some reassurance, knowing that he resisted anything to do with God. He was no longer in the room.

Chapter 46

The rest of the week flew by. Jacqueline was given minimal chores, which kept her under the very attentive and careful eye of Grammy. The woman was not about to let her out of her sight. Brian was right. She sported a beautiful black eye. The three of them had a chance to attend a state fair in the nearby town. She cheered until her voice was hoarse during the barrel racing, cattle wrangling, and other competitions.

"Jacqueline," Brian snickered at her, passing the popcorn. "That is how it is really done." He pointed to the cowboy, who had wrapped the rope around the saddle horn and leaped off his horse at lightning speed.

"No, I beg to differ. I think I got off my horse much quicker," she laughed and they joined her.

Sunday was a treat because they all piled into the new truck, just returned from the mechanic, and attended church. Brian even came with them, although he sat through the entire service outside on the front lawn. Sunday evening found them eating ice cream on the porch, watching the sunset.

"I want to thank you for the most exciting week of my life," she told them all and Grammy patted her hand.

"We are so blessed to get to know you. It has been a treat for Grace to have a friend and Brian has not complained as much as he usually does about doing his chores," Grand chuckled, and slapped his grandson on the shoulder.

"Hey, I don't complain... much," he replied, a mock look of hurt on his face.

She laughed and said seriously, "You have a wonderful family. I will miss that when I go home."

"Sweetheart, your parents are probably looking forward to seeing you. I'm sure they missed you," Grammy said gently, stroking her cheek. Jacqueline gave her a hug. It felt so good to have Grammy hug her. She didn't want to let go.

"You are welcome here again any time," Grand stated and grinned. "You will learn how to wrangle a cow correctly."

"I know I have wonderful parents. It's just the life we lead. It gets very lonely."

Granny nodded, understanding.

The next morning dawned and Brian helped Jacqueline load her suitcase into the back of the truck.

"This time we get to drive in style," Grace smirked, as she piled in next to her brother.

They didn't talk much on the way back to Billings. They stopped for a snack when Brian gassed up the truck and proceeded to the small airport where her plane was waiting. She sighed and tried to blink her tears away.

"We'll have to email, all right? It is much quicker than writing letters. And we are going to call, although I will be on a student budget." Grace hugged her fiercely.

Jacqueline nodded.

"I will call you, then."

"Thanks for breaking Grand's record. He was always a little prideful on owning it," Brian attempted to chuckle but it sounded hollow and flat. "We're going to miss you, Your Highness," he stated, and cleared his throat.

"Don't forget your hat," Grace yelled, and put her battered and dirty hat on her head. "It looks good on you. It will look a lot better on you once the bruises have stopped draining into the rest of your face." She gave her another quick hug and jumped back into the truck.

"Let me carry this for you," Brian offered, and grabbed her suitcase from her. They walked slowly to the terminal, where an attendant was already waiting for her.

"Take care, will you?" Jacqueline said, and went to shake Brian's hand. Instead she found herself wrapped up in his strong arms.

"You too," he whispered, and let her go.

She turned and walked away, but at the last moment, glanced back and waved. She was a little rattled and not in control of her emotions. The hug had been quite unexpected and had left a warm sort of feeling in the pit of her stomach. When she sat in her seat, she looked out the window. There was the truck, Grace and Brian sitting in the bed, waving at her. She waved back but was sure they couldn't see her. She sighed as the attendant offered her a quick drink before they took off. She sipped her soda.

Well, well, what do we have here, she thought, and decided that she enjoyed being hugged by Brian. She felt herself blushing when she thought about this.

"Please fasten your seat belt, Your Highness. We are about to take off," the flight attendant informed her.

She wanted to shout that she was not going back but she knew that she was expected to be home and to do her part in the family business. She felt the weight of it all over again. She felt her nerves tingle.

The engines roared and she glanced out the window one last time at her friends waving frantically. Tears were streaming down her face when she felt the acceleration of the plane pushing her back into her seat. She looked at the window, trying to keep her eyes on her friends for as long as possible.

The last weeks were a blur. So much had happened, that she could be thankful for. And she was changing. But one thing was for sure – she would miss Grace... and Brian... so much it hurt.

Acknowledgment

To the One, Who sat down to write this story with me, my Lord and Savior Jesus Christ. I am so thankful for this opportunity.

A great big thanks goes to my hubby, first of all, who went through the story with me and added quite a bit to it. Some of the comic relief came from him.

To my son, Logan, who listened to me read this story to him. And even though it is a chick story, he patiently indulged me, and made corrections as he saw fit.

To my daughter, Natasha, who designed the cover. Thank you so much Tash. You did such a lovely job. Thank you to Meara Small, who is just the way I imagined Jacqueline.

To my editors, Annie Omilian and Steve Place. Wow! I don't know how to thank you. So, I thank God for providing you for me. You have both been an encouragement throughout this process of editing.

Thank you to those who previewed this story, Aula Evans DeWitt, Jean Perreault and Theresa Little. I appreciate the time you took out and the encouragement you gave me.

Thank you to my friends and family, who prayed for every step of the way. It's been an interesting journey, and I needed those prayers along the way.

Author's note

Starting on this journey with Jacqueline and her friends has been exciting for me. Of course, when writing about her I had to make up a country, and thus created Lichtenbourgh. I wanted it to be a typical European country rich, in history. It has been fun to create this country in the heart of Europe.

Of course this is a work of fiction, and as such my characters are fictional. The journey Jacqueline has gone on is not fictional. There are many people out there who are extremely successful and who seem to have it all. But they could be dead on the inside. They try to do their best without the support that is out there for all of us. The support that comes from a relationship with Christ the risen Savior.

The great thing about Christ is that we don't have to have all our ducks in a row to approach Him for a chance of a good and full life. So many people think that they can't possibly approach God! That is the beauty of Christ. He knows! He walked on earth, and knows our problems, our hurts. When we come to Him, He promises not to take it all away but to make it better so that we can walk in the hurt and the problems that face us on a daily basis. That is the beauty of Christ. It's simple, really.

I hope that you have enjoyed this beginning. It has been very special to me, since it's been in my head for 30 years or so. When I asked God what was next he prompted me. He told me to write. I fought against it. After all, this story is a very personal one, one that has kept me sane, when I had nothing to hold on to. But He ended up convincing me to write it and promised to write it with me.

And He sure did. Alone I would never have written this. It is only because of the prodding from Him, the provision from God, and being sustained by Him, that I was able to write this. I pray that this story and the ones that follow will help you to come to know that He does love you dearly and wants you to come as you are. Naked and bleeding, if necessary.

May God bless you in every way.

Author bio

Anne Perreault was born and raised in Germany. In her early teens she moved to Dubai, UAE. After completing her studies at the British school there, she attended an American boarding school in Austria. After graduating from college in New England, she worked at a vet tech and riding instructor. Later on Anne became a certified Therapeutic riding instructor. She has a MA in Education, and uses it to homeschool her children. She and her husband are busy building their own home in Southern Vermont where they live with their three children.

Read an exciting preview of the next part of Jacqueline's journey.

Learning to Trust

The second book of

The Royal Skater Chronicles

by Anne Perreault

Coming 2016

That the trial of your faith, being much more precious than of gold that perisheth, though it be tried by fire, bight be found unto the praise and honor and glory at the appearing of Jesus Christ.

1 Peter 1:7

Chapter 1

Princess Jacqueline looked out the window as the wind whipped around the limousine, taking her to her home. The streets were drenched in inches of rain, still coming down from the gray and dreary sky .

"Well, that about reflects my mood," she thought.

After having been on holiday for over a month, and spending the last week with her friends, Brian and Grace, on their grandparent's ranch in Montana, she dreaded the loneliness waiting for her when she reached the palace outside Lichten, in the small country of Lichtenbourgh where she lived. But then another thought shot through her head.

In everything with prayer and thanksgiving.

Wow, where did that come from? she thought.

She was not being very thankful right now. Jacqueline was cranky and sad, missing her friends and the fresh Montana air. *I will have to be more thankful*, she thought. *I will also have to try prayer on my own now.*

Jacqueline took a deep breath and realized that she was not the same person who had left two month ago. Back then she had no time for God, whereas now, her life was in Christ's hands. She had met Him in the waters of the Persian Gulf, a both scary and wonderful day. Since then, she had come across some incredible people and given her life into the capable hands of Christ.

She blew a strand of hair out of her face and put on the battered hat she had purchased with her friends in a small store in Montana. It had gone through a lot when she had been dragged behind the heifer, leaving her battered and bruised. She didn't care if her parents didn't agree with her style, but the hat was here to stay.

She quickly leaned forward toward the front seat to check herself in the mirror of the car, taking her home. Jacqueline's face had seen better days and there were still scrapes and abrasions evident on her cheeks and chin, but the bruises and scrapes on the rest of her body were healing nicely. Most of the bruises were now green and yellow and didn't hurt anymore. The only evidence left of her black eye, were the green and yellow tinges, and she hoped that a quick application of makeup would disguise most of the damage. The car pulled into the gates of the palace, a stately building and a work of architecture, which loomed before her.

Jacqueline sighed as footmen hurried to have an umbrella ready for her and scrambled indoors as the wind picked up.

"Welcome home, Princess. Your parents wanted me to inform you that they had an emergency meeting and won't be home until late. They hope you had a pleasant flight and will see you tomorrow morning. They wish an audience with you at 9 A.M.," her parent's secretary smiled as she welcomed her in the foyer.

Jacqueline thanked her and made her way to her suite. To her surprise, she was welcomed by balloons and flowers decorating her room. This lifted her mood a little bit. She went in search of food, since she was starving. She proposed that eating a hamburger with French Fries one last time was not out of the question. As she made her way to the kitchen she bumped into Marie, her older sister by five years and the sibling she most longed to avoid.

"The prodigal returns home," Marie greeted her. "What on earth is that on your head?" she asked with a sneer. "And what happened to your eye?" She stared at her eye.

For a moment Jacqueline wanted nothing to do with her sneering sister. But then something tugged at her heart and she couldn't help wonder what would happen if she were nice to her, if she were to heap coals on her head to borrow Grand's phrase.

"Long story, Marie. I'm hungry so I would like to eat. Say, why don't I come to your room and I can tell you all about it after I eat. Or better yet, let's eat together down here in the kitchen."

"Nope, I have a date. See ya later, kid." Marie rushed past her.

Jacqueline felt the weight of loneliness. In the kitchen she ordered a burger and fries, and poor George, the head chef, almost passed out because she usually didn't eat a full meal at lunch time. She ate at the kitchen bar and told the attendants all about her wonderful and somewhat painful week at the ranch. The hamburger tasted superb as did the fries. Jacqueline rubbed her stomach, contemplating having desert of creme torte.

"I have to say, I never thought to hear those words out of your mouth," George sighed as he put a plate of torte next to her.

"I had this delectable smoothie overseas. You have to make it, George."

She proceeded to tell him about the healthy smoothies she had drunk and asked him to start stocking the ingredients. After eating, she meandered through the long corridors back to her room. She was weary but not ready to sleep.

Lord, I am lonely and have only been back a few hours. I don't know who to turn to, so I am trying to turn to You. Would You please help me not feel so alone? she prayed as she sat on her comfortable couch, staring at nothing.

A knock on the door woke her out of her thoughts. That was quick, she thought and opened her door to her brother. He was the oldest of the four of them and the crown prince of Lichtenbourg, a small country in the mountains between Switzerland and France. He was also the only one of her siblings she got along well with.

"Heard you were back," he grinned and flipped the brim of her hat. "Nice hat. And nice shiner too."

"Thanks, Jean. Do you want to come in?"

"I'm not standing out here because I have nothing to do," he smirked and sauntered past her. "So Jacqueline, how are you?"

"Are you asking because you are interested or are you asking because it would be the polite thing to say," she asked acerbically and flung herself onto her bed.

Her body was tired and a little achy still from the accident. The accident of being dragged behind a cow. Even though it was not a fully grown cow.

"A little testy aren't we?" he complained. "Seriously, you know me. I want to know how you are and how you got that shiner. Was there a riot in Montana?"

"Funny Jean. You really are interested on how my holiday went?" she asked not quite believing him. He looked at his sister in mock shock.

"Really, I have missed you around here. No reporters calling for an interview or fans waiting outside the gates. I really do want to know, because I care." He put a hand over his heart.

Jacqueline growled at him. She sighed. "All right, since you are here, I will tell you that I had a wonderful, incredible, fantastic, life changing time. How is that?"

"Well, proceed," he drawled and waved his hand at her lazily.

She told him about her time in the desert, when her friend Brian had become stuck and left her with sand between her teeth. He laughed out loud when she described her second time getting stuck. When she came to the part that she visited a house church, he held up his hand.

"Wait, please don't tell me, they converted you into a Christian?" he grumbled and glared at his sister.

"Why does that sound so derogatory?" she asked and went to get a bottle of water from her small fridge.

"We all know Christians are do-gooders who think everyone else is wrong." Jean looked hard at his youngest sister. "I can tell you Mother and Father will not go for that."

"Let us just say that I have been shown a better, a more perfect way to live," she answered tentatively.

Jean stood up and started pacing, running his hand through his hair.

"You might want to stop ripping out your hair. You may not have much left after this," she teased but Jean frowned at her.

"So, you believe all that stuff about Jesus being God and all that?" he finally asked.

"Yes, Jesus is God with us," she answered very assured. "I have no doubt about this. Sit down, Jean, I have to tell you why."

Jean sat reluctantly, muttering to himself. She proceeded to tell him about her incident in the raging sea, and how a Presence had been with her giving her the strength to kick and keep her hand above water until she was fished out of the water by men in a boat. Jean stared at her, disbelieving. She also told him about the revival meeting she had been privileged to be part of in Miami, where she had been prayed over and accepted Christ as her Lord and Savior. Jean continued to glare at her.

"So, now you are going to join a monastery and become a nun?" he finally asked. She laughed so hard, tears began to run down her cheeks.

"Not hardly. I want to live my life. And besides I could never be a nun. They can't marry. And I hope one day to have a family."

"Oh," he breathed and his face relaxed. "I thought we would be loosing our greatest public asset."

350

Jacqueline stared at her brother. How dare he! She resented being used for public relations. Just because she was now a hot commodity, after recently winning both the Olympic and World Championship in figure skating. She held her breath for a long moment and slowly released it.

"Are you serious about what you just said?"

"A little bit," he smirked cheekily. "Forgive me?"

She punched his arm and he winced. She proceeded to tell him about her time in Montana. He laughed when she told him about her sore muscles and the ornery mare she took for walks. He looked very concerned when she described being dragged behind an ornery heifer, earning her with the black eye and bruises all over her body.

"Wow, I can't believe you actually walked away from being dragged by a cow." He rubbed his forehead, a sign that he was clearly disturbed. "I have to say I'm glad you are back. It has been a little dull around here. Mother and Father have been busy and I haven't seen them much. I mean I have been so busy, but it is nice to have you back." He rose out of his seat and patted her head. "See you tomorrow. You look tired. Oh, by the way. I am engaged."

47215585R00195

Made in the USA
Lexington, KY
01 December 2015